THE BUFFALO ON MAIN STREET

C.W. BOOTH WYCHE

Copyright © 2020 by C.W. Booth Wyche

All rights reserved. No part of this publication may be reproduced, distributed or transmitted in any form by any means, or stored in a database or retrieval system, without the prior written permission of the author.

The characters and events portrayed in this book are fictitious, especially any illegal shit; none of it ever happened and is a creation of the author's imagination. Any similarity to real persons, living or dead, is coincidental and not intended by the author.

ISBN 9798626393415

Printed on the Planet Earth.

Contents

Preface   vii

Prologue   1

Part I
Prelude to Fuckery

1. Procyonids   5
2. Little Red Bows of Lace   20
3. Lawn Fairies Wear Boots   36
4. Slouching Toward Monogamy   49
5. The Smell of Perfidy in the Morning   65
6. Serial Killers in Prii   79
7. Bennett Family Values   90
8. As Gung as a Ho Can Be   105
9. Card Game   117
10. Cunnilinguist Lumberjacks   130

Part II
Fullblown Fuckery

11. Jurisdictional Clusterfuck   141
12. Teefies   151
13. Fellare Non Grata   165
14. Penises on the Marquee   173
15. Drug-Addled Eve Psychosis   181
16. Reaganomics   195
17. Tsk Fucking Tsk   209
18. Earholed   217

Part III
Post Fuckery Cuddles

19. Codeine   237
20. Winona Ryder's Boobs   243

21. Oklahoma Breakdown 257
22. The Buffalo on Main Street 268

Acknowledgments 277

Preface

This book is thirty-seven years in the making.

I was born a poor black child. I remember the days, sitting on the porch with my family, singing and dancing down in Mississippi.

None of that is true. That's the opening line to Steve Martin's story in *The Jerk*.

I was born a poor white child in the small town of Sulphur, Oklahoma circa 1982. And though the scenery of my childhood wasn't the most exciting, it was the type of upbringing that prepares one for the type of life that they might write about later. This book is full of experiences that I lived, characters influenced by people that I've known and the town in which I grew up.

When I was a sophomore in high school and Bobby, the oldest of our group of friends, got his driver's license, we were pretty shocked to find that an abandoned lot on Broadway was the hangout on Saturday nights. Kids parked their trucks, pulled out their lawn chairs and drank beer right there in plain view of the town — no one batting an eye. We soon got to know most of the local cops by name. As long as you didn't do anything too stupid, they mostly let you go about your business. I suppose that they preferred that we all got up to what we were getting up to out in the open.

Our lives revolved around football and girls. I was decent at one of those things. *Varsity Blues* came out during my junior year, and we wore out the VHS tape, treating it like our bible and watching it every week before games. We never put our wieners on the glass at the Alano Club while the ladies were rehearsing the Christmas pageant, but we tried our best. Our friend Daniel did call himself the Mad Mooner and ran around town showing everyone his ass for a whole year.

After high school, I became a college dropout pretty quickly, and that's when the monotony kicked in.

It's one thing to be in your hometown during high school when all of your friends are there and you spend most of your time trying to think of new ways to get into trouble. When you're an adult, it's decidedly less cool — especially when they make you stay the night in jail instead of calling your parents after you turn eighteen.

You still get up to stupidity, but you have to find new and exciting ways to do it.

That's where the inspiration for this book lies.

Dedicated to those of old-school MZP fame. Without that community, I never would have written a word.

"**D**aryl!" Megan's voice had rang out like a banshee. She had been a sheriff's deputy for a few years, and had discovered early on in her career that her booming voice was her best asset; it was particularly effective in frightening teenagers who thought that they might have more leniency with a female deputy than her male counterpart; and for attracting one's attention across large groups of people. She also swore like a sailor as a result of growing up with four brothers and working in a male-dominated profession.

Daryl sighed and turned to the find the source of the ridiculously loud voice that came in such a tiny package. He had been laser-focused in on Ainsley and getting a foot up on his competition that the last thing that he wanted was to have to fend off Megan and any attempt that she might have planned to outdo him. He saw people being pushed aside in the crowd, but couldn't yet see Megan where she was hidden amongst them like a lioness in the grass plains of the Serengeti. Finally, she emerged from the mass of bodies, slightly out of breath, but fully in control of her voice:

"Daryl," she continued.

"I'm right here, Megan," he responded, waving to where he stood a half-dozen paces from her.

"Oh," she responded, hurrying over to his side. "Sheriff Reynolds told me to come find you."

"I just talked to Sheriff Reynolds," Daryl replied, annoyed that the conversation didn't seem to be going anywhere.

"Within the last two minutes?" she asked.

"No, but—"

"Then shut the fuck up and listen," she scolded. "Some shit has gone down."

"I can see that," Daryl replied, motioning to the commotion surrounding them.

"Other shit. Different shit," she insisted. "Someone broke into and trashed the DHS office."

"Why," he asked. "Who the hell would breaking into the Department of Human Services building?"

"I don't fucking know," she answered with a scowl. "I didn't do it, did I?"

"Okay, after I talk to Ainsley—"

"And someone released the buffalo."

"What? Which buffalo?"

"All the fucking buffalo!" she yelled. "From the Buffalo Pasture! Some asshole broke the gate open and let them out."

"Jesus Christ," Daryl began.

"That's not all."

"There's *more*," he asked, dumbfounded.

"There was a sighting," Megan responded, quieter than she had been before.

Daryl could only imagine the words that were about to come out of her mouth. What sort of sighting? Alien? Terrorist? Jackalope?

"Sasquatch," she replied uneasily.

"Sasquatch?"

"Sasquatch."

"Are you fucking with me," Daryl asked, convinced that she had to be by that point.

"We got three different calls," Megan maintained.

PART I

Prelude to Fuckery

1

Procyonids

Troy Paulson.

That name used to mean something.

Sort of.

So it was never synonymous with the cure of a universal disease. People didn't get a Paulson vaccine, and there wasn't a planet named the Paulson-19874 Alpha. There weren't people who prayed to Saint Troy that weren't Dallas Cowboys fans in the 90s, but on Friday nights in Pine Creek and all throughout the following weeks during the entire fall semester, there were hushed whispers of immortality that followed the mere utterance of that name.

There were trophies and gaudy championship rings, write-ups in the state papers and national prep magazines, ridiculous prognostications of untold grandeur. Strangers took pictures with him. Strangers had sex with him.

Because he was Troy Paulson.

That name used to mean something.

But all that seemed like an eternity ago. Hell, it seemed

like another lifetime altogether — like one of those *E! True Hollywood Stories* that had been half-digested in between bouts of consciousness on a lazy Sunday afternoon. It was someone else's story: *that* Troy Paulson died in college. His story had been written. His eulogy had been spun. He was not pining for the fjords. He was no more.

And yet there were — in the zombiest of times — occasional resurrections. In the summer, when days were inevitably elongated and thinning strands of sentience were stretched to wit's end, the Troy Paulson of seasons past would rattle the chains of his ghostly existence, if for no other reason than to annoy.

Ghost Troy was quite cross with Corporeal Troy. There was no excitement anymore, no mystery. Everything was mapped out and color-coded to the point that they felt like a Master Goddamn Cartographer — and not the fancy sort from the days of yore who used their imagination to create Zelda-esque legends that marked the Fountain of Youth with otherworldly calligraphy. He was a Plain Jane, *Official Survey of the United States* mapmaker — the kind that used a compass to draw his circles.

A compass!

Real men freehand.

Such was the kind of alpha male thinking that Troy Paulson — the corporeal, living and breathing, version 2.0, everyday Troy Paulson — had to suppress now that he had joined the unfashionable ranks of the beta male.

Had it really come to that? All conventional reason had to conclude that it had. He was still good-looking enough: his teeth were white and straight, he had all his hair, he even sported a few noticeable alpha male scars for good measure.

But alpha males didn't work in their childhood friends' auto shop, nor did they meander repeatedly through the same shallow pool of female companionship or hang around their hometown when everyone with even the slightest hint of ambition had bolted for the proverbial door and tested the handle only once before kicking it in to escape to freedom on the other side.

These were the thoughts that held hostage the mind of a dejected Troy Paulson as he concluded the last leg of his walk-of-shame — or drive-of-shame, as it were. The cab of his truck was weighed down with random burger wrappers, dirty shirts, empty soda bottles, empty beer bottles, random chips and fragments of beef jerky. If a hobo hollowed out the shell of a 1997 Ford F-150 and squatted there for months on end with a family of pet raccoons that were perpetually battling a pack of rabid squirrels for rodent/procyonid supremacy, it would look about the same as Troy's truck did then. Despite his mood, the picture of such an epic, furry battle in his mind made him smile.

His hair was longer than it had been in recent years: brown greasy strands hanging slightly over his eyebrows before grudgingly ceding territory to his eyelashes. The slender scar on his right cheek, the result of taking a baseball to the face as a pitcher in high school, occasionally showed itself as the wind did the job that the truck's air conditioner hadn't done in years, blowing the aforementioned hair wildly about. Stubbly facial hair gave him the look of a stray dog, a bit bushy-tailed, but harmless enough. He was maybe fifteen pounds heavier than he had been in his prime, but only so much so that his abs had receded into a normal stomach. All in all, he was still a decent specimen, especially considering the locale.

WELCOME TO PINE CREEK: JEWEL OF THE SOUTH

So read the maddeningly familiar sign that stood just on the outskirts of town where light woodlands and rolling fields of crops gave way to the first signs of civilization. Troy scoffed as Cheryl approached the sign — Cheryl being the name of his truck, obviously — and perfunctorily flipped it the bird just as he did every time he passed it. For its part, the sign didn't seem to care one way or another, the sadist. It stood just as it always had for as long as Troy could remember, mocking those unable to escape its clutches and singing the connivance of the siren's song to lure unsuspecting modern-day sailors to its reefs below.

It had only been three days since Troy had last seen his arch-nemesis, the sign — three glorious days that he'd been out in the world, a man on his own, fighting the good fight: man versus nature and nurture and communism and estrogen and all the crap against which *Ghost Troy* campaigned.

It annoyed him to admit it, but it was *Ghost Troy's* incessant nagging that left him in the sorts of moods that led to his sabbaticals in the first place. Sabbaticals are what his friends called them, though Troy generally preferred to call them "trips" to play down their importance.

Dawn had come only an hour before, and some of the street lights on Main Street had yet to take the hint, flickering needlessly and fighting the sun to win an inch of space on the uniform, red-bricked storefronts as though they wouldn't be resuscitated later that evening.

Troy largely ignored the burgeoning hum of the morning as the worker bees left their hives to scurry to their respective daily tasks. He raised a forefinger from the steering wheel in a lazy response when the good townsfolk inevitably waved as his truck rumbled by them. They were never at a loss for audacity when it came to rubbing salt in the wounds of their former prodigal son. There he was, tail between his legs, gaping wounds in his pride, and they offered whole-hearted smiles and warm greetings.

The bastards.

Pine Creek was a quaint place, for the most part. Main Street was lined with businesses and divided by a grassy strip with a row of ornate, old-fashioned light poles that ran down the centerline. The barbershop anchored the line of storefronts where its hypnotizing, spiral pole bade that the random passersby pay attention. Just as Old Man Frazier liked it.

Troy pretended to be adjusting the buttons on his stereo as he managed to spot Mr. Frazier before Mr. Frazier had spotted him. The old barber would always wave more fervidly than the rest, demanding that Troy pull over to the curb so he could chastise him about the length of his hair. "This is Oklahoma, not California," he'd remind him each and every time, "and hippies are fags." Mr. Frazier stopped going to the VFW after the last of the local WWII and Korea vets passed away because he said that the guys who he served with in Vietnam were pansies.

Troy couldn't stand the old man, especially since he called Mr. Paulson on a regular basis to report on the sorry state of his son's hair and warn him of the depravity that can take hold of a man once he starts to ignore his basic grooming standards.

Troy rolled his eyes as he heard Old Man Frazier launching into his usual tirade and could just make out something that he was saying about his beard as he nudged the gas pedal forward and rolled safely past him.

A block down the road, where Main Street turned into Broadway, lost the dividing centerline and became four lanes, Troy's old friend, Pine Creek High, waited patiently to greet him.

It was a sordid ordeal, their breakup.

She had given him the best years of his life — and he had given her, for a short time, a place on the map to nestle her fleeting ego. But hers was a bitter heart in the end: on the very evening that he last walked her halls, Pine Creek High watched — with more than a smidgen of glee, Troy always supposed — as he had his heart ripped from his chest.

It was across the street from the high school and in front of City Hall where stood the Buffalo. Though the Buffalo was inanimate as far as the eye could tell — a bronzed statue that had been painted broadly black and then highlighted with a plethoric burst of color that was supposed to espouse some sort of inclusionary "shiny, happy people" mantra — Troy had come to the conclusion that it either had to be a tool of pure, unadulterated evil or a gravitational center for karmic activity. But he could never really tell which might be the case.

It was in front of this very Buffalo, at the age of sixteen, that Troy had found his first taste of love.

It was in the juvenile, *damn the man* sense of defiance that *Ghost Troy* and his friends had been drinking on Broadway in front of City Hall late one Friday night after a rout of a game just some two blocks away.

Hard to get wasn't something that he'd been used to. Hard to get rid of was closer to the normal game he played with the opposite sex. It was exasperating, chasing a girl that refused to play the game the way it was invented to be played. He was a superstar. Superstars didn't chase.

But something had compelled him, nonetheless.

And as they straggled behind the rest of the group that was roving in the general direction of the local park and its promise of late-night debauchery, Troy finally found a chink in the armor of his prey. And the chase was over.

Pine Creek High watched from her perch across the street.

She had seemed pleased at the time. She was the only witness to the moment in which the great Troy Paulson had fallen in love, after all. But two years later, Troy was leaving her in shambles, as if the kid behind him was going to be a superstar that would draw the national media to her doorstep. Instead she would be relegated back to the role of a modest Division 3A contender with nothing to offer the world, soon forgotten by all, even those who spent the better part of their formative years in her halls.

On graduation night, she conspired.

There was a lot of talk from his girlfriend about how she wasn't ready to settle down, didn't want to follow Troy to Norman, wanted to live her own life and not in the shadow of his. It was all a series of consonants and no vowels, as far as he could recall, a one-sided conversation that might as well have never been had.

Troy considered flipping the bird to the high school, but thought better of it: no sense in incurring the wrath of that vindictive bitch again.

So he continued his drive. He was only a few blocks from home now, after all, and he could put this trip down Memory Lane behind him for the time being and lock *Ghost Troy* back in his dungeon. He was just passing the Snak-Shak when his peripheral vision caught sight of something that he'd hoped to avoid this and all other mornings: the cold stare of a sheriff's deputy. Troy held his breath for the briefest of moments. Perhaps this wasn't the time.

Wishful thinking.

The deputy pushed down the brim of his dark, oversized aviators just long enough to wink at Troy and smile. Then he pushed them back onto his nose, tossed the fresh cup of coffee in his hand into a nearby trashcan, and broke into a dead sprint for his squad car.

"Shit." Troy wasn't in the mood for this.

He punched the gas and sent fuel speeding in the direction of eight bargain-bin spark plugs that were well past their prime. And though she, too, was far from her prime, Cheryl responded with a squealing of her tires before letting her pistons thrust her along Broadway.

Second Street. It seemed like as good a road as any other to take in the moment. Without ever setting foot to break, Troy cranked the steering wheel hard enough to the left that he nearly took Cheryl to two wheels, but she held on. Some of his various belongings that were not-so-well tied down in the back, however, weren't so fortunate and went skidding along Broadway, the various mementos tossed from their boxes and shattering on the pavement.

There was no time to grieve for lost memories, though. Safely onto the side street, Troy once again leaned his foot on the gas pedal. With some of his things now gone from the bed, he was able to take in the world through his rearview mirror. And in that mirror was a distinct lack of flashing lights, of smoke squealing from the tires of over-powered squad cars. Could it have been that easy? Perhaps Karma had seen the error of her wicked ways and would allow Troy to live out the rest of his life in peace.

Unlikely, but not unfathomable: he did recycle now.

As he edged ever-more-closely to a four-way-stop in a distinctively suburban area of the rural town, Troy began to ease his foot off of the gas. Not flipping the bird to the High School had been the right move after all.

He stopped at the intersection and sighed. He was in the *rich* part of town, which meant that he was where the few people in town that had stable enough incomes splurged on the only noisy houses around to brag about their status. School teachers — oddly enough — coaches, the town's only doctor, all the members of the city council, assorted local business owners, local cops and deputies — these were the inhabitants of the upper echelon of the Pine Creek social order who lived out their lives across the street from the golf course. While it would be wholly lower-middle-class in most any city or in a rural area with any sort of abundance of work, in a town like Pine Creek, there weren't many opportunities for employment and no opportunities whatsoever for advancement. Which is why everyone with half a brain found the exit the second that they turned eighteen.

And yet, even as Troy thought this thought, here was someone moving into the old Hinkler house. A moving truck sat at the curb in front of a well-kept, two-story house with perfectly lush green grass, despite the summer heat and the drought. All the lawns were like that in this neighborhood while the rest of town hadn't had to bother with mowing since May. It was as if God himself came out personally each night and pissed all over their lawns.

Troy wondered who would be moving to town to join the

crags of Pine Creek's elite. Another doctor? Dr. Stone certainly wasn't getting any younger. Another teacher? Doubtful. Pine Creek had a sort of buddy system that was on par with university tenure. Another cop? Pine Creek had three cops for every crime committed. It hardly required another cop.

Another cop.

Sitting stealthily behind the moving truck in front of the Old Hinkler house sat the smiling face of the same deputy that Troy had seen at the Snak-Shak. He wasted no time in flipping on his lights and sirens, and darted out in front of Cheryl just as she was passing by.

Troy pounded the brakes, narrowly avoiding the squad car with the smiling deputy inside. Cheryl was really on top of her game.

"Give it up, asshole. You're caught," came a gloating voice over the deputy's speaker system.

There was no question this time whether or not to flip the bird. Middle finger in the air, Troy had Cheryl in reverse and heading back in the direction of the four-way-stop sign, leaving a series of scruffy, black tracks on the otherwise pristine neighborhood streets. At the four-way, he pulled his best Jason Bourne impression, throwing the wheel again to one side and skidding sideways to get Cheryl into a position so that she might tear away in the opposite direction once she came to a screeching halt. In a very non-Jason Bourn-esque move, however, Cheryl clipped the side of one of the stop signs and sent it to the ground, its cement anchor embarrassingly exposed for all the world to see.

Un-miffed, Troy threw her back into drive and away they went, this time cascading down Williams Drive through the brilliance of water sprinklers, past the up-towners and into a slightly cheaper side of town, this time followed by the unrelenting wail of sirens and flashing lights. With the squad car gaining ground, Troy took another gamble and sent Cheryl headfirst down the narrow confines of a pothole-riddled alley, bouncing around her cab as he tried to steady himself enough to glance again into the rearview. And as he did, he smiled as the squad car sped past the alley and continued westward.

Convinced that any immediate danger had passed, Troy relaxed his foot a bit and allowed the craters in the unpaved back alley to only minimally affect Cheryl's shocks.

Stupid cops.

He let any pent-up momentum that Cheryl may have had from her initial lunge down the alley consume itself and gently applied the brakes before shifting the engine into park and removing himself from the vehicle to inspect any would-be damage that he may have incurred. One smooth once-over later, and Troy was feeling pretty decent about his driving abilities. No major damage that he could see — a tiny scuffmark on the fender from where he uprooted the stop sign — but nothing huge. Still, he felt bad about the scuffmark.

"I'm sorry," he started in his apology to Cheryl. "But you did great. And as soon as—"

But his apology was cut short when a siren shrieked its arrival. From his position at the rear of the truck, Troy sighed, raised his head, and glanced over the bed to where the deputy was standing proudly, leaning against his car, holding the mouthpiece of his speaker system and waiting for his presence to sink in before speaking. Troy hung his head, which was the deputy's cue.

"Nice try, douchebag, but you've been had." His voice was

a bit higher than one might suspect based on his looks. An ape of a man, he wasn't a typical small-town cop: the type that were typically a donut away from a new belt, or the type that poked holes in their existing belt to fit their one-hundred-and-five-pound frame. No, this guy looked like a cop. Broad, burly, and as hairy as Burt Reynolds on his most Chewbacca of days, his mustache had a mustache that would put a Wild West Marshall to shame.

Ghost Troy envied this mustache.

The deputy glanced at Troy at the back of the truck with a hawk's gaze, noting that it was taking him longer than was customary to surrender. "What's the problem, princess? You plan on—?"

But once again, a conversation between the two men was postponed when Troy abruptly bolted for Cheryl's open door.

"Don't do it!" the deputy's voice thundered, but Troy had already used whatever athleticism that hadn't bled out through years of beer sweats to get the door shut and the engine started.

"I wouldn't if I were you!" The deputy had his gun drawn, a round in the chamber, and the look of an angry Sasquatch in his eye.

Troy stared in the rearview at the open alley behind him, and then back to the unflinching deputy. He hesitated, even started to kill the engine at one point, but *Ghost Troy* was throwing giant handfuls of monkey shit against the walls of Corporeal Troy's brain, kicking holes in grey matter and biting through synapses.

This might not end so well.

That was the last thought Troy had before he put the engine in reverse and heard the gunshot ring out.

POLICE PRECINCTS AROUND the country not only require an ungodly amount of paperwork from officers that fire their guns in the line of duty, but it's also a fairly common practice to assign the guilty officer to a department psychiatrist or grief counselor. Daryl Lumley didn't find himself too concerned with either prospect in the immediate aftermath of the shooting. Paperwork didn't bother him as much as it did other cops — mainly because he supplemented his friend Kendrick's income by paying him to write the bulk of said paperwork. And as for the shrink, he definitely had no worries there: the closest psychiatrist to Pine Creek was nearly two hours away, and there was no way that Sheriff Reynolds would spring for that.

So he was all smiles as he holstered his sidearm, much to the chagrin of Troy and his newly flattened tire.

"Are you kidding me?!" Troy screamed at the top of his lungs from across the alley as he slammed Cheryl's door behind him and almost sprinted to her front passenger-side tire to inspect the damage. Just as he suspected: flat.

"You know, I'm just a lowly sheriff's deputy and not a fancy detective or anything, but I'd wager that bullet hole's your problem."

"Why? Just why? You know that bullet holes aren't covered by my insurance," Troy spewed matter-of-factly. "You know because you've done this on three separate occasions!"

"Last I checked, games weren't made to be lost, amigo," Daryl chuckled as he walked over to slap Troy playfully on the back — a move to which Troy didn't respond very well, slapping his hand away as hard as he might in his moment of exasperation.

"Barney Fief. In the fucking flesh."

Daryl laughed wholeheartedly. He knew that the guys threw the Barney Fief reference out as an insult, but he loved it, especially in moments like these when they were trying desperately to find something to tear him down.

"Well, you know what this means, don't you," he asked.

"That you're going to die old and alone with no one but your gun?"

"Everyone knows that. What they don't know — not yet — is that with this capture, this month's bar tab is on you." He snapped his fingers at Troy with that last bit and started heading back toward his car.

"But don't worry. I'll let everyone know."

"I don't have a spare." Troy knew that the fact wouldn't bother Daryl in the least, but felt that it warranted mentioning, nonetheless.

"What's that thing they gave us some years back? You know, when we walked across that stage and all the people were there—? Oh, that's right. A diploma!"

"Great. Yeah, that's hilarious."

"You're an educated man. You'll figure something out."

"I hate you."

"Love you, too." Daryl slammed the door to his squad car and started it before sticking his head out the window. "Oh, and Troy—?"

Troy, already on his way back toward Cheryl, turned around apathetically.

"You're going to need this." Daryl carelessly dropped a piece of paper on the ground.

"What's that?"

"Destruction of public property. You took out a stop sign, dumbass. Welcome home, Troy."

"Fuck you."

Daryl laughed again and drove away with a quick squeal of his siren for added effect.

Troy looked at Cheryl, hung his head with a sigh and addressed himself in his lowest octave:

"Welcome home, Troy."

2

Little Red Bows of Lace

Jackson was sitting on the front porch, sipping from a Budweiser and — well, not doing much else, frankly. There wasn't much traffic on 12th Street that day, so there was nothing to distract him from the soft sounds of chunky guitar riffs, thundering drum fills, and blood-curdling screams of the music drifting over from the nearby stereo that had been hardwired into the only duct-taped electrical outlet the porch had to offer. He glanced up the street, then back down the street, then, out of boredom, around at the house itself.

The sixty-some-odd-year-old Brose house had lost most of the luster from its younger years when it was under the care of Jackson's grandparents. After they had both passed away in the late 90s, leaving the house to Jackson and his brother, the upkeep had gone consistently downhill until neighborhood kids began to speculate that it was haunted. There was even a short period of pranks in which said kids utilized perennial favorites such as the flaming bag of poop, rocks through the window, and poop in the yard, but that was before they realized that Jackson Brose was crazier than Old Man Frazier. The first time, when a kid was shot mid-prank with a high-powered BB gun at precisely 3:47 a.m., there was talk in the middle school ranks that it might be a fluke. The second time, when a kid had the ass of his jeans eaten away by a Roman Candle, there was growing suspicion that something strange might be afoot. But by the time that a week's worth of bagged human excrement was dumped atop the head of the last kid that tried the flaming bag trick, it was widely accepted by all post- and pre-pubescents that the Brose house was off-limits when it came to tomfoolery.

The gray paint was chipped on virtually every board of the house, peeling off and flaking into the wind on a regular basis, and a few of such boards were hanging sleepily over the wraparound porch under which Jackson was sitting. Wall unit air-conditioners were hanging from most windows, and the hum from the nearest was shaking the floorboards beneath his feet. As he slowly observed the state of dilapidation around him, Jackson couldn't help but be struck by a moment of sheer, unadulterated pride. Some ten years after the fact, he was a homeowner. It was almost enough to bring a tear to his eye.

When he saw Cheryl approaching, Jackson was snapped out of his oddly inspirational dream-state. While he was proud of himself for owning a home, he was doubly proud of himself for managing to hang onto his friends for as long as he had. *Most people lose their best friends to college or marriage*, he thought, *but mine are big enough losers that we still have each other —*

well, except for Troy, of course. Troy was always the exception to the rule in Jackson's eyes.

He smiled broadly at Troy's approach, threw his hands in the air, and yelled at the top of his lungs: "Troy Motherfuckin' Paulson!"

Jackson creaked his way down the front steps, watching Troy limp to the curb on Cheryl's flat tire as he purposely avoided the trick step whose replacement had been neglected for the past several years. Jackson wasted no time bro-hugging it out the moment that Troy closed the truck door behind him.

"Welcome back, you smelly old bitch!" Jackson proudly exclaimed, then nodded to the flat tire: "I see that you ran into Daryl already."

"I did," Troy answered. "Let's just say that I'm more than a little certain that he was hanging out on Broadway on the off chance that I'd be coming by."

"Off chance," Jackson cackled in response. "Right."

Troy had left town the Friday before, which put the smart money on Monday for his to return. Typically, when he left town for good, the Monday after was when he returned. If he left on a Monday, he sometimes lasted into the weekend, making the odds a little more difficult to gauge. The irony of the situation was that Troy perpetually failed to see the pattern. Every time he waved goodbye to his friends for the last time, he believed that it was the last.

Jackson didn't see what the big deal was — why Troy wanted so desperately to get out. He had his friends, had his beer, had his pick of the litter as far as the women of the town were concerned. Everyone waved when he drove past. He was still a star. *What more could a guy want?* Sure, he could be banging Jessica Alba if he had gone pro, but he could also be getting ass-raped in prison for tax evasion. *Be careful what you wish for and such.*

Troy wasted little time in grabbing boxes, and Jackson was quick to follow suit. Troy had been a roommate of the Brothers Brose for nearly a decade; none of them made great money, so it made sense. There were times when things had the propensity to become contentious since they also all worked together as well, but the brothers tended to take it out on each other, which eased tensions all around.

"Can you believe he shot another tire," Troy asked indignantly.

"Eh, give him a break. The guy gets to legally carry a gun, just daring people to give him a reason to shoot it, but nobody ever does. I feel bad for him."

It was obvious from his *I'll choke you to death and bury your body in the yard* stare that Troy didn't agree with Jackson's point of view, but he didn't press the point.

As the two men started toward the house with their assorted boxes, Jackson's brother finally graced them with his presence. Jackson let out an audible sigh when he saw his brother Kendrick moving briskly toward them. That in and of itself was nothing new: the Brose brothers had been at each other's throats since anyone could remember, but this particular sigh may have been a bit more nervous than his typical annoyed groan.

Jackson and Kendrick Brose may have been the worst twins ever. They shared a womb, but that's about as far as the similarities extended. Whereas Jackson was husky — some might call him portly; and, in fact, some had: namely

Kendrick — and less enthused about personal hygiene than things like alcohol and thrash metal — his beard sporting both glistening droplets of beer saved for later and a braid in the longest of said facial hair beneath his chin — Kendrick was always precisely groomed to the point of preening, which was odd since he, like both Jackson and Troy, worked as a mechanic. His sandy blonde hair was always kept short, and the black glasses that framed his face never had the slightest hint that they needed to be cleaned.

Kendrick raised a wraithlike hand from pencil-thin hips when he saw Troy making his way toward him and waved wholeheartedly.

"Troy, my brother!" Kendrick rejoiced as he gave Troy an awkward hug around his box. "Welcome home."

"Thanks, Drick," Troy sighed. "Great to be home."

"I think you got the name wrong. Because, you know, I'm your brother. Your twin, in fact," Jackson noted.

"Yeah, but I like Troy better," Kendrick countered.

"I can see that you guys did a lot with the place since I've been gone," Troy nodded as he took a quick gander at the house. The Brothers Brose stopped alongside him to drink in the condition of their jointly owned property, taking a moment before beginning the opening stages of their retort.

"We were going to hang banners—" Kendrick started as Troy rolled his eyes, knowing that he'd inadvertently elicited an elongated tag-team response from his friends. Jackson and Kendrick were annoying when they were fighting, but when you got them on the same side of an argument, earplugs were a requirement.

"—maybe pick up some over-the-counter drugs. Nyquil, perhaps," Jackson chimed in.

"We were even thinking about getting a prostitute," Kendrick sighed with a shrug of his shoulders, allowing the overt pain of missing out on the phantom hooker to overtake his face.

"Prostitutes," Jackson corrected. "Three of them. Twins!" Jackson shouted, drawing a scowl from Kendrick the Grammar Nazi.

"—but that was only if we were feeling froggy," Kendrick reminded Jackson. "And if we had three of them, they would be triplets, not twins," he corrected, drawing a scowl from Jackson and a smile from Troy.

This is how it started, Troy knew. The seed of an argument had been planted. He only needed to relax, and the solid Brose front would devolve into name-calling and hair-pulling soon enough.

"—and of course, we were feeling froggy, as is our wont," Jackson continued, ignoring the correction of his correction. "But you know that a hootenanny like that takes time. Much longer than three days!" He threw his hands up in Kendrick's direction, looking for support, which he got without much of a fight when Kendrick went so far as to put an arm around his brother to cement the argument.

For a moment, they stood in awkward silence. Here the brothers were, agreeing with one another — touching each other, even — trying desperately to cling to their guns in defense of their very birthright; but it was nagging incessantly at Jackson, Troy could tell, which is why he never pushed his way forward toward the house, choosing to wait for the inevitable fireworks instead. After another minute-and-a-half, posed unevenly in their spots on the front lawn, he wondered if he hadn't finally stumbled upon a subject that could unite them.

But finally: "Twins are something that are the exact same. Twin towers, Siamese twins, twin...boobies! If we had three prostitutes that looked exactly the same, they would be twins," Jackson declared, pushing his brother back a few steps.

Kendrick, for his part, smiled and forced back a chuckle. "It's not a matter of likeness, dumbass. It's a matter of numbers. Two are twins. Three are triplets. Four are quadruplets. Five are quintuplets. Six are sextuplets. You should know this because you're a twin!"

"Bullshit! I call bullshit. There's no way that they're called sextuplets because that's just ridiculous," Jackson yelled, staring confidently back at Kendrick. Then turning to Troy: "Right, Troy?"

Troy just smiled. "I think my work here is done."

As he walked toward the house, the sounds of hair-pulling and name-calling faded blissfully into the background.

"What are you going to do? Huh?" Jackson began dancing around with the box in his hand, somewhat like a bee, nothing like a butterfly. Finally, when he was out of breath, and Kendrick was thoroughly unimpressed, Jackson quickly kicked his brother in the shin before running off in the direction of Troy and the safety of the house.

Kendrick let out a howl, but Jackson was already inside, catching up to Troy where he was unloading things onto the floor of his room. Once he dropped the box on the ground, Jackson looked back into the living room to make sure that Kendrick wasn't following, and then pulled the door closed, dropping all façade of a calm demeanor.

"Dude, thank God you're back."

"Yeah, I can tell you missed me." Troy eyed an empty spot on the wall, not covered by dust, where a poster was obviously missing.

"So I stole your Hendrix poster. Get over it. What you leave here on your sabbaticals goes to the dibs system." Troy rolled his eyes, but that didn't slow Jackson down. "Anyway," Jackson restarted, glancing back to the doorway, "like I was saying—"

Troy waited for a moment, watching Jackson as he kept eyeing the door.

"Well—?"

"I think he's gay," Jackson blurted out with a hint of panic in his voice.

"Who?"

"What do you mean 'who'?" Jackson was incredulous by this point. Who else would he be talking about — Rob? The guy got more ass than a Democratic Party memorabilia collector.

"Kendrick?" Troy was too tired for this.

"Fucking duh!"

"Three days! I've been gone for three days. How gay can a person possibly become in three days?"

"You haven't seen the way he's been acting, man."

"Three days!"

"I'm telling you, dude. He's been acting all weird. And every day, he leaves early for lunch at eleven o'clock."

"So?"

"That's when these fags go for their brunches or whatever," Jackson insisted. "It's not normal."

Troy sighed. He was tired, he was annoyed, but there was no way that Jackson was going to drop the subject, ridiculous though it may be, without further discussion. He rubbed his temples in preparation, took a deep breath, and said, "For the sake of argument, let's say that your brother has, in seventy-two-hours' time, started to mysteriously love the penis. Who cares?"

The look that Troy received implied some sort of mortal sin on his part — the kind of look that, in the old days, preceded a man pulling a sword or a pistol from his belt.

"What do you mean 'who cares'? I care! I'm his brother!" Jackson was not only fuming but searching desperately for words to support his case at this point. "We shared a womb, okay? If he starts wearing pink and, to quote Jack Nicholson, 'rubbing another man's rhubarb,' how long before I'm doing the same?"

Jackson was breathing hard from the fury with which he was delivering his argument. His breath was the only sound in the room as he stood, hands on his hips, waiting for Troy to respond.

"I'm speechless. Literally speechless." That was all that Troy could manage, and he was surprised that he could manage even that. Jackson was always coming up with inanity in its wildest forms, but this was out there — even for him.

"I just want—" Jackson began, but he stopped himself short, perking his ears up like a bloodhound being hunted by some sort of effeminate, death-dealing fox. "He's coming," he half-shouted, putting his finger over his mouth in some sheer desperation that Troy just couldn't force himself to share. "Don't say anything. You've got to promise me that you're—"

"Welcome to the Thunderdome, bitch!" Kendrick screamed in his best Native war cry as he swatted the back of Jackson's knee with a mini-baseball bat.

Jackson immediately folded like a professional wrestler, only it wasn't faked in the least.

In between bouts of surprisingly rhythmic writhing on the floor, he glanced up to his sibling and offered the only thing that he could in that moment: "I hate you."

To drive his point home and further wound the pride of his much larger brother, Kendrick put a recently washed forefinger in his mouth, leaned over him, and inserted said wet finger into an ear that could have used a little attention from a trimmer — an act to which Jackson was too tired to fight. He squirmed to get away, but couldn't, his ear left feeling sticky and violated. "Seriously, the Wet Willie? You sick bastard!"

"And now *my* work here is done," Kendrick smiled as he bowed in his best Kung Fu Master pose before backing out of the room.

Troy stood over the top of Jackson, arms crossed over his chest. Jackson was still trying to dampen the saliva from his ear with his own finger, but could feel Troy standing over him. Finally, he sighed and looked up from the hardwood floor.

"You're right," Troy mocked. "That's definitely the sort of thing that a gay man would do."

A COUPLE OF HOURS after the *Thunderdome Incident*, as it was to become known, Troy was unpacked and three of the four roommates were lounging lazily in their respective lawn furniture, feet propped up on the nearest inanimate object, beer in hand.

Whereas the more affluent members of Pine Creek had their country club, Troy and his friends had the foyer of Brose

Manor: the front porch. Troy had been caught up on the goings-on during his absence, which lasted about five minutes and was mostly a play-by-play of the more colorful shits that Jackson had taken. And with the defecating conclusion to story time, the day's activities had more or less been spent. All that was left was to ride the wave of an afternoon beer buzz and sparse conversation into the night and prepare oneself for work the next morning.

Luckily, growing up in Pine Creek prepared one for such an afternoon. In a town where absolutely nothing exciting ever happened, people had to create their own excitement. There were numerous ways to accomplish such a mission, and Jackson was certainly no rookie when it came to mischievous creativity; but he and his friends had found it prudent in their ever-evolving — though certainly somewhat stagnated — adulthood to limit such activities to the weekends. They were grownups now, after all, and it reflected poorly upon themselves and their boss when they showed up to work too hung over to finish something as simple as some minor brake-work. And since Jackson was the boss, he was doubly forced to follow the rules, which aggravated him to no end.

So there they were.

"Oh, and somebody changed the sign again down at the book store," Jackson mentioned with glee.

The local book store had an old marquee on the front of the building that the owner used to display literary quotes or to advertise events. Over the past few weeks, someone had been rearranging the letters to spell crass, inappropriate things — the sort of things that kids from the middle school would laugh about — but that hadn't stopped some of the *older kids* from enjoying it as well.

"They switched the words to spell 'choad thumper,'" Kendrick finished with a roll of his eyes as Jackson chuckled nearby.

"What does that even mean?" Troy asked.

"Who knows?" Jackson answered with a smile. "But it says choad. Right up there for all the world to see."

"Where's Rob?" Troy inquired, shifting the subject from male genitalia to a more pertinent matter.

"Haven't seen him," Jackson admitted with a shrug of the shoulders.

"Last I heard, he was shacked up with What's-Her-Name over at her place."

"Her name would be Jenny, you Neanderthal," Kendrick corrected, yet again.

"Whatever." Jackson rolled his eyes more outlandishly than normal.

"That's borderline strange, isn't it? Rob, doing what some people might consider dating." Troy mused on his own thoughts before Kendrick offered his own:

"Maybe our little boy is finally growing up."

"He's getting laid!" Jackson cried. Not content that he'd cleared the issue up: "That's all there is to it. Case closed. End of discussion. Speak no more."

"Says the man who's still sleeping with his ex-wife," Kendrick tacked onto the conversation.

"What? That's just— Shut up," Jackson snorted. "Bringing Reagan into this is just a dick move, by the way."

Jackson and Kendrick shared another round of threatening glances, but were taken out of it when Troy interrupted them again.

"So, what do we have lined up tomorrow, boys?"

This time, Jackson shared a small, nervous smile with his brother, worrying Troy that he'd breached another subject over which the twins could forge an unlikely alliance. Jackson was the first to respond: "You mean 'we,' as in the two of us, and then 'you,' as in the guy who quit to move to California without giving two weeks' notice?" Jackson answered.

Despite the mock tones of resentment, Troy seemed to hardly concern himself with the question. Jackson knew that Troy's sabbaticals numbered well into the dozens by this point in their lives, and any sort of veiled threat of future unemployment was rendered null and void by the sheer number of times that Troy had come back to work for him in the past. The word resignation had become synonymous with vacation as far as their relationship as employer and employee were concerned. Besides, it didn't really bother Jackson or Kendrick. They were never so busy that they actually needed the help. It was just nice to have someone there as a buffer to their fighting to allow them to get things done.

Furthermore, Jackson's derisive answer had only been a stall tactic. He'd hoped to move Troy from the subject so as to avoid the topic of conversation that he was desperately hoping to avoid, but Troy didn't take the hint.

"I mean 'we,' as in the three of us, the way it's always been, and, God willing, the way it'll always be. Can I get an amen?" Troy asked in his best Southern Baptist voice. "No?"

The concern sprung back onto Troy's face, suggesting that maybe he thought that Jackson would fire him this time. Jackson loved to blaspheme, and any time that he passed on a mock "amen" or "hallelujah," something must be wrong.

"We've got some bodywork to do on a Caddy tomorrow,"

Jackson said through his best fake smile. "You've...got the day off."

"The day off?" Troy couldn't believe what he was hearing. Something strange was definitely afoot. "Did the Ghost of Christmas Past crawl up your ass or something? You've never given me a day off — not without putting up a fight, anyway."

"Yeah, well, let's just say that you're going to need it," was his only answer from Jackson.

Finally, Troy turned away from what was otherwise fated to be a ritualistic bitch-slap on his behalf to look at Kendrick. "Your brother's apparently lost the ability to speak in any language other than vague innuendos, so I'm going to need you to translate."

Kendrick shuffled uneasily in his chair, moving his weight from one side and then back to the other again. Up until this point, he had remained thankfully aloof from the dreaded conversation, but now, against his will, he was being sucked into it as though a Kraken had grabbed him by the foot and was dragging him beneath the waves.

"What Jackson's trying to say is..." Kendrick let the sentence taper off, tasting a bit of seawater at the back of his throat. He glanced back over at Jackson for help, but there was none forthcoming.

"Are you guys trying to kill me?" Troy bellowed. "Death by spontaneous combustion of the curiosity gland? I'm going to stick a size thirteen shoe up somebody's ass if I don't get an answer."

Jackson couldn't help but smile. Troy was a funny guy. *Spontaneous combustion of the curiosity gland*, he was snickering to himself before he looked up to catch Troy's glare.

"What we're saying is—" Jackson started, but he couldn't

bring himself to finish it. He looked over to Kendrick: "Tell him!"

"You tell him!" Kendrick defied.

"No, you tell him!"

"You—"

"Size thirteen, right here!" Troy growled, pointing down to the black sneakers on his feet.

Knowing that there was no further ado to be had, Jackson mumbled, "Eve's—"

"—back in town," Kendrick finished.

Troy smiled a dull smile. "I'm sorry. It sounded like you said that Eve was back in town."

"She is," Jackson nodded, keeping his eyes to the floorboards to avoid Troy's gaze.

"Eve?"

It was Kendrick's turn. "I'm sorry, buddy, but yeah."

"*My* Eve?"

"I hate to break the news to you, dude." Jackson bit his lip and muttered a silent curse. "Actually, I was hoping that Daryl would tell you since he saw you first, but—"

"—apparently she's more like *Ian's* Eve now." Kendrick made it a rule not to help his brother unless the situation was dire, indeed. And he counted this a dire situation. They may yet have to take the mini-baseball bat to subdue Troy for all they knew.

Troy had that crazy Tom Cruise look about him that he sometimes got when his brain was running in overdrive to wrap itself around a particular subject. There was a smile on his lips, but it wasn't so much a "knock-knock" smile as it was the smile that a serial killer got when he looked at the trophies he kept of his victims.

In his calmest voice, Troy inquired, "And who is Ian?"

Kendrick could visualize him sorting through a shoebox of bloody, severed ears and strands of hair tied with neat, little, red bows. He looked back over at Jackson, but by this time, Jackson had fallen back on his most reliable of defense mechanisms: pretending that he was asleep.

So Kendrick was forced to answer: "Ian's her husband."

3

Lawn Fairies Wear Boots

"I'm going to kill that fucking moving guy," Evelyn Hayse huffed as she slammed the front door of her new house. The wind from the force with which the door was closed propelled waves of hair across her shoulders and into her flustered face, forcing a quick, Big Bad Wolf-esque puff of air from her cheeks to clear the bangs from her forehead.

She was normally considered a very pretty woman, but during rare bouts of unabashed hostility, she tended to take on an aura of exaggerated evil, during which auburn hair turned blood red and fangs protruded from cracked gums. It was a woman's scorn that scared most, which is why she hid her fury from others like a teenager hides his pornography.

Fortunately for Evelyn, however, there was no one around to witness her outburst. She stood alone in a room full of neatly stacked boxes. It was the type of scene that would have typically thrilled her: an entire house full of things for her to organize, to place, to control. She wouldn't call herself a control freak, per se, but there was a certain way that she liked things, and she didn't apologize for that. Why should she? It was entirely reasonable for a person in a chaotic world to enjoy an amount of sanity in their home-life.

But now that she looked around the room — a room that was a box short, no less — the wind began to leave the sails of her frustration. After all, just how chaotic of a world did she live in now? This wasn't New York City, where she'd spent the last half-decade of her life. She wasn't a wrong turn away from a mugging or a slip-of-the-tongue away from a life sentence for one of her clients. This was Pine Creek. She wouldn't have to lock her doors at night if she didn't want to, and she would be defending people against traffic tickets and neighbors with trees growing onto one another's property. There hadn't been an honest-to-god felony committed in Pine Creek in over two years, and that event had been such an outlier that the trend was unlikely to repeat itself.

Maybe she didn't have to be so controlling anymore.

To test her theory, she pushed a towel from atop a nearby box and casually watched it tumble to the floor. She stared at it for what felt like an eternity. The towel stared back at her, refusing to blink.

"Blink, damn you," she commanded before glancing at her watch.

Less than a minute had passed.

She sighed a dramatic sigh as she picked the towel up from the polished hardwood floor and began to fold it into crisp corners. Moving back to Pine Creek after so many years might be harder than she had originally thought. Almost nothing had changed since she left after high school, which was just weird. She saw some of the same people on the same streets that she had seen on the very day that she left. And she couldn't be sure, but she could have sworn that the high school was watching her when she passed. It was only in her peripheral vision that she thought she noticed something, because she could hardly take her eyes off that goddamn Buffalo the whole time that it was within her line of sight.

She had done some fairly impressive things in her life for a small-town girl — not the least of which was having the good sense to leave the life of a small-town girl behind. She had graduated near the top of her class from law school, spent a summer backpacking across Europe, had a blooming career as a big-city attorney. She had done so many things by the age of twenty-nine that women would line up to strangle puppies for, but when it came to the biggest moments in her life, she could trace them all back to that stupid Buffalo.

It was before the Buffalo that she'd had her first taste of love, her first taste of heartbreak, her first taste of petty larceny; it had even been in front of the Buffalo that she'd decided that she was going to become an attorney, though drunkenly so in response to the way a particularly overzealous cop handled a simple act of public inebriation, but still.

And now, here she was: back at the scene of the crime, so to speak, living a few short blocks away from the stupid thing, and across from the golf course, no less. It was just...weird.

She gazed around the room one last time, took her hands from her hips, and offered a curt nod to the god of blind resilience. Second thoughts or not, she'd made a decision, a commitment, and there was no point in crying over spilled milk — or some other applicable Southern colloquialism that she might have ingested from the food network. Before grabbing a box labeled "garage," Eve made a mental note to try and find some Paula Dean DVDs online — colloquialisms would go over well in Southern courtrooms.

Forsaking the comfort of central air, she stepped through the doorframe that separated the blissful silence of her world from — well, the blissful silence of the outside world. The same grounds crew mowed all the yards in the Southern Comfort Addition of Pine Creek, and the odds were better of snagging the Loch Ness Monster with a Snoopy fishing rod than to catch a glimpse of the mythological grounds crew in action. Eve wasn't even sure that there was human involvement when it came to mowing there. She was simply told when she bought the house that the yard would be "taken care of." As far as she knew, a gaggle of fairies descended from the forests with an eternal hatred for towering blades of grass and waged a one-sided war on neighborhood lawns. If so, they also harbored an irrational hatred for scuffed pavement because the street in front of the house bore no evidence of activities from the day before.

Eve unlatched the lock from the gate of her picket fence, sliding the weight of the box in her hands onto her hip and glancing to her right where the car chase had taken place the day before. She had only caught a quick glance as the sheriff's cruiser had squealed away after the truck. She had opened the front door just in time to see a cloud of smoke spring up from the pavement, the black and white of the squad car and an altogether familiar forest green of a decade-plus-old truck tip over a stop sign. Though she had just caught the last few moments of the altercation, her heart didn't stop pounding for several minutes thereafter — partly because it was her first day back in Pine Creek and she was witnessing a police pursuit; but also because that truck had reminded her of someone from her past: namely, herself.

She wondered who drove that truck now. Some high school kid, no doubt, playing a kid's game with one of the new, clueless deputies. She remembered those games: the type of excitement that would land you in a cell in New York City with a felony charge, but in Pine Creek would get you a call to the parental unit and a scolding from Sheriff Reynolds. And when it happened again the next week, there were more slapped wrists and chided ears. *There's no use in ruining a kid's future over something that kids are apt to do, anyway*, Sheriff Reynolds had concluded years (and years) ago. It was partly due to the aging sheriff's lax view on juvenile delinquency that perpetuated the pattern, but his wasn't a minority view in rural towns like hers. People liked a quiet neighborhood, quiet streets, and they liked to know that they were going to find their kids asleep in their beds on Saturday and Sunday mornings.

Sheriff Reynolds would keep a closer eye on and berate to no end the more troublesome of teenagers — which Eve well knew — but they were just as probable to find themselves being punished by parents as opposed to those in uniform with tin badges.

Eve's stomach tightened as a laugh made its way up her body, her mind dancing between this memory and that, remembering times when she thought that her mother's hue would forego the human concept of color altogether and take on a demonic shade when she had received the latest call from Sheriff Reynolds. It hadn't been quite so amusing at the time, but the thought of her mom taking something so minuscule, in the scheme of things, as a public intoxication citation to mean that her first-and-only daughter would become Pine

Creek's first-and-only hooker was wildly amusing. Of course, it wasn't so much the alcohol as it was the combination of the alcohol and a certain boy whose reputation had preceded himself in the Hayse household.

That boy, of course, was:

"Troy Paulson."

Eve had been so caught up in her own thoughts that she hadn't heard the heeled footsteps approaching from across the sidewalk.

"Excuse me," Eve spat as she hurled herself around, nearly dropping the box in the process.

"Troy Paulson and Daryl Lumley acting a fool again," Rosemary Hyde responded. The woman was pushing sixty years old and refused to admit that it was over a hundred degrees outside, dressed in her Sunday finest: a flower-speckled blouse with a skirt that nearly skirted the diminutive blades of grass at her feet.

She watched curiously for a moment as Eve took her hand from her chest, which Mrs. Hyde noticed was rising and falling more quickly than it rightfully should after such a small surprise as a neighbor visiting. This would require further investigation: "I couldn't help but notice that you were looking down the street where all the damage was done yesterday," Mrs. Hyde slowly observed with a thicker-than-most Southern drawl. "Must bring back memories."

Eve smiled politely to the retired English teacher. Mrs. Hyde had been always been one of the most outspoken of teachers at Pine Creek High, and it seemed that the years hadn't affected her sense of impropriety. She had had a particular inclination toward chastising her students for things that happened neither in her classroom nor should have been any of her concern. Most students were simply embarrassed by her in-class tirades about political correctness and moral certitude, but some were unfazed to the point of boredom by the ramblings of a middle-aged widow who had always been rumored to sleep with her students, while a few went so far as to declare themselves enemy combatants.

That's all behind me now, Eve reminded herself before responding. She was a lady now, insofar as her post-high school friends were concerned: she went to the ballet, read classic literature, moved in the upper strata of social circles. Moreover, she had been the subject of vicious, Hitler-esque rants at the hands of opposing attorneys; she had learned to keep her cool, and if she could do it in a courtroom full of people and through the eyes of a television camera, she could fake her way through a few minutes of artificial civility with the old woman who lived next door.

"Mrs. Hyde, how nice to see you!" Eve feigned with her most sincere of insincere smiles. "Especially since I assumed that your crusty, old ass had died years ago!" Her smile faded momentarily as she flicked her tongue across her upper row of teeth to check for fangs.

Eve had surprised herself with the outburst, but her surprise was nothing compared to the utter indignation smeared heavily across the face of Rosemary Hyde. She may have been rude, insincere, and asinine in her comments to her new neighbor, but at least she had been civil! Mrs. Hyde opened her mouth to respond, but all she managed was an elongated, immutable sound that an old lady makes when she's been so boldly insulted — rightly so or otherwise.

Eve wasn't sure what the appropriate reaction was to her situation. The strong desire to laugh uncontrollably for minutes on end was difficult to quell, but she really didn't want to start one of those illogical, decades-long neighborly feuds for which small towns throughout the South were known. Hatfields and McCoys be damned: the rest of the world wasn't familiar with the Whitley/Hail rivalry.

Olivia Hail had been the heart of a small group of friends over on the east side of town. She hosted book clubs and card games, oversaw neighborhood watch and planning organizations, and was generally known for her overall sunny disposition. But a small nothing of a tiff between Ms. Hail and her neighbor, Ladonna Whitley, set off a chain of events that eventually led to Ms. Hail becoming locally known as Old Lady Hell. No one even remembered that her surname was Hail; to the younger generations of Pine Creek, she was simply the old lady that stood on her front porch, carelessly cursing the neighborhood children for this imagined insult or that, and generally despising the world until the day that she died.

Eve didn't want to curse the neighborhood children; she rather enjoyed children, not to mention the fact that that spiteful old bitch next door, with her thirty-year head-start, would probably still outlive her like a vindictive zombie so the feud could never die. This really wasn't the new start that she was looking for now that she was back in town, so, pain her though it may, things would have to be made right.

"Mrs. Hyde, I would like to apologize," Eve began. She smiled, somewhat more convincingly than her last attempt, and took a deep breath. "What I meant to say was—"

"No, I think that pretty much covers it!" a voice declared to interrupt the apology that Eve hadn't quite mapped out yet. Daryl was striding from his cruiser, a bottle of wine in his hand and a smile beneath his mustache. When he finally made his way to the fence to stand before the two ladies, he held out the bottle toward Eve, never taking his eyes off of Mrs. Hyde.

"Crusty old bitch?" Daryl chuckled in question form. "Sounds like a fairly accurate description to me. And I take down descriptions for a living, mind you."

Mrs. Hyde silently cursed herself for not hearing Daryl approach. There were two things in the world that she hated to admit: that she was getting older, and that she was unable to keep a snide remark prepared for each and every opportunity. She was a student of literature, after all! Would Dickens be caught without a quip? Would Twain or Wilde? Hardly.

She watched Daryl and Eve exchange something of an awkward, *trying too hard to be friendly* hug, fighting to both note the exchange for future reference and investigation, and also to continue trolling the depths of her wit to ably form a retort before that delinquent deputy had the chance to think that he'd gotten the better of her.

"Daryl Lumley!" Mrs. Hyde reprimanded. "Does your mother know that you use that type of language with upstanding members of the community? And even if she doesn't, do you know who will? That's right, mister. Jesus!"

Daryl handed the bottle of wine to Eve, then went to his default move that worked to frighten deviant juvenile offenders and annoy uppity old ladies: placing his right hand on his pistol where it hung in its holster from his belt. Mrs. Hyde didn't seem overly amused by the gesture, so Daryl went to the next-best thing: unfastening the button that held the pistol firmly in said holster. Though the old woman merely rolled her eyes, Daryl felt as though he'd proven his point.

"Mrs. Hyde, if Jesus was going to engage in any sort of

brimstone on my behalf, he'd have done it a *long* time ago," Daryl replied, putting an emphasis on the word "long," as he let his Southern drawl become a bit too *Deliverance* for Eve's liking. "Like that time I had sex with my eleventh-grade English teacher!"

Mrs. Hyde didn't bother to even put her hand on her chest to feign any sort of indignity this time. It was a quick, military-esque about-face, followed by the timeliest walk-of-shame that high heels would allow, past the various blooms of her garden and through an oversized, gothic front door.

Eve stared for what seemed like an eternity, mouth agape and bittersweet victory in her eyes. *What the hell just happened?* After the front door of Mrs. Hyde's house slammed with all the indignity that she hadn't been able to voice herself, Eve turned her gaze to Daryl without so much as bothering to alter the ridiculousness of the expression she wore. There were words, she was sure — words that could express…something — but they were whirling about the vortex that was her brain in something that resembled what she assumed would be an LSD trip.

Daryl, for his part, played the part of a seasoned Deadhead, so long now impervious to the delusions of the lysergic experience that the feeling was merely quaint. He continued on with the greeting that had been interrupted: "Finally decide to grace us with your presence after ten whole years? Those hippies in New York must have been something else."

Eve smiled — at least she meant to smile. What had happened, more factually, was that her expression went slightly askew by some four degrees to the left, and her head tilted more forwardly as a chuckle escaped from between her clenched teeth. She was becoming increasingly aware of the fact that she must have sported the countenance of a Down Syndrome patient, but there wasn't a tool within the repertoire of her nervous system that had the authority to do anything about it.

It was a bit later, after the conversation had run its course and she was, again, standing in an otherwise empty room, surrounded by boxes full of her new life, that Eve realized the cause of her momentary spasticity: it was way too easy to slip back into her old life. The way that she had been jilted so effortlessly into becoming that girl from high school would merit some introspective Lara Croft-ing at some point; but for the time being, she would have settled simply for the ability to control the useless oratorical device on her face.

Finally, as Daryl raised something of a bushy eyebrow and pushed the chrome-framed aviators to the brim of his nose, something inside of Eve snapped. Just like that, the muscles in her face defaulted back into standard operating procedure; with the motor functions, along came speech, and Eve was free to move about the cabin of normalcy as though nothing out of the ordinary had occurred.

"It's New York, Daryl, not California," Eve laughed, pushing a stray strand of hair from her face to behind her ear. "They're not hippies."

"Are they liberals?"

"Most of them."

"Then they're hippies."

Eve smiled wholeheartedly as she quickly snatched the glasses from his face, sliding them over her own to shield her eyes from the sun that was gleaming from over Daryl's shoulder. Without further ado, sensing the smallest of lulls in the conversation before he could change the subject, Eve punched

Daryl as hard as she could in the shoulder, receiving a yelp that shouldn't rightly have come from such a sizable man.

"You never told me that you had sex with her!"

"Who?"

"'Who,'" Eve mocked. "Who do you think? The dinosaur from next door! I didn't even know those rumors were true!"

"Most rumors are," Daryl laughed as he stole his recently stolen sunglasses back from Eve's head. "Like you moving back to town with a new fiancé."

Eve laughed again — a bit less enthusiastically this time. "You heard about that, huh?"

"I did," he nodded. "A lot of people heard about that."

Daryl let the conversation taper down with the last remark, watching as Eve momentarily eyed the ground, ostensibly because of the fact that the bastard had bogarted her glasses; she even held a saluting posture when she raised her head to sell the ruse, but she knew that tiptoeing around the inevitable was pointless.

"How is he?"

"You tell me," Daryl quipped.

"What's that supposed to mean?"

"He found out about your homecoming yesterday evening — plus-one and all — hopped in Cheryl, and no one's seen him since. The way I figure, he came to talk to you, you killed him and hid the body in your basement."

"You are such a goddamn drama queen."

"Or he just got drunk and did something stupid. Come to think of it, that's probably the more likely of the two."

"You think?"

"I don't know. You mind if I look in your basement?"

They shared another round of laughter, each getting more

awkward by the moment, before the police radio that Daryl wore attached to his shoulder like *Robocop* exploded with a burst of nearly inaudible screeches. Eve had a sneaking suspicion that it was the dialect of the Lawn Fairies coming over the radio, coaxing one of their human subjects into doing their evil bidding, but she hesitated to say anything on the off-chance that they'd given him a license to kill. It wasn't a long wait for an answer, though, because Daryl was apparently fluent in Lawn Fairy:

"Yeah, so he got drunk and did something stupid."

With that, Daryl turned and headed back toward his cruiser. Eve waived halfheartedly as he stepped across the sidewalk and into the car.

"Thanks for the wine," she added, but a quick wail of a siren was all that she received for her effort.

"I'll be back to check that basement later!" Daryl yelled as he squealed away from the scene.

"Goddamn drama queens," Eve muttered to herself with a shake of the head.

Out of the corner of her eye, she caught a glimpse of a curtain fluttering from a first-floor window of Mrs. Hyde's house, and she knew already that her recently forged nemesis was on the phone with some old biddy or another around town.

Moving back to Pine Creek after so many years might be harder than she had originally thought.

4

Slouching Toward Monogamy

*I*t's *raining really hard.*

It wasn't a really complex thought in the scheme of things — monosyllabic, for the most part, and on the toddler side of the vocabulary spectrum — but, at the time, it seemed a miracle that Troy was able to pluck the words from his skull to complete the thought: mostly because he suspected that his skull was in a million-and-one pieces.

What had happened the night before wasn't particularly clear; it was awash in a haze of variegated pandemonium and polluted by the unrelenting aftertaste of cheap, stubborn whiskey that refused to cede the battle and follow its fate down the esophagus to the stomach. It was hanging around the back of his throat in a knot that threatened retribution, and against his will, Troy was forced to open his eyes in an effort to stop the room from spinning.

The room, as it turned out, was the cab of Cheryl, none the cleaner from a day home than she had been on the road; more cluttered, in fact, than she had appeared in Troy's last conscious memory by a further assortment of beer bottles — most of them in the floor now, the apparent result of a sudden loss of momentum. The rain, as it turned out, hadn't been quite what Troy had expected either. There were raindrops, and then there were gushing torrents of liquid cascading from the sky as if an angry deity were preparing a flood.

As his eyes slowly began the cumbersome process of coming into focus, Troy, too, tried to focus, throwing every ounce of energy at his disposal toward the windshield. He was starting to reconsider his initial assessment of this also being the work of God, because it was becoming apparent that it was the work of aliens. An assortment of colors were being levied into the cab through the flowing water, creating an insanely chaotic fractal masterpiece like a Pink Floyd laser show, making it all the more difficult to concentrate, but simultaneously lending credence to the alien theory. Like a cheap liquor store camera that had been trying to focus upon the faces of the men who were robbing it, only to finally focus on the backs of their heads as they made their escape, Troy's eyesight finally righted itself.

With all of his might, he flipped the windshield wipers on, and, in between tides, he saw two local cops, guns drawn, approaching Cheryl from their respective positions beside the flashing lights of a squad car, yelling some theretofore uninterpretable commands in Troy's direction.

Immediately and instinctively, Troy turned the windshield wipers off. He wasn't sure why, but it seemed like the right thing to do, all things considered. It didn't necessarily make him invisible, but, if nothing else, it might lay the groundwork for his insanity plea some months down the line.

"Shit, shit, shit!" He looked around the cab one last time,

frantically searching for something — anything — that might help him in the situation. Unless he planned on clubbing the officers with empty beer bottles, however, his options were pretty much limited to grabbing the grease-stained white shirt from the floorboard and waiving it in the most docile fashion imaginable to avoid being shot.

As he contemplated whether or not the empty beer bottles may be the better alternative, something happened. A series of sharp noises. The cessation of the Pink Floyd lights. Then the calm of running water.

Down in the floorboard, grasping the white shirt meant to be his ensign of surrender, Troy was a bit befuddled. He was jumping ship on his alien idea and swimming back to his original divinity theory. There had to be some sort of cosmic influence in the most inane set of circumstances that he could imagine. There was a god. And he was fucking with Troy.

Once more — with a bit more caution this time — Troy pulled himself up eye-level with the steering wheel before gently flipping the windshield wipers back to their *on* position.

No good. The lowest setting didn't do nearly enough to turn the tide of the maelstrom that was bombarding the windshield. Almost hesitantly, as if not wanting to anger whatever — or whomever — was influencing events, Troy slowly turned the switch another dial, again and again, until the wipers were working at full force. Peeking over the steering wheel and into the dewy distance at nothing in particular, he was beginning to think that he was still asleep until:

"What's up, cracker?!"

The voice was that of Troy's friend Rob, entirely harmless in octave and intent, but a voice for which Troy wasn't particularly primed in that moment; a long, vulgar honk of Cheryl's horn was the response when Troy tested the strength of the welds holding her door closed, pushing hard with his legs in the direction away from the unexpectedness of Rob's voice and inadvertently triggering the horn in the process.

"What the fuck is wrong with you?" Rob inquired, an amused smile on his face at finding his friend in such a stupor.

"Me? What the fuck is wrong with you, sneaking up on a man like that?!"

"Oh, you mean a man that's tactfully parked on top of a fire hydrant in the middle of town in front of his favorite statue?" To prove his point, Rob opened the door further behind him so Troy could see the Buffalo.

Rob, for his part, had come prepared, dressed semi-appropriately, as he was inclined to do, in a red raincoat over a white tank top with some shorts and his trademark sandals that he wore regardless of season, a bit Goldilocks-ian with his shaggy blondish hair hanging down into his eyes. His otherwise plain, pallid face was accented by a silver hoop eyebrow ring that he felt that he'd outgrown years ago but had trouble removing. No one in the group thought that he was great-looking, but it was widely agreed, though hesitantly so, that it was between himself and Troy in the looks department, if only he would drop the hippie garb. Troy, however, didn't find himself currently concerned with Rob's mode of dress.

"Stupid Buffalo," Troy panted. "I should have known he had something to do with this."

"Yeah, it was the Buffalo that drank and drove, you selfish prick."

For the most part, drinking and driving hadn't taken on the degree of wickedness in rural parts of the state like it had in its urban parts. It was frowned upon, to be sure, but there were miles upon miles of open dirt roads out in the country that were a veritable redneck playground. A thirty-pack and a tank of gas, getting lost in the absolute middle of nowhere: that was the way to stay off the sheriff's radar. As long as they kept well enough to themselves, Sheriff Reynolds preferred them out in the proverbial boondocks rather than drinking at the Watering Hole — Pine Creek's only bar — because the town didn't have a cab system, a public bus, a trolley or a horse-driven buggy, for that matter. The only public transportation home from the bar was in the back of a squad car, which is why Troy and his friends always played rock, paper, scissors to designate a sober driver. Of course, that rarely worked, as Jackson was notoriously bad at the game, and he would usually end up far more intoxicated than the others by the night's end. So they often walked back from the bar.

To Rob's point, Troy hung his head, knowing that he'd been had: "I know."

Rob allowed a moment to pass so Troy could wallow in his own self-induced misery, reflecting on the irony that he, the town drug dealer, was dealing in the currency of moral superiority.

"Well, are you going to sit there and mope until they come back or are we gonna get the hell out of here?" Rob half-yelled, not content that he'd gotten all he could out of the moral superiority experience that he so rarely got to enjoy.

"I—"

"Shut up, and let's go!" Rob was three-quarters drill sergeant by that point. "And you should stop cheating on your taxes!" So that last point wasn't particularly pertinent (or true, insofar as he knew), but after he told Troy what he did to get the cops to leave the scene of the crime, he'd most likely lose the high ground and the mountain that he was standing upon — and, as Old Man Frazier said, you always milk the cow until it's dry.

TROY HAD SHUFFLED HIMSELF loose of the conscious coil as soon as they got back to the house. Rob did his best to fill him in on the details of his evil, master plan, but Troy — adrenaline rush and all — had barely kept his eyes open through the prologue, much less the specific, evil details. To ensure that said (evil) master plan had a decent chance of survival in spite of Troy's hangover and subconscious rumblings, Rob wrote a bare-bones version onto a sticky note and stuck it to Troy's forehead; not the most impressive method of delivery, granted, but it wasn't like he had access to any Inspector Gadget-esque exploding notes; plus, he was a sticky note kind of guy, so it seemed appropriate.

Closing the door behind him, Rob quietly left Troy's room and ducked through a dingy, unlit corridor into the living room, a rather nondescript dwelling for the most part, with the exception of the oversized television and various gaming systems. The carpet was verging on shag — not quite of the era, but in the same vein — a dirty, brown mess of a floor that was covered sporadically by this broken-down piece of furniture or that. The ultimate bachelor pad, given that said bachelors were poor: money spent on entertainment, typically of the technological variety, and skimped on everything else.

With a sigh, Rob rolled himself lazily across the back of the couch and into the waiting arms of his girlfriend, "What's Her Name." Jenny, he reminded himself — Jenny was her name. In the beginning, he remembered solely based on the *Forrest Gump* annunciation, and he would employ a deeply Alabaman, deeply over-the-top Southern drawl when he said it in his mind. Jenny wondered why he would sometimes cackle when he said her name, but she assumed that it was the weed. In the months since, however, he had become somewhat attached to Jenny and, for the most part, had no problem remembering her name; and if he did, he blamed it on the weed.

She was an attractive girl, this Jenny: plucked from the tallest trees of the Pine Creek rainforest, far above the rabble on the forest floor where the sun hadn't the slightest chance to shine. She sat upright with Rob's head in her lap, pushing the hair first from her face, then his hair from his, to offer a kiss for no reason whatsoever. Her hair was longer and darker than Rob's, straight and the darkest of browns that verged harrowingly close to black. Where he was a perpetual whitey, regardless of season, she was moderately-to-well tanned. She was also quite short. He liked them short, for whatever reason — maybe it was to make him feel more masculine, but he liked it when she stood on her tippy-toes to kiss him. It was the tanned skin and the hair, though, that did it for him the most; maybe because she was the opposite of him and he liked that, but it could be just as much about the dark allure and mystique that she conjured in his mind, like an old-world gypsy; or maybe it was her legs, come to think of it: thick and profound in all the right places. Or maybe, yet again, it was the tone with which she delivered her discourse against his own fountain of bullshit that he found difficult to suppress from spewing forth from his lips. Even with Jackson in the group, Rob was considered the resident bullshitter, and Jenny was the kind of girl that called him on it every time. He liked that, too.

That is where Rob found himself: unable to narrow down precisely what it was that he liked about this girl. He had even found himself naming features aside from the physical ones that he appreciated about her, which was worrisome.

"I can't believe you called the cops on Grady Byers," she said with a half-laugh, playfully slapping Rob across the cheek.

"I didn't call the cops," Rob answered. "I mean, I *did* call the cops, but not specifically on Grady. I didn't mention names or anything."

"You might as well have."

"I could have been talking about anyone walking around town in the general vicinity of that playground with a loaded rifle."

"You told him that you saw a twelve-point buck wandering around the park!" Though she put up quite the convincing argument, Jenny wasn't mad — quite the opposite, actually: growing up a preacher's daughter in a preacher's town, the excitement of dating the closest thing to a bad boy the town had was the closest she could get to her father disowning her.

"That I did," Rob laughed. It's not like Grady was going to prison or anything. It was deer season, after all, and it was legal to hunt in the park. With the media focus on gun violence, however, the police could hardly ignore a call about a crazy man with a gun roving about town, could they? Did Rob like piggybacking on the misfortune of others? Not so much — but he liked it better than his standing by as his best friend went to jail.

"What am I going to do with you," Jenny asked in a faux tone of disapproval. "It's like I'm dating a high school boy."

"Yes, but a high school boy with a well-above-average penis," he reminded her. "I feel that that the extra length cancels out any immaturity that you may have to occasionally deal with."

A muffled laugh was her response.

"What are you going to tell Sheriff Reynolds about Troy's truck being there?" she asked.

"Don't worry your pretty little head about it. Just let the master work."

Another muffled laugh.

These muffled laughs of Jenny's had the propensity to become annoying under the wrong circumstances, and they had signaled many a beginning to many an argument in the past. As far as Rob was concerned, they were her only truly annoying quality. In this particular instance, however, Rob was willing to allow them to float safely past the safety nets of civil conversation. Anything that he could do at this point to discourage her from asking about Eve would be well worth the forsaken masculinity discarded by allowing a small penis joke to pass without correction. Eve — and Eve in regard to Troy and his obsession with her, in particular — was a topic that was better left un-broached, as it inevitably drew questions of commitment and eternal devotion which would inevitably follow a well-tread roundabout to come back and bite him in the ass on the subject of his own inability to commit and/or devote.

On cue, as if she'd been privy to each hopeful little thought that he had thought in vain, Jenny broached the un-broachable:

"Tell me about Eve."

Her voice was inquisitive, seemingly without malice or

forethought — certainly without implied foreshadowing of an impending clusterfuck that would echo into a federal investigation. Still, it wasn't the questioner, but the question that was inherently evil. She had stumbled upon the Necronomicon through no fault of her own, and it was tugging incessantly at the loose threads of her soul to ask the un-askable.

"What about her?" Rob had played this game before.

"She's got to be some sort of awesome for Troy to still be hung up on her after ten years."

"She's okay."

"Okay? Ten years. That's a decade!"

"I'm familiar with the western convention of timekeeping." If he didn't win the game this time, there would never be any winning to be had.

"I mean, would you still be hung up on me in ten years if I broke your heart?

So close.

Ours is a spiteful god, Rob thought. *Goddamn Troy*. This is how it always happened: eventually, someone in the group would let the story of Troy and Eve slip (Jackson, in this case); then the sewn seed would germinate in the mind of whomever Rob was dating at the time (Jenny, in this case) until it became this magnum opus of a love story to which Rob was attached; and in their minds, Rob, by association, played the dual role of both himself and Troy in this tragedy: the perpetual stoner with a perpetual dedication to his woman. Now, with Eve in town and Troy basically a puppet with a drunken puppet-master, the fairy-tale ending was pretty much guaranteed to be the least enjoyable iteration of the debacle to date.

"I've got to take a leak," Rob answered. It wasn't quite a declaration of undying love, but it also wasn't a resounding *no*.

Besides, Jenny knew that he was weird, so, at the very least, it could buy him a few minutes to think in the bathroom.

Just as snakily as he'd slithered onto the couch some minutes before with thoughts of mid-morning monogamy on his mind, so then his body flowed, seemingly without effort, off the couch, onto the floor, and across the room — with thoughts of monogamy on the mind, still, but with far less erotic flare than before. The noose was tightening; he could feel it sliding ever-so-gently across his Adam's apple, teasing effortlessly what was sure to be the most violent of finalities that a manhood could endure: *monogamy*. The word had taken on a sadistic resonance within the last few moments, free-falling from playful coital suggestion to an evilly cadenced repetition of phrase that hyenas howl to one another in the mighty jungle.

Monogamy.

He was halfway down the hallway, cursing his luck and fighting off fits of hysterical laughter that kept trying to force themselves from his esophagus against all reason. Focused on the obvious, he was hardly in the mindset for:

Monogamy.

Rob slipped through a door, pushing it soundly closed behind him with as little force as possible to avoid making any sort of noise with which Jenny might make some sort of snap inference — or notice that he'd ducked deftly into his bedroom instead of the bathroom.

Standing softly in the serene darkness that only tinfoil-covered windows would allow on a bright summer morning, Rob leaned back against the recently shut door and sighed heavily. Muscle memory had always proven the definitive tool in Rob's arsenal for the few skills he had: guitar, video games, and — well, those were the only skills that he had acquired so far in life, but he was still young...in some cultures. Annoyed that he had opened the age door at that particular time, it was at least comforting to learn that said set of skills also applied to Scooby Doo-esque moments of joint-lighting in what amounted to the total darkness of space. Inhaling ever-so-deeply, Rob held his breath as long as his lungs would allow before releasing what he imagined was an insanely impressive smoke ring. Still, he hesitated to flick the nearby light switch on the off chance that said smoke ring had actually spelled out the word *monogamy*.

Finally, after any possible ethereal wordplay had dissipated — and with a few random swipes in the air around him to assist said dissipation — Rob ran his hand morosely across the wall, fumbling to find the light switch that he had found in similar conditions a thousand times before. After a few annoying moments, and with less satisfaction than was normal, the dim bulb hanging clumsily from the ceiling hummed to life, revealing the contents of Rob's brain in a world of sticky yellow notes.

His obsession with sticky notes had begun in high school — roundabout the same time that he'd discovered marijuana, oddly enough. It had seemed that he had always had the most pristinely sublime ideas when he was stoned: symphonic deliriums of uninhibited genius that would rival the thoughts of Einstein with a Shakespearian turn of phrase. But that genius was never long for this world, as it was inevitably whisked away in sobriety's wake, lost in the annals of time, a sacrifice to the gods of deviance and mind-altering drugs.

It was only after he had awoken one particular afternoon — feeling a rush of vast confidence that he had successfully rebutted the theory of relativity the night before — that Rob had begun the process of jotting down his thoughts whilst high. As a result, his room had become a shrine to otherworldly certitude, random half-thoughts strewn wildly about and stuck to every crevasse with aging adhesives.

As he was a traditionalist, yellow was his color of choice, a nod to those who had come before him in the community of forgetful brethren, stoner or otherwise.

Once Rob had made his way safely through the minefield of assorted junk that was his bedroom floor, he thrust himself in one crude motion into the waiting arms of a collection of plush bedspreads and pillows. He didn't bother fighting the throngs of layered blankets as he usually did in an effort to place himself in a catlike coma position so that he could float calmly away from the shores of consciousness. Instead, he sighed as he pulled a pillow from beneath his back and placed it behind his head, grabbing at a stack of sticky notes from a nearby nightstand. With a purposefully placed pen from the windowsill, Rob scratched a single word onto the pad.

Even with the soothing combination of black ink on the bright yellow paper, Rob could barely stand to ingest the word into his consciousness without feeling as though he would vomit it back up through his ears at any moment.

Monogamy.

Fuck.

There was a reason that Rob was so averse to the term that had recently overtaken his life and everything that it implied. It wasn't so much that he could be categorized as an outright misogynist that saw serial dating as a way to besmirch the female gender. He wasn't even the Johnny Appleseed type who just wanted to spread his seed (affected by THC to the point of impotence, though it may be). His aversion stemmed from somewhere much deeper than the superficiality of cultural peer-bonding. It pained him to admit it, but Rob had a full-on Freudian complex. It was nothing so bad as an Oedipal obsession, though, at times, he wished it were something so simple.

The fact of the matter was that Rob was the product of a whiskey tango household. Even in his head, it was hard to bring himself to think of his upbringing by using the words white trash: whiskey tango, the McCormicks, Joe Dirt — white trash by any other name would still smell just as god-awfully horrid, but at least funny nicknames and fictional characters, cartoon or otherwise, lugged with them entertaining anecdotes with which Rob might later amuse himself while comparing them to his own life.

There was a difference between poor white people and poor white trash that Rob liked to distinguish amongst those with whom he was close enough to actually discuss the issue — a group comprised solely of Troy, Daryl, Kendrick, and Jackson — and that was that poor white people generally viewed their station in life with a healthy dose of disfavor and, thus, used every tool at their disposal to improve said station. White trash, however, was a breed peculiar in its inability to realize that it was at a disadvantage, one whose denizens, when left to their own devices, would perpetuate generation after generation of uneducated, hapless souls who not only tolerated their inborn lifestyle but reveled in it. They also liked NASCAR. Rob's family, much to his chagrin, was of the latter camp, NASCAR and all.

It wasn't the fact that they were poor that formed the grudge against his parents that Rob still harbored to that day.

He, himself, could hardly be confused with the bourgeoisie of Pine Creek, much less any other more affluent community. It was that he had been alone in his quest to uproot himself from the tainted soil from which he and his whiskey tango forbearers had been conceived in an effort to ascend through the social ranks to the modest status of poor white person.

His parents weren't bad people; they were just content to cope with their meager existence with the few mechanisms at their disposal: predominately recreational drug and alcohol use. Rob's friends thought it a bit hypocritical that he had created this chasm of resentment between himself and his parents over a practice in which he, too, took part. The difference, he explained, was that he wasn't responsible for another life. Insofar as Rob was concerned, he could smoke himself stupid, snort this substance or that until white powder spewed from his eye sockets, and shoot heroin into his testicles to his heart's desire — not that he indulged in any of such things, with the exception of the smoking-himself-stupid part — as long as it was solely his own safety and well-being that required his full attention He had vowed at a very young age that, much like Johnny Cash, he, too, would walk the line if ever a moment occurred in his life that he found himself plus wife and kid.

When the issue was completely boiled down to its base components, the crux of the matter was that Rob didn't see himself as the father type at that particular point in his life — not that Jenny was pushing for a ring and stroller, but the mating dance of the stoner only required one false step to collapse into the mating dance of the soccer dad.

And Rob hated soccer just about as much as he loved smoking weed.

Tossing the sticky note onto the floor, he took a final hit from the joint that he had carelessly laid upon the nightstand within arm's reach and mused momentarily on whether or not his moral quandary would make sense if explained to Jenny. While she was a cool chick, to be sure, he wasn't satisfied that she would understand his dilemma — or would she?

There was something about her that Rob couldn't quite explain that produced a sense of calm about him. He laid back more fully onto the pillow beneath his head and dove deeper into the abyss of blankets covering his bed, allowing himself the luxury of a fantasy in which his quandary was solved. Though Rob had quickly concluded after their conversation earlier that his and Jenny's relationship was fast approaching an untimely, Wyle E. Coyote sort of end, in his fantasy, there simply was no such end in sight. In his fantasy, he continued to gallivant joyfully through the wonderland that was Jenny's body, Jenny's mind, Jenny's soul. Toward the end of the fantasy, Rob frowned: even in his fantasies, he was unable to concentrate solely on sex.

"What the fuck is wrong with me?" he asked to no one in particular. And though no one in particular was his intended audience, someone in particular had evaded his Spidey sense and entered the room with the furtive grace of a master ninja.

"I don't know," Jenny replied. "What the fuck is wrong with you?"

Rob sighed.

This would require some sort of scheme.

5

The Smell of Perfidy in the Morning

Daryl had been a sheriff's deputy for going on eleven years, having joined shortly after he graduated high school, and he absolutely loved his job. There were, of course, downsides to a vocation in public service, as there were with any job, but the lax atmosphere in which rural law enforcement was approached always outweighed the negatives, as far as Daryl was concerned. It allowed him to be involved with the community in ways that an urban cop might not: clocking the speed of high school kids on the quarter-mile as they drag-raced on Old Highway 51, for example, was a favorite pastime that ingratiated him toward the town's youth; rescuing cats from trees and ushering fugitive livestock back into their respective homes nearly always earned him a baked good of some sort from the village elders; not to mention that being a man in uniform never hurt when it came to wooing the female population of Pine Creek.

There was the occasional annoyance that he had to deal with that soured his mood on the job as a whole, but they were mostly few and far between. For instance, someone had been rearranging letters to spell dirty words on a local business marquee; and though it wasn't specifically Daryl's job to take care of and was hardly the end of the world, certain members of the public at large felt that Daryl should be the one to take care of it nonetheless and wouldn't allow him a moment of silence until he had promised to look into it.

Aside from that, he wrote a few speeding tickets here and there — mostly to out-of-towners or the assholes that he hated in high school who had, likewise, failed to leave Pine Creek — and every so often he got the opportunity to arrest one of the village idiots who got a bit too cavalier in their disdain for authority while standing a bit too close to this legal gray area or that. There was also the local scumbaggery that regularly required his attention: all those smalltime drug-dealers, big-time alcoholics, teenage vandals, and white trash domestic disturbances that cropped up with the consistency and familiarity of crop circle patterns. All in all, however, the sheriff's deputy game was a quiet one in Murray County, Oklahoma.

There was a predictability about the job that Daryl liked. There had only been one major incident a few years prior that had rocked the community, but it was the exception to the rule and was really the only blip on the radar during the whole of Daryl's career. He considered it a perk to know that he'd probably be arresting Lawrence Boggs on Friday Night at the Watering Hole and that he'd spend the bulk of his Mondays sleeping in his cruiser on Main Street, pretending to clock speeders. There was, though, one large question of possible malleability in his future that concerned him: Sheriff Reynolds would be retiring next year at the end of his current term. Daryl had worked exclusively for Sheriff Reynolds, but a new sheriff would be sworn in soon enough — one that could not only upheave the entire system of law enforcement that the sheriff's office had operated under for the past twenty-some-odd years that Sheriff Reynolds had been in charge, but one that could fire the lot of deputies and bring in his own group of subordinates.

This was worrisome to Daryl.

He ran his fingers across the whole of his mustache, flattening out the individual hairs as best he could where they stood wily and defiantly away from the others like narcissists craving attention. This was the routine through which he achieved his modicum of chi when he found himself agitated, usually when Troy evaded his arrest attempts while playing their beloved game of cops and robbers. Having been part of the weekly poker game with his co-workers for a decade-plus had made this routine common knowledge amongst the ranks of the sheriff's department.

"What's crawled up your ass?" Sheriff Reynolds grunted in the form of a question from across the cruiser, noting the plight of the mustache with a nod.

Daryl glanced across the cruiser from the passenger seat to Sheriff Reynolds where he navigated the car along sleepy city streets with bullish apathy. The old man was puffing a cigarette — which was against policy both while a) on the job and b) in the cruiser, not that he cared — as he waited impatiently for an answer to his question.

"Nothing," Daryl answered half-heartedly, as he continued to thoughtlessly stroke his facial hair.

"Uh huh." That was the typical response from the grizzly old sheriff: a truncated gruff of a syllable or two, especially when he knew that he detected the taste of bullshit.

The old man's hair had been gray for as long as Daryl had worked for him, had started graying shortly after he'd first been elected to office, in fact. Like Daryl, Sheriff Reynolds liked the slow pace of the job, but that didn't mean that it was without its headaches. There was the city council, the county board of officials, the local cops — reasons, all, that he had been graying for the better part of twenty years. He also blamed them for the extra weight that he had been carrying around for the past several years, though that could as easily be explained by the fact that his divorce had left him eating fast food more often than not for most every meal. The buttons on his uniform clung for dear life to the thread that sustained them while the fabric of the uniform sported various coffee and food stains. There was a time when a shit was given about such things, but that time had passed long ago for all but the most formal of occasions. At that point in his career, a number of things took precedence over a clean shirt. One of those things was keeping control of his town in the face of belated teenage angst.

"Are you going to have a problem with what we're about to do?" the sheriff questioned.

It took some effort for Daryl to contain a smile that wanted nothing more than to curl up with his mustache for an afternoon of passion. Sheriff Reynolds knew, of course, about Daryl and Troy's ongoing game of vehicular pursuit and their lifelong friendship. He worried that forcing Daryl to possibly arrest him might be a conflict of interest and he could have brought someone else along to question the Paulson boy. Sheriff Reynolds — unbeknownst to his deputies, however, including Daryl himself — was hoping to convince Daryl to run as a candidate for the office that he would soon vacate.

Before he could throw his support behind Daryl publicly, though, he needed to know that he could handle the pressure of having to do the right thing when the right thing needed to be done, regardless of to whom it needed to be done.

Unbeknownst to Sheriff Reynolds, Daryl had absolutely no problem whatsoever arresting his friends when they were in the wrong. He had arrested them several times when they hadn't fucked up — just for fun. And arresting Troy for drunk driving — in town, no less — was something that Daryl was actually looking forward to with no small smidgen of glee. He knew that, with Eve back in town, someone needed to get out in front of Troy's behavior before it was allowed to spiral out of control and into full-blown fuckery, which was more of an inevitability than a possibility.

"No, sir," Daryl answered. "The job's the job."

"That it is," Sheriff Reynolds agreed between puffs of smoke. "It's been a while since Mr. Paulson has been in my crosshairs. This wouldn't have anything to do with our new lawyer in town, would it?"

"I couldn't say, Sheriff," Daryl answered falsely. "I haven't talked to Troy in a few days. I don't even know if he knows that she's back."

"I like my balls, son."

"I'm sure you do, sir."

"If I had to pick a favorite, I'd say that it was the right one. Don't know why. I'm just partial to it."

"That's a fine choice, Sheriff."

Though the conversation might seem somewhat unconventional to someone from outside Murray County Sheriff's Department or from outside the population of adult males throughout the South in general, Daryl was comfortable with an in-depth conversation about his superior's testicles. This was typical of how conversations were had and points were made, and there was a point to be made shortly, he felt certain — or at least he hoped.

"I'd bet my right nut that Mr. Paulson found out that Mrs. Hayse is back in town, went on a bender, and did something stupid."

"I can't argue with that logic."

"It's not logic. It's common sense. I never had any more trouble from Mr. Paulson than I did from you before that girl shit on his heart," Sheriff Reynolds released along with the last breath of smoke from the cigarette that he was tossing out of the cracked window of the cruiser as it pulled up to the curb of the Brose house. "Let's get this over with."

THE TIRED KNOCK of a soon-to-be retired sheriff wasn't enough to shock Troy out of the coma that he had induced the night before. The ensuing knocks of a yeti-esque, possible sheriff-of-the-future, however, were a different story, echoing throughout the house with the ferocity of a beanstalk-descending giant hitting the ground.

Troy bolted upright in bed from the depths of what he assumed must have been a nightmare, judging from the amount of sweat that was coursing from the pores in his forehead. Though he didn't suspect it possible, his head was pounding even worse than it had when he found himself so rudely awakened earlier that morning in front of the goddamn Buffalo. An initial moment of panic set in as a brief blindness scare gripped the whole of his consciousness, but a quick swipe of his hands pulled back a sticky note covering each eyelid.

With that crisis averted, Troy took to the task of reading each note, but it wasn't an easy task based solely on his blurred vision, much less due to the fact that the sweat had caused the ink on the notes to run. He could only make out the words "Cheryl," "Reynolds" and "jail" on one note and "Jackson" and "blowjob" on the other.

The first note didn't bode well, but the second held disturbing consequences.

Another round of world-shattering knocks at the front door caused a cessation of Troy's heartbeat and caused him to quickly devolve into full-on panic mode.

SHERIFF REYNOLDS WAS BECOMING IMPATIENT, as evinced by the old-school scowl growing across the breadth of his face, leading Daryl to briefly consider whether or not he should show some initiative, feign probable cause, and kick the door down.

Here, he was torn. There were few things that Daryl loved more than the rush of virility that pumped through his veins when he was allowed to dislodge a large piece of overpriced wood from its hinges and watch it slide across the floor on the other side. It was a love affair that had started in high school when he, Troy, and the others had discovered the joys of kicking down doors when they came across abandoned homes on the back roads of Murray County and would drunkenly take turns closing and kicking in every door in the house. It was just as cool as they made it look on that show COPS —

until the time that they found a home that they thought was abandoned only to find that it was, in fact, an occupied home with little emphasis put on exterior upkeep. That was the last time that Daryl had illegally kicked a door down, but one of the many perks of being a sheriff's deputy was that he was on occasion given a license to kick. It really was his calling in life.

Before Daryl was able to make any sort of decision, pro-destruction or otherwise, the front door slowly creaked open to reveal a squinting Troy, shirtless and pantless, standing unapologetically in nothing but the glow of his tighty-whities against the blinding sun rays.

"Oh, hey, man. I'm glad you're here," Troy greeted Daryl warmly before nodding in the other direction. "Sheriff Reynolds."

With pleasantries out of the way, Troy tried to grab Daryl's sunglasses from where they hung from the collar of his shirt. Daryl slapped his hand away with a warning glance. Why did everyone think that his sunglasses were communal property?

"You're glad I'm here?" Daryl asked inquisitively with a tone of disapproval. Already, it was clear that Troy was going to try and pull something out of his ass.

"Yeah, you didn't, by chance, happen to take my truck last night, did you?"

Sheriff Reynolds, by this point, too, realized that Troy was in the midst of laying some sort of story on the two of them. This was precisely the type of bullshit for which he wasn't in the mood, and he wasted no time in answering, "Let me get this straight: you're accusing Deputy Lumley of grand larceny?"

Troy scratched his head in answer to the tone with which the sheriff asked his question.

"Well, I wake up this morning, my truck's not where we left it. I figure either one of my friends is playing a little 'welcome home' prank on me or someone stole the shit out of it." Troy laughed. When it was clear that neither man was going to return his laugh, it was time to put on his serious face. "You really didn't take it?" he asked Daryl.

"You say the truck wasn't where *we* left it?" Sheriff Reynolds asked, not giving Troy the satisfaction of any further misdirection.

"Right."

"We, being you and...?" Sheriff Reynolds asked impatiently.

"Me and Rob."

"Mr. Douglas?"

"That's right," Troy answered before putting on his best poker face. He turned again to Daryl. "Wait, are you saying that you really didn't take it?"

"Did you report the truck stolen, Mr. Paulson?" Sheriff Reynolds grilled.

"I was just about to, actually."

"Your truck was stolen this morning and you wait until," Sheriff Reynolds began before checking his watch and continuing, "one-thirty in the afternoon to report it stolen?"

"It was kind of a late night last night, to be honest," Troy confided rather convincingly. "I just rolled out of bed a few minutes before you guys knocked, actually."

Sheriff Reynolds exchanged a questioning glance with Daryl, which was Daryl's cue to get involved.

"Yeah, we heard about your late night down at the station," Daryl began.

"Caused quite a ruckus down at the bar, I understand," Sheriff Reynolds finished.

"Uh, yes, sir. Not by choice, though. I was a victim of circumstance."

The sheriff didn't seem to be overly impressed by Troy's answer, which was nothing new. This had been an ongoing dance between the two for nearly a decade; less so now than in the past, but Troy hadn't forgotten the steps.

"I had a personal problem or two that I needed to work out, sir," Troy continued. "My friend Jack and I went a few rounds, and before you know it, I was in something of a predicament."

"You mean Jack Brose?"

"No, sir. I mean Jack Daniels."

The sheriff's expression didn't change, but Troy knew that he was about to explode with rage on the inside.

"And after I got thrown out of the bar, I still had enough sense about me to call Rob. He came and got me, then drove my truck home."

"And Rob can confirm that?" Daryl asked.

"Of course," Troy answered with a deep breath before yelling, "Hey, Rob!"

He smiled politely back at the "before and after" standing on his front porch and waited patiently as they exchanged annoyed looks. Thirty long seconds passed as Daryl stood angrily on the front porch, first with his arms crossed, but soon thereafter with his hands on his hips. This was typical Troy, but more so than that, it was atypical Rob. He wished, in the moment that he faked a polite smile back to Troy, that the sheriff wasn't standing alongside him; he could get to the bottom of it all if he was by himself. He'd un-holster his gun, maybe slap Rob around a little bit, and chastise Troy into a shameful apology.

Sheriff Reynolds sighed when he saw Rob coming around the corner. As much as he disliked Troy, he hated Rob and his drug-dealing. He had it on good authority, though, that Rob never dealt anything other than weed and that he never dealt to kids, which was enough to label him as a low-value target most days. If it wasn't Rob selling weed, it would be someone else and they would probably have fewer scruples, so he typically overlooked Rob's activities as long as he kept to the shadows and back-alleys.

"Alright," Sheriff Reynolds conceded to Troy. "Alright, I believe you. But if Mr. Douglas drove your truck home, as you say he did, how exactly did his car end up here?"

"Oh, that," Troy reacted, sharing a bemused look with Rob for a split-second. "How *did* that happen," he mused in Rob's general direction.

"That was Jenny!" Rob exclaimed, mentally wiping a bead of sweat from his forehead.

"Jenny," Sheriff Reynolds asked with a hint of *I got you, motherfucker* at the back of his throat.

"Yeah, Jenny," Troy answered. "Rob's girlfriend."

Sheriff Reynolds looked to Daryl for confirmation, which was quickly forthcoming with a nod of his head. It still wasn't enough to quench his curiosity, though: "And this Jenny will say the same thing?"

"Absolutely," Rob answered this time.

"And where can we find this girl of yours?" Reynolds

asked, pulling a pen and notepad from his pocket before being interrupted by a yelling Rob.

"Jenny?!"

The sheriff sighed, putting his notepad back in his pocket. Daryl, for his part, rolled his eyes — this was beginning to get ridiculous, and the more ridiculous that it became, the more trouble was going to come of it later. Sometimes he really hated these assholes for the situations that they put him in with his job. The next few seconds, though, weren't the worst of his career to that particular point when Jenny emerged from the darkness of the house in nothing but a frilly pair of boy shorts and a lavender bra that left little to the imagination. Goddamn Rob and his indescribable ability to pull top-shelf women wherever he went.

Daryl was beginning to suspect that he was staring a bit too intently, but that was before he was able to pry his stare away to glance over at his superior officer. Sheriff Reynolds had been divorced for six years now; he hadn't seen a woman in her underwear, outside of porn, in six years; and he wasn't sure that he'd ever seen anything to rival this, even in porn. For a moment, he was tempted to call in backup to take the whole lot of them in, including Daryl, the young bastard, and burn the whole building to the ground with everyone in it, himself included.

"Let's get the hell out of here," he finally groaned in Daryl's direction.

"So, should I..." Troy started.

"You can come pick your truck up at the impound yard!" Sheriff Reynolds answered in an irate tone.

"Thanks, guys!" Troy offered as his last words before ducking back in the house.

Once they were in the car, Sheriff Reynolds lit another cigarette, took a long drag, and put the car in drive. "I don't believe a goddamn word of it," he began before taking another drag. "I should bring all of them in and charge the other two with obstruction."

"I don't think you'd be wrong to do it."

"But..." the sheriff replied, deep in thought. "It would be a huge pain in the dick to track down people to refute all three stories. Besides, there was no real damage done, not to mention that he's your friend. I'm gonna let this slide. Cite him for destruction of public property and fine him the cost of fixing the damn hydrant."

"Whatever you think is best, sir."

"You better keep an eye on him, Daryl. This is his one *get out of jail* free card. Whatever you do, keep him away from that girl. If this comes back to bite me in the ass as a murder/suicide, I'm going to ask which nut is your favorite before I put it into a goddamn vice."

"Yes, sir." *Goddamn Troy.*

STANDING IN THE darkness on the other side of the closed door, Troy smiled the smile of a man who had just escaped the hangman's noose as he leaned giddily against the door and let his legs fall out from under him and slide down to the floor.

"That was a nice touch, by the way," Troy said by way of thanks to Jenny. "Coming in half-naked was a stroke of genius."

"Thanks," Jenny laughed. "Just doing what I can to help the bad guys."

"I don't know that I'd necessarily consider us the bad guys, but I'll take it where I can get it," Troy answered.

"Me, too," Rob added, putting his arms around Jenny and burying his face in her neck. Though it had only been some minutes earlier, the awkward conversation that they had only barely avoided was thrust onto the back burner, thanks to the excitement of collusion against the local authorities.

Troy, relaxed though he was at the moment, began to feel the awkwardness of the situation when Rob started to tease his fingers underneath the waistband of Jenny's panties. This was coming far too close to a pervert's voyeurism for his taste.

"I think I'm just going to take a walk," he announced, pushing himself to his feet and receiving very little reaction from either party for his trouble. "So I'll just..." he continued before realizing that anything further could be considered participation. "Right."

Without another word, he opened the door and quickly made his egress before sheepishly showing his face a moment later with a laugh:

"I should probably put on some clothes first," Troy announced again before he noticed that his roommate and acquaintance were only moments away from penetration.

"Or I'll just go like this."

He wasted no time in closing the door behind him, immediately aware of the fact that he was in nothing but his skivvies for the world at large to see.

"Way to lay low, Troy," he mused aloud.

6

Serial Killers in Prii

"**H**oney, don't forget what I said," Eve reminded in her best non-threatening, mousey voice. It was an effort to chide her husband without sounding as though she was chiding her husband, as he was preparing to step out the front door of their new home, past the manicured grass and into the inviting seats of his beloved Prius.

"I know," Ian replied in a very specific tone. It wasn't an annoyed tone. He didn't really have much of an annoyed tone in his repertoire insofar as the traditional American understanding of the word was concerned. What he did have was the ability to project a sense of civility with a slight tinge of displeasure in a ploy designed specifically for its conversation-ending propensity — a quintessential British trait that could occasionally come off as condescending in the wrong hands. Ian, however, held a fairly tight grip on the execution of his mannerisms, and it only rarely seemed to bother Eve.

"I'm just saying—" Eve began before slowing to consider her words more carefully. "Try not to get excited too easily or get carried away in the first few days. I know how much of a grammar Nazi you are, but this isn't a private school in New England — or even England, for that matter. You know how you hate ebonics, text-speak, and all the so-called 'pseudo languages?'"

Ian did know full well how greatly he hated ebonics, text-speak, and all the so-called "pseudo languages," being that they were so-called because he was the one that called them so. He smiled politely, followed by a simple: "I do."

"You haven't heard redneck yet. 'Ain't' is a word here. The sooner you accept that, the better things will be."

"Darling," Ian began, "I love you. You know that I love you. And I'm sure that I will grow to love my students, however profane and ignorant they may be. But, having been well-acquainted with the Queen's own English for going on thirty-four years now, I can assure you that 'ain't' is not a word, regardless of geography."

He smiled, gave her a quick, perfunctory kiss on the cheek — having thus bid her adieu — and closed the door behind him to leave her standing with a wide smile on her face.

They're going to eat him alive, Eve thought to herself with a smile.

Ian took a quick glimpse around at his neighborhood as he busied himself shuffling a stack of papers from one arm to the other — where they should have been in the first place, had Eve never began waxing philosophical about the culture shock that he was about to endure. She was well-intentioned, this wife of his, but she misjudged his ability to compartmentalize and adapt to his environment. Besides, he was from a rural part of England, himself, and had made the transition from said rural environment to London before New York City, so her warning hardly seemed warranted.

For the most part, people in Pine Creek so far had seemed to be of the pleasant sort, despite the broken English that seemed to plague even the bulk of the adult population. Their neighbor, a Mrs. Hyde, had been one of the few people with whom he had spoken to prove an exception, but she had stopped speaking to him shortly after they moved in for some reason or another — which could only be chalked up to xenophobia, as far as he could tell, as nothing else of note had transpired insofar as he knew.

Papers now in the correct arm, Ian used the other to adjust his tie as he headed down the walk toward the driveway. Eve had warned him that he was overdressed for the position of high school English teacher in Pine Creek, but he both suspected that a) she was basing her opinion on a jaded, decade-old schoolgirl's perspective, and b) his father would roll over in his grave if he knew that his only son belonged to a vocation that did not require formal dress.

Ian had been an associate professor at NYU while in New York, so salary alone dictated that his wasn't the garb of a Fifth Avenue socialite, but he would soon learn that suits in general were reserved for funerals and funerals alone in Pine Creek — making his conservative choice of only a quasi-expensive (considering his salary) black suit over a white shirt with a black skinny tie seem like he had stepped out of an advertisement in *GQ*.

He had started to bald only slightly, which would have been quite a bit worrisome to him in his youth, but now that his forties were beginning to peek over the horizon, he felt that no one would take seriously an aging professor with a full head of hair — which wasn't all that problematic now that he found himself an educator at what equated to a primary school back home. He wasn't bitter about that point, though; it had been his idea to move to Eve's hometown, after all. She hadn't said as much, but Ian felt as though she was beginning to tire of the lifestyle that they had led in New York.

After placing his briefcase in the passenger-side seat and his cup of coffee in the cup-holder in the center console, Ian closed the door of his Prius and began the walk back around to the driver-side door that he had, after years of positive reinforcement from Eve, begrudgingly accepted to be his side of the vehicle. Inside, he buckled up, started the engine and adjusted the volume of the BBC World station on his satellite radio. Having thus prepared himself for both travel and intellectual stimulation, he checked the rearview mirror one last time and put the car into reverse.

"Ain't is a word," he harrumphed.

Nearly at the end of the driveway, and with a bit more speed than usual due to the mild agitation of his mood, it was only at the last second that he caught a glimpse of what appeared to be human skin in the rearview mirror. Though his reaction time left little to be desired in applying the brakes, Ian still noticed something of a thud when the car came to a complete stop, throwing him into a hysterical daze.

"Good Lord!" he exclaimed, making to jump immediately from the car before being dragged back to reality by his seatbelt.

When he had finally negotiated the release of the death-grip that the seatbelt had laid into his torso, Ian scurried as fast as trembling nerves would allow to the rear bumper of the car, where he almost heaped over atop himself at finding a half-clothed body lying in his driveway. He would later find himself intrigued by the speed with which his mind began devising ways that he might dispose of the body. He wasn't a fan of horror movies — nor did he partake in much of the action genre outside of the Bond series — so it was something of a surprise to find the answer to his dilemma squirreled just beneath the surface of his subconscious: a vat full of battery acid! But how in the bloody hell was one to pull acid from a battery?

Before he had a chance to act upon his initial felonious impulse, however, and start ransacking the neighborhood stores for their battery supply, the body groaned and pushed itself up from the ground. Ian leaned back against the car and released the sort of sigh that involved the whole of his body; from toe to bald spot, the panic evaporated like pheromones into the ether; save the off-chance that this man was, in fact, a human corpse-turned-zombie, things were going to be alright.

Thankful to see that the man was not, in fact, a zombie, Ian rushed over to take him by the hand and profess his sincerest apologies: "Oh, thank god you're alright," he began.

After departing from his house of ill repute, barely missing the opening act of *Rob Bones Jenny*, Troy had found a pair of Jackson's shorts on the front porch that had been taken off after spilling an inordinate amount of ketchup on them while the group had enjoyed an outdoor dinner a week-and-a-half earlier. Instead of throwing them in the washer or even going inside to change, Jackson had merely taken them off and continued to eat his fries. They were big on Troy to the point of 90s Jinco Jeans, but, luckily enough, Jackson had also left his belt on the front porch as well, so at least they would stay around Troy's waist so he could proceed down the street —

though shirtless and apparently on his period — without worrying about adding a lewdness charge to the day's activities.

So it was on the verge of frontal male nudity with a series of bleeding scrapes from the pavement that Troy met the husband of the woman for whom he had spent the better part of his adult life pining after. As things stood, however, Troy was blissfully unaware as to the depth of humiliation that the universe was throwing his way. He had, after all, not hung around long enough to hear the whole of the story from Jackson and Kendrick when they had first informed him of Eve's return to Pine Creek. He had reacted in the way that any man in his right mind would have reacted: he had gotten drunk and done something stupid. To Troy, this was an encounter made uncomfortable simply by the fact that he had survived what Ian had originally thought to be a case of vehicular manslaughter.

"Yeah, I'm fine," Troy laughed, taking the time to realize that he'd just been knocked from his feet by a car and had only a few scrapes on his back to show for it. He wiped the dust off his hands on Jackson's shorts and smiled back at Ian. "Thank god this thing isn't an F-250, huh?" he asked, pointing toward the Prius.

Though Ian's limited understanding of Southern vehicles precluded his understanding the reference, his was too jovial a mood to not share Troy's laughter.

"Quite right," he answered nervously. "You sure you're okay?"

"Yeah," Troy answered. "Ain't no hill for a high-stepper, right?"

While Troy used as many contractions as the next man in

Pine Creek, ain't was a word in his lexicon which was typically reserved for prudent Southern adages, the result of being the son of an English teacher who would slap his mouth any time he let loose the dreaded "A" word. To that day, he still took a quick survey of his surroundings to ensure that she wasn't lurking in the shadows before he would let one slip through his lips.

Ian wasn't sure that the adage was right — or what this strange, half-dressed man was doing casting furtive glances about the neighborhood for no apparent reason — but he nodded along. The two men shared an elongated, awkward moment of silence in which the eternity of time might have passed. Troy was starting to suspect that he had stumbled upon some sort of aspiring international serial killer who had tried to use his car as a murder weapon, only realizing too late that a few hundred pounds of plastic was insufficient to kill a man.

"Well, I'm sorry to hit and run — so to speak — but I'm off on my way to work," Ian began, finally breaking the godawful silence that had persisted longer than good manners dictated that they should. "Again, you're sure that you're alright? No broken bones or anything of the sort?"

"Broken bones?" Troy laughed, again making reference to the Prius with a wilt of his forefinger.

"Right," Ian answered, peeved slightly that Troy seemed to be implying that he couldn't have possibly done any damage with his car.

With no more ado, Ian got into the car, double- and triple-checked the rearview mirror, and fully departed from his driveway this time. *What a strange man*, he thought as he put the car in drive and stared at Troy in his rearview.

Goddamn, that dude was weird, Troy thought to himself, *even for a Brit.* Troy had spent a few days on vacation in England and Wales in his younger years before his father had left his mother, thus leaving them less affluent and incapable of trans-Atlantic travel; and though he had found them to be a peculiar people, none had seemed as peculiar as the one that he had just watch drive away in his peculiarly Japanese Prius.

He turned back in the direction in which he had been heading before the incident, which was nowhere in particular, before being startled by the unexpected:

"I'm not sure that you'll need it," Ian added, "but you can get my insurance information from my wife. If you need it."

Troy released a deep breath, recovering from the fact that he hadn't heard the Prius on its re-approach and had momentarily thought that the car had been a diversion and that Ian was about to bash him over the head with a cricket paddle.

"Yeah, thanks, man."

"My name's Ian, by the way," Ian offered. It had seemed natural to give the man his name, in the event that he had, in fact, desired to collect his insurance information from Eve, but the look on Troy's face made him think that he had happened upon some sort of cultural taboo at some point during their conversation. Maybe Eve was right. This might be more difficult than he had thought.

Without another word, he rolled up the window and drove away in the direction of the Buffalo and Pine Creek High.

Though serial killer was still within the realm of possibility, Troy was suspecting that maybe Ian had just been attracted to him, which actually worked to momentarily brighten his day.

"I still got it," Troy mused, looking down proudly at his naked torso.

His glory was short-lived, however, as ever-so-slowly, from somewhere above his head, Troy noticed the dim buzz of an old-school Edison light bulb as it began to illuminate the expanses of his otherwise clueless brain.

Ian.

Where have I heard that name?

Then it all came crashing home just in time for:

"Troy?"

MUCH TO HER CHAGRIN, Eve had been informed that the office space that she had rented to be the Bat Cave of her law practice would not be ready for at least another week. Meanwhile, at home, she had unpacked all of the boxes, arranged all of the knickknacks, put away all of the silverware; she was a high-functioning type A personality with a lull in her professional and home life. If she didn't find a client to defend or a leaky faucet to fix, Eve was worried that she might slip back into *Vengeful Teenage Eve* and stoop so low as sneaking next door and spelling the word "pedophile" in gasoline on Mrs. Hyde's yard. Not convinced that it had come to all that, she still found it prudent to push open the curtain from the corner of her kitchen window just enough to gauge the distance between the two houses — just in case.

Two days!

It had been two days, and Eve was ready to vandalize property of a neighbor to settle a ten-year-old grudge against a senior citizen. She needed a distraction. And as if she had prayed to the Lawn Fairies themselves, a distraction appeared outside of her window and on the other side of the freshly manicured grass.

For a moment, she actually lost her breath. It wasn't as though she had spent the past decade yearning for a return to her childhood home so she could have a second meet-cute with her high school boyfriend, but she had spent more than a few minutes in contemplation on how she would comport herself when they inevitably crossed paths. She just hadn't expected it to be so soon — or when he was so scantily clad.

For God and all the neighborhood to see, Troy Paulson was standing in front of her house in a pair or ridiculously large jean shorts and nothing else, looking like a backup dancer for a 90s boy band. Was he about to *Say Anything* her with a rendition of a *Backstreet Boys* song?

Eve caught her breath just in time to lose it again as her heart skipped a beat at seeing Ian's Prius backing up to stop alongside Troy. Her smartly dressed husband was talking to her barely dressed ex in some sort of lewd cosmic bastardry. Whatever the two of them had to say to one another was able to be conveyed in ten seconds of conversation, and as Ian drove away, Troy was staring proudly down at his body. If her ex-boyfriend had just been propositioned by her husband, she was *so* burning her house down and leaving Pine Creek immediately.

Finally, unable to corral her curiosity, she opened the front door, stepped uneasily onto the top step, and prepared herself for something just this side of abnormal.

"Troy?"

When their eyes met, Eve felt a rush of familiarity in which time itself began to drag against the winds of providence and flirt with the possibility of reclusion. Whereas she had experienced a similar feeling in the broad sense just the day before with Daryl, the current iteration of nonlinear existential crisis was more acute; floating between a memory and a dream.

Just as she began to think that she would be unable to shake herself free from the throes of timelessness, the invisible machinery of the cosmos righted itself and Eve was thrust into the *Here and Now* so quickly that she felt a case of phantom whiplash for several hours thereafter. And no sooner had she realized that some sort of conversation would have to be had than she was saved from hanging to do so by the fickle hand of panic.

After Troy had gotten past his initial deer-in-the-headlights moment, he had apparently realized that he, too, was ill-prepared for any sort of conversation. And when he broke into a dead sprint across the golf course, holding the oversized shorts up with one hand and trying to maintain a semblance of runner's form with the other, Eve watched with a sense of pure bewilderment until he disappeared over the seventh hole green.

"Goddamn drama queens," she sighed.

7

Bennett Family Values

The Bennett family had as long of a history in Murray County as any other could claim. The area, like most areas in the state, had been granted as Tribal lands as part of the relocation process in the early 19th Century, and the area that Pine Creek would eventually inhabit had originally been granted to the Choctaw Nation in 1820 under the Treaty of Dancing Rabbit Creek; in the first of several changes of hands, however, it was subsequently granted to the Chickasaw Nation in 1855 under the Treaty of Doaksville. Of course, this was all done without taking into account the fact that there were already Plains Tribes living in the areas that the government had granted to the relocated tribes. Between 1824 and 1851, the government built a succession of forts in the area in an attempt to quell the conflict between the tribes, and had largely been successful by the time the American Civil War began.

The Civil War, however, not only left a swath of the country devastated, but also gave rise to a series of outlaw gangs who were sewn into the fabric of the Midwestern lore by leaving thousands of battle-hardened young men without homes or families to return to even if they did wish to be part of Reconstruction with the scalawags and carpetbaggers who had descended into the South after the War – carpetbaggers like Henry C. Warmoth, who had become Governor of Louisiana in 1868. And the natural inclination of these gangs was to head west into the unsettled territories where they could evade authorities.

Henry Benoit was of Cajun descent from a well-to-do New Orleans family who had been part of Jackson's ragtag band of brothers at the Battle of New Orleans. Upon returning home from the war to a mood of suspicion — and one that only grew worse at Warmoth's election in '68 — it seemed that he was going to be drawn into another civil war before he was ever able to set about regaining his family's wealth that had been lost during the war he had just fought.

There was a lot of family lore about what happened between the time that he left Louisiana in the spring of 1869 and the first time that he appeared in the property records of the newly-established Pine Creek in the early 1882. The popular story was that he had made it as far west as Missouri and had fallen in with the James-Younger Gang, who made use of Indian Territory as a refuge while on the run from the law, and that Henry had earned the money that he used to establish the family in the territory by digging up the fabled James treasure buried in the Wichita Mountains a day's ride to the northeast; another had it that he had made it as far west as New Mexico where he had ridden with Billy the Kid back and forth to Nebraska and Old Mexico time and again until his death. Ramona's grandmother had told her that her 3rd great-grandfather Henry hadn't gone so far west as north, and that he had been a rambler who had made his living as a gambler as far north as Deadwood, South Dakota, where he remained for several years before leaving in the late '70s when the unruly outpost began to feel the long arm of society creeping in to suffocate its feral nature. He'd then traveled supposedly across the plains to Texas before happening upon the plot that would eventually become Pine Creek, centered around the natural springs that would be dedicated as a national recreation area in the early 20th century.

By the time he had arrived in Pine Creek, he had Anglicized his surname from Benoit to Bennett to avoid the suspicions that one bestowed upon an outsider, and thus the Bennett tract of land was purchased in the spring of 1882, six-hundred-and-forty acres north of town; of course, it was a shady agreement at best, being that he had purchased the land from someone who had claimed the land that had been claimed by the Chickasaw Nation that had been claimed by the United States Government; but the government recognized his claim when Oklahoma attained statehood in 1907 and a patent was issued posthumously to Henry Bennett for his 640 acres. And that land had remained undeveloped and in Bennett hands for the next one-hundred-and-thirty-five years down to the present day.

Whether Henry had been a bank robber or a gambler, he had definitely been an outlaw. And as Pine Creek grew, so did his small backwoods empire. Before statehood ushered in the rule of law, he ran a saloon and brothel that was passed down to the family when he died. Though he had shed most of the family habits that the Benoits had brought with them from the old country, Henry was a firm believer in primogeniture, as his view was that it took a strong person to head a family and conduct its business. He had left the family business in the hands of his wife upon his death to be passed on to his eldest child John Bennett; but upon her death, John's brother Samuel had killed him in a heated disagreement about dividing up the family land. It was just as well, insofar as the family was concerned, because when Samuel took over the family business was again stabilized and preserved for future generations.

Ramona's great-grandfather Herschel Bennett had transitioned the family business heavily into bootlegging and whoring in the '30s, moving away from the saloon model, as it had been considered impolite during the progressive era to do such things in public. And it was Ramona's own grandfather, James Bennett, who had been head of the family when it had been on the verge of collapse during the '60s when the FBI had swept through the region with its KKK task-force whose sensibilities seemed to be far more incensed by the bootlegging and the whoring than the institutional racism upon which they were supposed to be focused two states over. Most of the Bennett men were sent to prison around that time, and a lot of them died there, including James Bennett. It was Ramona's grandmother who took over the family business at that point as one of the last few on the outside who was capable of doing so.

Ramona Bennett liked to ruminate on her family origins from time to time. She never bothered with the "way back" origins, which were supposed to be some even more distant great-grandfather coming to Louisiana in the mid-18th century from France to a considerably more distant great-grandfather coming from some barbarian tribe to settle somewhere in Gaul in the early BCs. None of that mattered. *Her* family started with Henry Benoit.

And it was *her* family.

Grandma Carolyn taking over had been a tad controversial in her day — not so much because she was a woman as much as it was that she was only a Bennett by marriage. There had never been a female head of the family up until that point, but with most of the men away, there wasn't much to do about that except to make some boy-king out of one of the grandchildren. The controversy ensued because James Bennett had a first-born daughter from his first marriage who could have — and was more than willing to — take over the business. For a while it seemed that history was doomed to repeat itself and that stepdaughter would kill stepmother to settle the dispute. Carolyn Bennett, however, turned out to be more than capable of both handling business and unruly stepchildren and had headed the family until her death in 2007.

During her time, Carolyn steered the family away from the sorts of things that would outwardly rankle the feathers of the Baptists who dominated the county denomination-wise. Gambling was the big no-no de jure in the Baptist world, but was more of a lip-service no-no that everyone from the Old Bingo Ladies to the young card sharks enjoyed; thus, underground card games, sports betting, and loan-sharking became the modus operandi for the Bennett family with the occasional toe dipping into other underworldly waters when the crime suited the need.

So it was a wholly different family business that Ramona Bennett inherited in the fall of 2007 when her grandmother named her her successor. Though it had been fifty years since the last transfer of power, it was the second controversial transfer in a row – mainly because Ramona's father was alive and out of prison, as was her aunt who had challenged Carolyn for supremacy in the late '60s. People were unsettled because Henry Benoit's vision of primogeniture was being replaced with a flavor of despotism in which the outgoing ruler chose their successor, but, really, Henry's vision equated more to survival of the fittest and was predicated upon the chosen person being able to hold onto power – or so argued Ramona after her first display of dominance that sealed her position as head of the family for as long as she wanted it.

Ramona was first-generation college, and had not only spent some time in the world as a result, but had proven that her brain was worth its weight in gold during her twenties when the family was under another statewide RICO investigation during the formative years of the methamphetamine epidemic. The family had never been involved in the drug trade, but any time the federal government came sniffing around, the scent of a crime syndicate produced the sorts of erections in ambitious junior officers that required medical attention. And out the few people who made known that they wanted to contend with her for leadership, it was Ramona's father who pushed the hardest – the father whom she barely remembered because he had been imprisoned early in her childhood and spent only short stints of freedom in between longer vacations in McAlester State Penitentiary.

He had pushed and pushed until Ramona convened a family meeting to settle the issue once and for all. Sitting at the head of the table, Ramona listened to the concerns of every family elder and to the lambasts on behalf of her father and aunt who both assumed that they would be able to turn the tide of opinion and that Ramona would be forced to cede power to either of them. When her father finished his rants against his sister and daughter, he went to the head of the family, leaned over it with both hands on the table in as menacing a pose as he could muster, and demanded that the girl in her 29th year step aside for someone with more experience.

Ramona later boasted that if her father had been half the man he thought he was, he would have known that threatening the head of the family was a bad idea in and of itself, but doubly so when she had Henry Benoit's ceremonial hatchet nearby that every head of the family held to symbolize their power. She hadn't expected so much blood, but in retrospect, with her father as full of adrenaline and testosterone as he would have been, his heart had definitely been pumping at near full capacity; and when he pulled back the nub where his hand had been taken off at the wrist, the blood had spurted like a water hydrant that had been mowed down by a truck.

In the ten years since, no one had so much as questioned an order, much less challenged Ramona's authority. Business had been good, arrests had been minimal, and portfolios had even been diversified into local businesses that laundered money to keep the federal government from poking around. Of those businesses, Ramona's favorite was where she made her base of operations for reasons that were twofold: a) it just made sense for the head of the family to work out of the one legitimate business that didn't take in much money or rouse suspicions; and b) she loved the snakes. The Snake Farm was, as its name suggested, a reptile house on the outside of town where the Bennett Plot butted up against Highway 177. She had dozens of species of snakes, lizards, and various amphibians in terrariums lined along a labyrinth of hallways, which she charged $5 a head to visit. For another $5, she would allow patrons to feed the snakes. Since it was the sort of business that rarely drew repeat visitors — you've seen the snakes once, you've seen them a hundred times — it was the perfect home base for Ramona who only saw a handful of legitimate customers a week and could conduct business with a modicum of privacy.

Now thirty-nine-years-old and an old hand at the business world, there was little that surprised Ramona in those days. She could expect a few visits from employees — almost always members of the extended Bennett family, with a few exceptions — delivering money that had been collected, and then a stray drug addict or two looking for loans that would almost always be denied unless they held some sort of collateral, making her not unlike a pawnbroker; there were also the legitimate clientele looking for money for genuine reasons such as just trying to make it through tough times when the oil and gas industry was down, but the loan sharking was a tricky business that shouldn't draw too much attention, as the propensity for federal involvement was high if performed recklessly; so it was a fine line that she walked between scumbags with something to lose and squares with a likelihood of making good on their debt — at a high interest rate, of course.

She had high-priced attorneys on the payroll who had created shell corporations that owned a significant amount of property in the county because Ramona had branched into home loans; most didn't default on their home loans, and she acted almost as a legitimate bank in that regard and enjoyed the fact that she was actually helping locals attain homeownership when they were unable to get one through traditional means — but business was business, and when they missed that payment, she took it back.

When Kendrick Brose walked through the door of the Snake Farm, Ramona was flipping through a magazine in which she wasn't fully invested, thinking about what she wanted for lunch and who was going to bring it to her; and though she wasn't surprised often, she was surprised to see a Brose darken her doorstep. The Brose family didn't have as illustrious, if not infamous, a past in Pine Creek as did the Bennett family, but there had been at least one Brose in town for most of the past century when Kendrick's 2nd-great-grandfather Elijah Brose settled in Pine Creek just before statehood and shortly before he was killed by Samuel Bennett over a contract dispute. Theirs wasn't a blood feud by any stretch of the imagination – and, in fact, both sides were more or less cordial down to the very day – but there was bad blood, nonetheless, and small towns were nothing if not nostalgic. The two families had never since conducted business with one another.

"Hi, Ramona," Kendrick began with a nervous smile.

"Kendrick." She smiled a cautious but warm smile in his direction. While it couldn't be a particularly auspicious thing to have a Brose in front of her, she was at least glad that it was Kendrick and not Jackson, as the latter was notoriously bullheaded and unpredictable. She would definitely have had to deny Jackson whatever he would have asked, and would probably create more bad blood from the fallout; Kendrick, though — Kendrick was interesting.

"How's Wylie?" Kendrick asked about the only thing that each held in common with the other.

"Wylie is fine. He's in New Mexico, bound for Abilene tomorrow. So what can I do for you?" she asked. "You just wondering how Wylie is or are you here to see the snakes?"

"I saw them in high school," Kendrick responded, hands in his pockets and fidgety in a way that made Ramona feel like a snake herself.

"So you're here to talk to me about business?"

Kendrick nodded.

"This really isn't a place for law-abiding citizens," Ramona answered, coming out from behind the desk and circling her prey. "What could a Brose possibly need from a Bennett?"

"I need a loan."

"I was afraid of that," she answered, taking a small box from a nearby counter. "Loans are a tricky thing. You need the money now, I'll need the money later and a little bit of money on top of that. I'll need it in a timely fashion. You might not have it, but that doesn't stop me from needing it. You see where I'm going with this?"

Before Kendrick could respond, she opened the box and pulled a tiny, white mouse out by the tail.

"I do," Kendrick answered with an audible gulp. He fucking hated snakes, and he was pretty sure that Ramona was about to feed one in front of him to both intimidate him and discourage him from taking a loan.

"Why do you need the money?"

Ramona began walking toward one of the nearby terrariums where she planned to feed one of her snakes in an effort to both intimidate and discourage Kendrick from taking a loan. This was a dance that she had done many times, and it helped to test the mettle of a prospective business partner and to drive home the point that this wasn't a simple loan from a friend that was being discussed; and with Kendrick, it was probably best that she not extend a loan — not only because of the bad blood between the families and the propensity for having to deal with Jackson — and possibly Daryl — if the time ever came that she had to collect.

"I'm going back to school."

"Fucking mazel tov," Ramona exclaimed while dropping a mouse into a nearby snake's den. She wiped her hands off on her shirt, turned back around, and got down to the nuts and bolts of the situation. "You're aware that there are student loans through the government, right? And that their terms are favorable to mine in that they won't show up to your house for your car keys if you don't pay them back on time."

"I really messed up my credit and I was technically expelled from school the last time I was in it. I checked, and I'm ineligible."

"Why go back to school in the first place? Tired of being a grease monkey?"

Ramona waited a few seconds for an answer, but Kendrick was fixated on the mouse where it was sniffing the edges of the glass, seemingly oblivious to the fact that a snake was coiled motionless nearby.

She snapped her fingers to bring him out of it.

"Yeah, I just need to—" Kendrick started, glancing at the mouse and then back to Ramona before continuing. "Did you ever feel like if you didn't get out of Pine Creek at that exact moment, you never would?"

"Lots of times. You think I didn't want to leave Pine Creek with Wylie when he started out? Or that I don't want to leave now and meet him at the show in Abilene tomorrow night?

But what are you gonna do, right? My cousins are idiots, and my one-handed, dumbass dad would run the family into the ground before I hit the Panhandle. I'm stuck. Family's family, right?"

"Right."

"Speaking of which, how's that brother of yours handling the fact that you're leaving town?"

"I haven't actually told him yet."

"He gonna be a problem?"

"What do you mean?" Kendrick asked just before he noticed a bolt of movement out of the corner of his eye. Before he could bring himself back into the conversation, he had to mentally deal with the fact that there was an evil-ass snake with a mouse in its mouth not more than a dozen steps from him in that very moment. He wanted nothing more than to leave what was beginning to feel like a demon's lair and go back to work at the shop with his dumbass brother. He had half-decided that that was what he would do, preparing the formulations of an excuse in his head for leaving so abruptly and to thank Ramona for her time so he didn't offend her; but when she slid her arm around his neck in an unexpectedly friendly embrace, he felt as though her arm was scaled.

He froze.

"What I mean is when I go into business with someone, I go into business with everyone that they know." She moved from where she stood at his side to his other side, her arm slithering from one shoulder to the other as she used her free hand to nudge Kendrick's face toward hers. "If your brother becomes your problem, there's a possibility that he becomes my problem. I don't like problems."

"He's not a problem," Kendrick answered, knowing that

Jackson would almost always be a problem in some form or another, but he was unsure why Ramona would think that he could end up being a problem for her.

"Then I think we might be able to come to some sort of understanding," she said, uncoiling her grip and walking back behind the counter. "You were going to school to be a doctor before, right?"

"Yes."

"And that's what you're going back for?"

"It is."

"Then that means, what, six years of school?"

"Eight."

"That's a long-term investment. I'm going to be upfront with you. This isn't the sort of thing I normally take on. Don't get me wrong, I try to help out locals if I can, but what you're asking is that I give you a couple hundred thousand dollars to be paid back in – what? – a decade?"

"Roughly."

"Roughly," she repeated with a flip of her hair behind her shoulder. "Something that risky is going to require more interest than I normally charge. Forty percent."

"Forty," Kendrick managed in between breaths. "So roundabout a hundred-thousand dollars."

"Roundabout."

"Holy shit."

"That's not all," she cautioned. "You're going to have to work for me. Don't worry: I'll give you minimum wage that will go toward your debt. You're good with numbers, yeah? I need you to run a sports book for me wherever you go to school – East Central or OU. We'll set the lines, you just need to bring in new clients, take their money and so on. We'll handle collection if it comes to that, but try to make sure that it doesn't. I know shit gets rough when you hit med school, so you only have to run the books while you're an undergrad. Next six years, worry about your education, but during that time, if I have need of medical services, that's you. Guys need to get patched up, I get ass cancer, you're my primary physician. And even when your debt is paid in full, me and mine still get seen for free."

"That's— Holy shit, Ramona."

"I'll also need the deed to your house."

"I can't give you my house. It's not even *my* house. It's mine and Jackson's house."

"Which is why I said he could be a problem," she said with a sarcastic raise of her eyebrows. "Besides, you're not giving me your house. You're giving me the deed to your house that I'll put in a drawer for safekeeping in case you're not good for your end of the deal. Most people who come to me, they want things, they have collateral, or they want to buy a house and the house is collateral. You, you're offering me a theoretical med school degree for a quarter-million dollars."

"I don't know. If I can talk Jackson—"

"Look, you do or you don't. What happened here was just two people talking. You decide you want to do more than talk, bring me the deed and I get one of my attorneys to create a scholarship fund the next week and you're good to go."

Kendrick had unceremoniously ushered himself out the door with a half-hearted goodbye shortly thereafter, leaving Ramona to ponder the proposal she had just made. Forty percent was a sweet deal in and of itself, and the whole book running aspect bringing in new clientele in other areas would have its value, but if she could get a family doctor for life, that was where the real value of the deal would lie: bringing universal health care to the Bennett Family. She half-suspected that Kendrick would turn it down, anyhow — or that he would be forced to turn it down because of the need for Jackson's involvement – but she couldn't bring herself to offer a deal, no matter how sweet the possibility of reward, without the sort of collateral that made the other party realize who held the stick and that there was no such thing as a carrot in the Bennett World.

WHEN KENDRICK LEFT, he had been in something of a hurry, attempting to shake off the shudder that he had been holding back ever since walking into the place. He was so caught up in wondering if he had made a mistake by attempting to elicit Ramona's help that he hadn't managed to spot Jackson where he was trying — and failing miserably — to blend into his environment across the street. Jackson watched Kendrick as he drove away before hurrying across the street to peek through the front glass to see who was in the building. He saw Ramona's car out front and hadn't seen anyone else go in, but why would Kendrick be visiting Ramona? She was a good-looking woman, about ten years their senior, and Jackson himself would certainly go there, but it seemed like she was lacking something that a recently converted gay man might desire.

"What the fuck are you up to?" Jackson muttered before attempting to disappear into plain sight.

8

As Gung as a Ho Can Be

Troy had sprinted all the way across the golf course in a throwback to peak high school performance — sheer horror and humiliation coursing in place of testosterone and fueling adrenaline by the bucket load. Once he had cleared the golf course, however, he began to doubt his initial suspicion that Eve had been chasing him the entire quarter mile like a Jesus Lizard. When he finally stopped, his body immediately began to seize with cramps, having had no suspicion that it would be called into action. Just to be sure that he wasn't about to be bushwhacked, he grabbed his aching side and glanced back to his rear to assure that he hadn't been followed.

Satisfied that he was alone, he doubled over at his hips with a hand on each knee before grudgingly beginning his walk of shame the few blocks back to Brose Manor — though at least it would afford a cool-down period so that his muscles wouldn't keep yo-yoing from idle to 5,000 RPMs. His transmission wasn't able to handle such extreme spikes like it was in his youth.

When Troy finally turned the corner from Pecan onto 12th Street, the relief flowed through his shoulders and worked its way down through his back and all the way to his toes. *Ghost Troy* was claiming that pride would demand they get drunk and do something stupid to honor tradition, but the sprint across the golf course had drained the energy out of both of them and his shouts were barely a whisper, easily ignored. Troy could hole up in his room beneath layers of blankets for at least a few hours, allowing both his subconscious and pride time to heal themselves sufficiently so that he might again face the world.

Before he was able to follow through with his plan, however, he was immediately thrust back into panic mode upon seeing a familiar car. A silver SUV — a silver SUV strikingly similar to the one that had been parked in front of the house that Eve had emerged from some ten minutes ago, in fact — had just pulled into the driveway at Brose Manor. Troy prayed in that moment that there had been a run on silver SUVs at the local dealership and that *anyone* other than Eve was about to step out of the vehicle — be it IRS, Men in Black, his hot third cousin Amber he had complicated feelings about.

When Eve stepped out of the car, Troy's first instinct was again to flee like a small child, but no sooner than had the thought crossed his mind, his hamstring began to tighten as a warning against it: *do it and I'll rupture.*

With the risk of a major sports injury hanging overhead, Troy had little choice other than to accept his fate to be devoured by the masculinity-ending force of the successful ex-girlfriend. *Ghost Troy* had surreptitiously sidestepped the indignity by sidestepping his way back into his cell and hiding beneath the blankets.

Eve spotted him just as she had exited the car and ended up meeting him in the middle of 12th Street.

"Eve," Troy began, not sure what else to say in the moment.

"Troy," she countered.

"You caught me in the middle of a workout," he lied, hoping that she would have the common decency to allow it to pass.

"In a pair of huge jean shorts and no shoes?" she asked.

Who wouldn't just let it pass, Troy was fuming on the inside.

"I've outgrown classic methods of training," he lied again, assuming that she would let the second one slide. "I find that to stay in peak physical fitness, I've got to get creative."

"By running barefoot in a huge pair of jean shorts?"

The balls on this woman.

"Precisely," he replied. "The need to hold up the jean shorts with one hand creates an odd running style that focuses the exertion on the obliques. And the being barefoot forces you to use the heels of your feet."

Troy was beyond proud of himself and absolutely sure that Eve would have little to no confidence in the subject matter to try and rebuff his assertion — even if she were wicked enough to call him on a lie a third time.

"That sounds made up," she responded with a raise of the eyebrows.

Motherfucker!

"Unless you became a kinesiologist since the last time I saw you, you're not really in a position to comment, are you?"

"Touché," Eve conceded with a smile, seemingly content to finally let the point lie.

"So, did you just come here to ask about my workout routine?" Troy asked, elated to finally change the subject, but still stumped as to how to proceed with the rest of the conversation.

"I was just worried about you," she replied with a seemingly sincere expression. "I looked out the window, saw you nearly butt-naked and talking to my husband, and when I went out to say 'hi,' you took off running like a crackhead down an alley in New York City."

"Thank you for your concern, but I'm not smoking crack. Just exercising," Troy concluded firmly. "Plus, your husband hit me with his car, so if you're going to be drug-testing people, you should probably start with him."

"He hit you with his car?!" Eve nearly yelled.

"Like a goddamn serial killer," Troy confirmed with a vindictive flair.

"Are you fucking with me?"

"Does it *look* like I'm fucking with you?" Troy spouted, turning to show her the scrape on his back from where he hit the pavement. So it wasn't as gruesome an injury that he wished it was in that moment — an exposed lung or a hole through to the other side where she could see his beating heart — but he felt that having even the tiny scrape gave him the moral high ground.

"*My* husband did that?"

"Yes, *your* husband did that.

"Well, if that's the case, I'm sorry."

If that's the case, Troy thought with a shake of his head. The gall of this woman! In that moment, he hated the he still occasionally thought about her when he masturbated. He could even feel *Ghost Troy* beginning to stir beneath his blankets. He couldn't suffer this indignity lightly any longer. It was time to come in over the top like Stallone and then bid her good day.

"I'll be sure to have that noted in the lawsuit," Troy Stallone'd.

"You know that I'm an attorney now, right?"

"Not a kinesiologist?"

"A good one."

"Kinesiologist?"

"A *fucking* lawyer!" she exclaimed.

"Good, then I'll see you in court," he curtly concluded with a nod.

"But I—"

"Good day," Troy further concluded before turning and walking toward Brose Manor.

"Troy—" Eve tried to continue.

"I said good day!" Troy yelled with a dismissive hand as he kept his back to her and his stride long. Though his hamstring was *really* tight, he made sure to maintain said stride all the way until he made it through the front door and could wallow in shame and misery.

TROY OPENED THE FRONT DOOR, slammed it behind him with a malcontent's ferocity, and slid with his ass against it toward the floor, just as he had done some hours earlier. But whereas the previous ass-slide had been a celebratory one, born from elation and the fidgety limbs of adrenaline-fueled muscles, now his slide was one of abject failure. He sighed the sigh of the dejected and hoped against hope that a freak tornado would drop from the sky and carry him away in a blaze of righteous glory. Before the skies had a chance to open up, however:

"Fucking tell me about it," Rob replied from spaces unseen.

Troy screamed at the top of his lungs for what seemed like the hundredth time that day, throwing his hands in front of his face to shield them from any would-be-attacker that might be skulking about his living room in the daylight hours on a weekday.

"What the fuck is wrong with you?" Rob inquired, though unable to find the smile that had been produced on command in an eerily similar circumstance earlier that morning.

"Would you please stop doing that," Troy yelled, still clenching his chest.

For the effort that Troy put into the question, he felt that he at least deserved an answer, but it was beginning to appear as though none would be forthcoming. Another quick sigh, this time in the guise of a grunt as he pushed himself up from the floor, and Troy was ready to press his case more forcefully — until he saw Rob lying dangerously across the couch as though it were his deathbed. Extremities strewn about in unnatural angles, one across the whole of his face so that he might be hiding the fangs of a vampire for all Troy knew; nothing good could come from this position, and Troy very nearly decided that he didn't want to press the matter any further on the chance that it could make his own mood any worse than it already was; but *Ghost Troy* was intrigued.

Ghost Troy always took advantage of Troy's ill moods.

Whenever he became depressed or anxious, it was easy to let the remnants of his alpha male past take the wheel; and though it usually ended in circumstances that were less than desirable, it felt better than the alternative, which was to tuck tail between shivering legs and admit defeat: page one of the of beta male handbook.

At least when *Ghost Troy* came springing from the depths of Troy's consciousness like Rambo emerging from beneath the waters of an otherwise calm river, spraying not only waves of water but a hail of thundering bullets, he was able to feel like he was in control of any situation. And after the events of the past hour, he really needed to feel in control of *anything*.

"What the hell's wrong with you?" Troy asked with a light kick to Rob's shin.

Rob didn't answer, but slapped wildly in the air without removing his other arm from his face to find the source of the kick. But finally, after Troy continued to intermittently poke and prod, Rob bounded from his place on the couch, all the while screaming:

"Monogamy!"

Troy looked up from the ground a few inches to his friend's face where Rob had landed atop him following his war cry and subsequent attack.

"Monogamy?"

"Monogamy."

It was an inescapably strange moment that grew weirder by the second — neither side particularly sure how to proceed without making it even more awkward or escalating the situation. Troy wasn't sure that Rob was finished with his sudden desire for violence, and Rob wasn't sure that Troy wouldn't silently call dibs on the first kick in a revenge match of Rochambeau.

But finally Troy found a solution: "You're at least going to buy me dinner first, right?"

The silence lingered a bit longer, echoing down the hallway and returning in a wave of defeat before being replaced by a round of hysterical laughter on the part of both men who struggled to release themselves from the entanglement that the inertia from Rob's lunge had created. When Troy began to feel as though he might pass out from the lack of oxygen from both the laughter and Rob's weight, he gathered the last of his energy to bench press Rob off him and allow him to fall where he may; Rob rolled over onto the floor with a thump, ignoring the pain and laughing until he nearly cried, occasionally glancing over to Troy in between gasps for air where he was doing the same.

It felt good.

Finally, when abdominal muscles would no longer tolerate the continuation of laughter, when tear ducts had begun to dry and when it was beginning to feel more than a little bit gay that two men in their thirties were rolling around on the floor, giggling like schoolgirls, each began to push themselves up from the floor.

"I take it that your situation has something to do with Jenny?" Troy asked, dusting himself off.

"I take it that yours has something to do with Eve?" Rob countered.

Each man nodded to the other with a defeated grin.

"Women," Troy mused.

"Right?" Rob was becoming animated as he paced the living room floor. "This chick is fucking me up on the inside, man. You think Daryl would really arrest me if I just said 'fuck it' and killed her?"

"Probably. Murder/suicide is really your best bet."

"I'm on board with everything you just said. Except for the suicide part."

"I could come along and kill you after you killed her. Can't say for sure, but Daryl definitely likes me better than you and he might let me go with a warning. Worth a try, at least."

Troy laughed again, grabbing at his stomach where it still wasn't prepared to allow such a thing.

"I've got to get out of this town," Rob moaned.

"Preaching to the choir, brother," Troy answered. "Preaching to the fucking choir. Eve is back in town. *My* Eve! Only she's *Ian's* Eve now. And as a thirty-year-old man, I should be over this high school shit, but all I want to do is take my dick out and piss all over the whole goddamn world." Troy leaned back against the door, which was beginning to feel way too comfortable for his liking, ashamed of both his helplessness and puerile desire to urinate over the entire universe. "But, in case you haven't been paying attention to my travels throughout the years, getting out of town and staying out of town aren't exactly the same thing."

Rob sighed and looked at Troy as he dropped truth bombs all over the floor like raindrops.

Then, in a moment of pure animation, as if a muse had spoken directly to him from her perch on high and he was trying to say *thank you* with his facial expression alone, Rob's eyebrows shot up toward the heavens. Without explaining himself, he sprinted from the living room and down the hall from Troy's sight before he could be bothered to ask *why*.

When Rob came running back into the living room

toward Troy with sheer purpose in his eyes, Troy stood erect and readied his fists in case he needed to punch his friend in the face to keep from being tackled again. Instead of tackling him, however, Rob skidded to a stop and held out a yellow sticky-note inches from Troy's face — so close in fact that Troy was unable to read its contents.

"How gung-ho are you about leaving town?" Rob asked, nearly breathless.

"I'm as gung as a ho can be," Troy responded, slapping at Rob's hand, tired of having sticky-notes tacked to his face like a bulletin board. "But unless you've got a trust fund that I don't know about, I think we're fucked."

Unconcerned with Troy's gloomy statement, Rob reached into himself and pulled out a yard's worth of resolve, smiled a heinous smile that only an Evil Master Plan could produce, and retracted the sticky-note back a few inches where Troy was able to make sense of the letters; but whereas the letters now made sense in and of themselves, the words that they composed accomplished no such thing.

Piggy.

Piñata.

Angels.

"Is that supposed to mean something?"

"It's code," Rob answered. "In case anyone was snooping around my room."

"Code for what?" *Ghost Troy* was beginning to lose interest, and so Troy was looking for a reason to slip out of the house to the Watering Hole where he might engage in the dance of the alpha male.

"Bank. Juan. Los Angeles," Rob answered with a confidence that would sell an abortion to a Baptist.

"Yeah, so, I'm going to go," Troy began as he reached for the door handle.

"What, no! It's my EMP," Rob exclaimed, slamming his hand against the door to block Troy's exit. "Juan is my supplier's supplier. He brings piñatas full of all kinds of shit across the border and sells them wholesale."

"Why is weed your answer to everything?" Troy asked accusingly as he rolled his eyes and started to pull the door open.

But Rob stood firm, slamming the door closed where Troy had managed to open it a few inches. "It's not the *answer*, my friend, just a means to an end." Rob resumed his Evil Master Plan smile until it was clear that Troy wasn't buying in. "Fine, what's your big plan, then?"

"Get drunk and do something stupid," Troy answered. "Never let me down before."

"We can get drunk. No one said we couldn't be drunk for my plan to work!"

But it wasn't working. Troy's expression hadn't changed in the slightest, a stare that oozed a viscosity so vile that Rob thought better of blocking the door any longer. He stepped back, forced a smile, and opened the door for Troy.

Troy, for his part, forced an impolite smile of his own and went to leave, until:

"Winona Ryder's boobs," Rob replied with the knowing countenance of 1,000 Buddhist monks.

"You son of a bitch." Troy closed the door and glared at Rob.

It had been a tradition amongst the group since time immemorial — which had really been just some several years prior, but they liked how dramatic time immemorial sounded so they used it whenever possible — when Jackson had a dream that turned into a cautionary tale about life and negativity that they applied to just about everything.

The gist of the dream was that Jackson had been back-roading alone and stumbled upon a quaint little town on the outskirts of the county and had, on a whim, decided to explore its surroundings, only to discover that there was a movie being shot nearby; and though the filming of a train hijacking had been thrilling to watch, the life lesson had come when he snuck a little closer to the set to notice one of its stars. Not only was Jackson thrilled to see that the film was starring Winona Ryder — who had been one of his masturbatory go-to's in his pubescent years — but he had happened upon the set just in time to catch them filming a nude scene.

So the sage wisdom that everyone had taken from the prophetic dream that Jackson had dreamed in one of his infamous drunken stupors was one of positivity toward the possibilities that life presented. And while it had initially been used as a motivational tool when anyone in the group faced a moral or potentially life-altering dilemma, it had quickly devolved into a means of blackmail by insinuating that whomever it was being used against was behaving contrary to the group's guiding philosophy; and would be used to publicly shame said person by pointing out the fact that by behaving in such a cowardly manner, they would never be worthy of Winona Ryder's boobs.

"I don't think her boobs apply here," Troy pronounced.

"Her boobs always apply," Rob countered.

9

Card Game

Since the late '70s, it had been a weekly tradition that the assorted business owners of Pine Creek's Main Street district would come together for a gentlemanly poker game. There had been whispers about it throughout town for going on thirty years, but it was no casual affair that would allow for loose conversation on the part of the townsfolk. After an alleged incident during one of the games in which the money purse was said to have been stolen (supposedly at gunpoint, if the legends were true), outsiders were forbidden and the rules strictly forbade speaking of the event under any circumstances. Refusing to speak of the game was widely accepted as the reason that Old Man Frazier's wife had filed for divorce some years back, but she had also been strangely quiet about her reasons — which only added fuel to the fire of speculation.

Nearly a decade had passed since Jackson had taken advantage of the connections that his grandparents had with the Pine Creek Community Bank to get a loan to buy the

Auto Repair Shop from his uncle. Though it wasn't the warmest of receptions, custom dictated that an invitation be extended for him to join the game.

The first few games were beyond surreal — like being allowed into the chocolate factory — or, being a member of the last generation of Cold War Children, like spying one's way inside the Kremlin. It may have just been an old storeroom in the back of Old Man Frazier's barbershop and the extent of the Cold War gadgetry was a rectangular, sliding peephole on the alley door to verify identity before entry, but Jackson was being granted a peek behind the curtain of Pine Creek's inner workings. As far as he was concerned, he had, that day, become a made man.

It was a tenuous relationship at first, given that he was the youngest member of the group by some fifteen years — and that the other members all hated him. Jackson's reputation in those days had been cast into the very lowest valleys of the social order. Though his grandparents had been well-regarded during their lives, and even Kendrick had been seen as an up-and-comer due to his high-school intentions of med-school, that regard hadn't been transferred onto Jackson, who was generally seen as the smallest of steps above drug-dealers (with whom he was known to freely associate).

But it turned out that his crude sense of humor, lower-class though it may have been, played well in a card game setting. And in the early days, when he was in his early twenties, Jackson was a valuable source of information into how the younger generation of Pine Creek citizens would behave, shop, and vote — all of which was of vast importance to the other players, as they comprised the bulk of not only the town's economy, but also its city council.

So while appearances must be maintained outside of the card room — Jackson thumbing his nose at the snobbery of his presumed betters and the snobbery looking down their noses at him — inside the card room, they considered one another equals. Jackson had a full vote in all matters — the city council meetings were a public affair, but the vote was almost always decided beforehand during that week's game — and he had eventually found himself, if not well-liked, then at least well-tolerated.

Kendrick had left him alone an hour before with an unsatisfying excuse of going to see their mother, and Troy had been somewhere with Rob so far as Jackson was aware. Typically, he would find himself both concerned about Kendrick's whereabouts and Troy's spending more time with Rob than himself, but it was easier to get out of the house. Jackson had never broken the cardinal rule of talking about Card Game with his friends, as the group had a zero-tolerance policy and Jackson wasn't about to be on the outside looking in after seeing how the sausage was made. The guys had hounded him relentlessly for the first few years about Card Game, but Jackson went out of his way to make certain his secret was kept, and eventually the hounds lost interest.

"What the hell is wrong with you, asshole?" Old Man Frazier asked through a puff of cigarette smoke where he was setting fold-up chairs around the card table.

Though Old Man Frazier absolutely loathed Jackson's appearance with every fiber of his being, he still enjoyed the younger man's sense of humor and general demeanor. Something about it reminded him of the few men he had considered brothers in Vietnam, given that Jackson cursed like a sailor and didn't seem to adhere to any sort of ethical system which might preclude the killing of men, women, or children, if necessary. He found that comforting. And Jackson, for his part, had resigned himself to the fact that he was just a younger version of Old Man Frazier, less concerned about hygiene but just as borderline insane and inordinately forthright.

"I don't like we're doing tonight, Crane." Jackson had found it amusing to refer to the older man as Frazier Crane since the idea of an urban psychiatrist with their whiny, touchy feelings was the embodiment — even more so than Jackson — of what Old Man Frazier considered wrong with America.

"We're not doing anything. We're considering someone, and that's it." Old Man Frazier dropped the last of the chairs in place, cracked the top of a cold beer, and sat down across from Jackson. "Besides, what are the odds of the other guys letting a goddamn woman into the game? Pretty goddamn slim, I'd say."

Aside from his affinity for using the word "goddamn" at least twice in any given reply, Old Man Frazier also had history on his side. Jackson, so far along in his tenure, had heard all of the stories from the old days and knew the history of the game well enough, and so he knew that there had never been a woman allowed into the *He-Man Woman Haters Club*. It was a combination of two parts sexism and one part lack of opportunity; even if the men of Card Game had been willing to consider a woman, the only local business that had been owned by a woman had been the beauty parlor that Old Lady Hell had run in the '80s and '90s, and no one was about to consider that mean old bitch for a place at the table.

Still, Jackson was uneasy. And although it was forbidden to

discuss Card Game outside of Card Game, everything from outside was fair game once Card Game had begun; and the weekly imbibition of alcohol into the wee hours of the night between the same few participants meant that there were very few secrets left between them over the years.

"What is it—? You think your friend Paulson is going to be pissed off at you for voting on whether or not his old girlfriend can join the game?" Old Man Frazier took a long drag from his cigarette before extinguishing it into a nearby ashtray and taking a generous drink from his beer before exhaling and continuing his conversation. "Even if she did get voted in, which would be a goddamn abomination — let me just say that right now — Paulson would never know about it. So what's the goddamn problem?"

Jackson rolled his eyes, knowing that he was being unreasonable but unable to shake the feeling. "I feel like I'm cheating on Troy."

"Kids these days," Old Man Frazier scoffed as he began shuffling one of three decks of cards on the table. "Always worried about your goddamn feelings."

"I'm twenty-nine years old, you old coot."

"Kids," he maintained.

It didn't help to assuage Jackson's guilt knowing about Eve's return, by way of the Card Game pipeline, for almost a month before she actually arrived in town. Judge Collins had received a friendly call from Eve to inform him that she had recently passed the Oklahoma Bar Exam and that she would be practicing in Murray County. While it hadn't been discussed at the time, Jackson had borne an inordinate amount of guilt ever since by assuming that there might be a future vote, during which he would be expected to cast a *yay* or *nay* for or against Troy's dream-girl based solely upon the merits of her status as a potential asset to card game.

"Or are you still worried that you're a fag like your brother?"

Jackson sighed with a glance over at Old Man Frazier, who was nonchalantly waiting for an answer. Being otherwise preoccupied with the mental gymnastics of trying to navigate the minefield of his allegiances, he hadn't recently had time to worry about becoming a homosexual by association.

"Fuck you, Crane. I never should have told you that."

Old Man Frazier responded with a lazy middle finger and a vindictive smile.

Later that night, when the other nine members had arrived, the cards had been dealt and booze and money were flowing freely, Jackson still hadn't shaken himself from the sense of impending doom over what was to come. He usually refrained from touching any hard liquor until later in the night, as Card Game custom was to spend the first hour or so of the evening welcoming a mood of combined merriment and beer-fueled camaraderie with cards before an intermission to deal with any business at hand; that night, however, Jackson had been hitting the whiskey early.

Judge Collins, befitting his rank as county magistrate and senior member of Card Game, was the one who decided when it was time to get down to the matter of business. Having just beaten Jackson in a heads-up showdown over a decently sized stack of crisp twenty- fifty- and hundred-dollar bills, amounting to some three-hundred-dollars or so, and in the midst of dragging the currency across the table toward an impressive stack of money sitting before him, Collins decided to start the intermission on a high note: "Well, what do you boys say? Shall we take a break and get down to business?"

As there were no objections, he continued: "There are a few things to talk about tonight. As you know, we've got a new attorney set to start practicing next week. There's also the matter of the Southern Comfort Homeowner's Association President using illegal workers again."

"Tell me he hasn't gone back to using retards," Jay Collins chimed in with a laugh coiled at the back of his throat in anticipation.

Jay Collins was Judge Collins' younger brother by some thirteen years, and was also the only practicing attorney in town, which was somehow never seen as a conflict of interest by anyone interesting enough to make any sort of fuss about it. His current cheerful demeanor was due to the assumption that HOA President of the nicest housing development in town had been caught using the mentally handicapped to do yard work again, which had been a ruse developed by said president to keep HOA fees low by "borrowing" the clients from the nearby home for the mentally handicapped for the purposes of maintaining the pristine conditions of his housing development. It wasn't illegal, per se, as he had had an under-the-table agreement with the director of the home to provide his clients with exercise, which he technically did.

The only snag in his plan came when the family of one of his "employees" had caught wind of the scheme and the fact that her brother was performing manual labor in exchange for candy. The families had all gotten together and determined that they really didn't mind that their loved ones had been assigned menial labor under the recognition that it could be good for them to have jobs like normal people; the sticking point came when they demanded that said loved ones be paid in standard federal reserve notes at minimum wage instead of handfuls of the stale Halloween candy that he had bought in bulk and handed out throughout the year. He had heard that some of his former employees really missed being landscapers afterward — not to mention their candy ration — and the residents, rich though they were by Pine Creek standards, complained endlessly about the increase in HOA fees, but the professional landscapers from Ardmore were really something.

"No retards this time," Judge Collins replied. "Mexicans."

A collective sigh went out across the room.

Undocumented immigrants meant the possibility of federal participation, which was never a welcome endeavor under any circumstance. Though it was somewhat less dramatic than a Hollywood thriller, this shadowy government body was going to be forced to bring down a sitting president — granted, the president of a Homeowner's Association — but Jackson, especially being well down the road to inebriation as he was, found himself exceedingly excited by the prospect.

"Finally, I've also gotten a heads-up from the soon-to-be former Sheriff Reynolds that, due to the aforementioned new attorney coming to town, we should probably expect some sort of shenanigans from Jackson's friend, Troy Paulson," Judge Collins concluded with an annoyed groan. It was at that point that Jackson began to realize that he had drunk far too much whiskey far too early in the evening when all eyes turned to stare in his direction.

"Nay," Jackson answered, ignoring the fact that there was no vote in progress and that he wasn't particularly sure as to what he was objecting.

Daryl had more in common with Jackson than he knew.

Any time the dudes did anything, it reflected poorly on both of them; and though it was often Jackson who was reflecting poorly upon Daryl, there, in that circle, Jackson was in good standing.

"Nobody called a vote, Brose," Old Man Frazier spewed with a smoker's cough at the end for dramatic effect.

"I know," Jackson hurriedly offered. "I was saying nay—" he began again before stopping himself and collecting whatever drunken wit he could. "I'm saying no — that you won't have to worry about Troy doing anything stupid. I know Troy. And...you don't have to worry about him. He's good people. Known him all my life. Good people."

"Reynolds said that he ran over a water hydrant this morning."

"Because it was slippery out. And his tires were bald, Jay," Jackson nearly yelled with an annoyed tone barely concealed beneath his breath.

He needed to catch himself before there was a repeat of the 2012 incident that nearly came to blows between the two men when Jay had spoken too liberally about the alleged indiscretions of Jackson's acquaintances and the ill esteem in which he had held them. Jay was the next-youngest member of the group, and at forty-seven, some sixteen years Jackson's senior, he had still somehow managed to allow something of a rivalry to develop between them.

"Calm down, son," Judge Collins cautioned. "There's no witch hunt here. No one's interested in your friend. Our only concern is that if a rash of petty crime crops up this close to the election, and if Sheriff Reynolds were to solve said crimes, we might find ourselves stuck with the good sheriff for another term."

Though theirs was an unfounded concern — given that Sheriff Reynolds had already decided not to stand for re-election, but hadn't divulged that information to anyone outside of a few of his deputies — it was enough to rankle the feathers of Card Game in a way that few other things might.

Over the past several decades, it had become the predominant practice of small municipalities throughout the South to fund themselves not by raising taxes, but by raising revenues. Though the words technically meant the same thing, they had very different meanings for those who uttered them. Raise fines — not taxes. Tax increases were evil things, decreed by God himself and spoken through his vassal, St. Reagan; fining the populace for not obeying arbitrary rules, however, was the pinnacle of small government.

And therein lay the problem with the good Sheriff Reynolds in the eyes of the city council — and, thusly, the members of Card Game: he saw his role as a peace officer as opposed to a tax collector. The city cops, all beholden to the mayor, were on board with their duties as the town's biggest revenue stream: traffic citations, DUIs, public intoxication, civil seizure; anything they could get their hands on was fair game, insofar as the city council was concerned. However, if a sheriff's deputy was first on the scene or if something happened outside of city limits, given that it wasn't severe, it was typically handled with discretion — meaning that it rarely ended with a jangle in the city's coffers. If a deputy pulled someone over for a minor traffic citation and during the course of the stop found that they had been drinking — assuming that they were well this side of shit-faced and little threat to public safety — more often than not, he would confiscate the beer, follow the driver to their house, and take their keys to the station where they could be picked up the next morning.

This was an abomination against their lord and savior, insofar as the city council was concerned.

"So you see, son," Judge Collins continued, "it's better to be safe than sorry in this instance."

Jackson, not wanting to cause any more of a scene than had already been caused, was trying to formulate an exit strategy. If he could feign an aneurysm or diarrhea, then there was a chance that he could still make it out with his dignity intact. He wasn't sure which option he'd settled on yet, but he felt certain that the face for either would be more or less the same, so he took a deep breath, crinkled his nose and readied himself for the role of a lifetime.

The Academy, sadly, would never see his performance, nor would the members of Card Game. As Jackson opened his mouth to imitate the guttural noise of the wildebeest, the barbershop door swung open with seemingly unnatural force.

Before anyone in the room had the chance to adjust their demeanor to whatever new reality had befallen them, a man entered the room in a desperate haste, wearing a baggy hoody over a ski mask and a pair of thick gloves that each brandished a pistol.

"Everyone be cool and no one has to die!" the man shouted.

For their part, the people of Card Game just moaned and groaned with a teenager's fervor. Their lives weren't flashing before their eyes and there were no last thoughts of loved ones before an untimely demise. It seemed likely that it would be difficult to avoid losing whatever money they had on the table, but more importantly, Card Game had been compromised.

The fan had just spattered the entire room with a generous helping of shit.

The newcomer produced a burlap bag from the giant koala pouch on his midsection and threw it on the table. "All of the money on the table, your wallets and jewelry."

"We're men. What kind of goddamn jewelry do you think we're wearing," Old Man Frazier growled.

"Shut up, old man! Wedding rings, watches — anything you've got! In the bag!"

Slowly, the bag filled with bills, wallets, and a nearly full ashtray, which Old Man Frazier tossed in along with his wallet. A hush fell across the table, a calm before the storm that might mean that Old Man Frazier could well be put out of their misery right in front of them.

Instead of a gunshot, however, the members of Card Game were treated to sounds that were very similar to those Jackson had just been prepared to feign moments beforehand, as the would-be-robber let out a growl of rage and dissatisfaction that would make Bruce Banner jealous.

"I hate you old bastards!" he screamed at the top of his lungs.

And there *was* a gunshot.

But it wasn't fired from the most obvious of guns.

While the would-be-robber began eyeing Old Man Frazier and swinging his pistol in his direction with all the hatred he could muster, Jackson, who was sitting directly across the table from Old Man Frazier, had un-holstered his own pistol that he wore underneath his jacket.

With little hesitation, Jackson pointed the gun and fired a single shot. The whole of the room had already begun diving for cover in the event that a shot would be fired toward Old

Man Frazier, so they assumed the worst from the various locations on the floor. When the smoke cleared, though, they were pleasantly surprised to find the would-be-robber lying face-first on the floor, a gunshot wound spilling blood from the meat of his ass.

Before anyone could voice their satisfaction, Old Man Frazier had already begun to assault the man with a series of kicks to the ribs before one final insult in which he stomped his boot on the cheek that bore the wound, laughing as the would-be-robber let out a yell.

"Shit, Brose!" Judge Collins exclaimed, pulling himself slowly up off of his knees. "Hell of a shot!" The others began exclaiming themselves until one exclamation was indistinguishable from another, each man laughing at their good luck and congratulating Jackson on the lifetime achievement of ostensibly saving all their lives.

"I was aiming for his head," Jackson uttered under his breath, thankful that the room was too abuzz to notice his confession.

10

Cunnilinguist Lumberjacks

Reagan found herself that evening behaving in an atypical manner for a woman in her position: sleepily reviewing documents for an ungrateful boss who would inevitably find something to complain about in her work — despite both the effort and time that she had wasted doing something that he, himself, could have done — if he hadn't spent the night playing cards with his dad, that is.

Jay Collins hadn't told her about Card Game, obviously. He was cordial with her, as she was his paralegal, but he had developed a well-earned, bulletproof reputation over the years as something of a legendary dickwad in legal circles — which had resulted in their relationship being predominately professional with little to no personal information being exchanged by either side.

Her relationship with Jackson Brose, however, was decidedly less professional. They had been high school sweethearts, and though it hadn't been under the most traditional of trajectories — and could be called worse than dysfunctional by judgmental parents — theirs was the sort of oddball relationship that had spanned a decade-and-a-half. After a pregnancy scare during the summer after they graduated high school, the two had gotten engaged; and though it had been diagnosed as a simple scare some weeks later, much to the chagrin of both of their families, the short engagement continued and ended in a marriage; true enough, that marriage had ended in divorce less than a year later, but the *Titanic* ending, tragic as it were, was unable to sink the semi-platonic relationship that defied logic to persevere through her attending college in another state, her getting re-married then re-divorced, and Jackson being a bona fide man-child.

There were times Reagan hated herself for allowing the only "successful" relationship she had ever been in to be one-part Wookie, but there was part of her that felt like it had to be fate — that the only explanation for her undying attraction to and inescapable need for intimacy with *that man* was that it was preordained by some sort of cosmic influence. She had dated so much higher on the food chain — married so much higher on the food chain — yet she always found herself drawn back to the portly, foul-mouthed metalhead who made her laugh and feel like the queen of her very own mountain — Shit Mountain, as it were, but a mountain over which she ruled, nonetheless.

She was annoyed by the fact that she was thinking about Jackson so late while trying to finish what little work was left in hopes of actually catching a few hours of sleep before going back to her thankless job the next morning. Annoyingly enough, he, too, would be playing cards — with her damn boss from her damn thankless job, no less; that said, she was pleased by the thought of Jackson endlessly aggravating him to the end of the known world, well beyond that into the spirit realm and into the infinity of multiple dimensions. Jay hated Jackson almost as much as Jackson hated Jay. Though it hadn't been explicit, Reagan had spent the better part of the past several years fostering an unrelenting hatred of her boss in Jackson, knowing that it was the only way she had to spite him: forcing him to play cards once a week with a Neanderthal who would ruthlessly berate him on any given subject, hopefully to the point of suicide.

She really hated her boss.

She was smiling at what she thought Jackson might be complaining about at that very moment — Jay's hair or his cologne, speech pattern, his bald spot, his taste in music; the possibilities were endless, and they were enough to bring a smile to her lips, despite both her mood and exhaustion. Her smile, and thusly her newfound joy, was short-lived, though; interrupted by a loud, incoherent knock at her door, followed by the unmistakable sound of glass shattering across the hardwood floor.

At the first knock, she had assumed that it was Jackson looking for something that she wasn't in the mood to give, despite being rather smitten at the thought of him in that moment, but after the shattering glass, she hoped that it wasn't the local scumbaggery. Reagan's dad had drilled into her head for years the importance of keeping a weapon nearby in case of emergency, and her relationship with Jackson aside, she had always been daddy's girl; she reached to the side of the desk where she kept holstered a loaded .45 Ruger for situations just like these. A quick check of the chamber and a flick of the safety switch later, and she was heading toward the front door and whomever was stupid enough to be standing on the other side of it.

Before she could even glance through the broken glass to see the other side, however, it became obvious that the stupidity required to be standing on the other side of the door could really only belong to one man.

"Shit," Jackson was cursing loudly to himself as he attempted to pick up shards of glass from the front porch.

Reagan rolled and then rubbed her eyes. She was too tired to deal with this. She flicked the safety back up on the pistol, emitting a loud click and startling Jackson in the process — for a moment he thought that she might have actually decided to shoot him this time. She opened the door, pistol still in hand, to find Jackson standing sheepishly on the other side, making sure to keep the pistol within his periphery while he began his apology. The apology, however, wasn't readily forthcoming — due almost exclusively to the degree to which Jackson was obviously inebriated.

"Yeah, that was—" he began before pausing to allow for an ill-timed hiccup. "—my bad."

For added effect, Regan loosed the clip from the .45 and ejected the round in the chamber, catching it with the other hand before turning away from Jackson to lay the pistol down on the coffee table. With her back turned, Jackson tried sneaking his way into the house with the stealth of an ox; however, back still turned, Reagan reached an omniscient arm out across the doorway to block any attempted entry as would a wizard on a bridge.

"What the fuck do you think you're doing?" she asked, putting a pin in what Jackson clearly had planned.

"I brought you flowers," he managed, holding out a

makeshift bouquet that had obviously been pilfered from someone's yard or front porch that very night, fresh dirt falling from the roots onto her hardwood floors.

"And as custom dictates, broke the glass on my front door to signify their arrival?" she countered.

Jackson took a long look down at the flowers, collecting what thoughts hadn't abandoned him before offering: "Aren't they pretty?"

"They're stolen."

"You're pretty," he smiled with a drunk's countenance.

"You're drunk," she frowned with sobriety's authority.

"You're drunk," he replied. It had sounded just fantastic in his head, but now that he had heard it out loud, he was beginning to suspect that he might be drunk. "Yeah, I'm drunk."

"And there it is. The love of my life, ladies and gentlemen." She stopped the conversation with a glare when Jackson tried to continue the charade of a conversation, allowing him to stew in his own debauched state of mind for half-a-minute or more until she was ready to continue.

"You're not coming in."

"I don't want to come in."

She started to close the door in his face before he grabbed the corner of it to prevent it from doing so.

"Wait, I do want to come in," he admitted. "I'm thinking that I do want to come in. Now that I think about it, coming in would be nice. Wasn't feeling it before, but feeling it now."

She shook her head defiantly.

"You're pretty."

"Jesus Christ, Jackson. What are you even doing here? Card Game shouldn't be over for hours."

With a drunk's charm, he bumblingly ran his hand across

her face in awkward circles before dropping the other three fingers and thumb, leaving only his index finger placed inappropriately up to her lips. "We don't talk about Card Game."

"I hate you," Reagan responded with the smallest of smiles — small enough that she hoped he wouldn't notice and thus cue his mind in its highly inebriated state to initiate Protocol Zero, which is what Jackson called his flailing attempts at seduction. She actually found that he could be remarkably charming when he wanted to be — in his own weird, hyper-inflated egotistical manner, but the heights to which hyper-inflation would soar when he was drunk were ridiculous.

"Sorry about your door," he began, playfully pushing his way through her arm. She finally yielded and allowed him to pass.

"You're fixing my door."

"I'll go get my tool belt from your garage right now."

"I don't have a garage, dumbass. And I meant in the morning." She stood and waited for a response while he stared very determinedly at the floor. "So what do you want? It's too late for a booty call. I'm telling you that right off the bat. I'm tired. I still have work to do. And I'm not loaning—"

"I need to borrow five-hundred dollars," he blurted out, cutting her off.

"—you any money," she finished. She sighed again and walked back toward her desk to holster the pistol that she had picked up from the table, unsure as of yet whether she should just shoot him and put herself out of his misery.

"I don't know why I'm attracted to you. You inadvertently break shit in your Hulk-like drunken stupors, the sex is just okay, and you're a horrible poker player," she finished, raising her eyebrows to let the fact that she just questioned his manhood in so many ways sink in.

Jackson, meanwhile, had recently borne a smile — realizing that she had begun to magically soften before his very eyes from enemy combatant to possible agent of collusion. She would probably loan him the money until payday to cover his poker debt, which was a bit of a knock to his manhood, to be sure, but he always paid her back and that made up for it, he thought. He had also begun to suspect that it may not, in fact, be too late for a booty call, based upon the eyebrow game that she was throwing his way.

Jackson began to stalk toward his prey, his own eyebrow game one step short of crazy eyes in bedroom-eyes mode. Being of a single mind, he had also managed to focus his speech into something coherent, if still nonsensical.

"One, I break things on occasion," he began, "but that door sucked, anyway. I did you a favor, darling."

Reagan couldn't help but drop her eyes and laugh to herself before looking back up to this man-child coming toward her with the most unappealing of looks on his face, trying hard to be sexy, but managing to look as though he may need to bum a ride to the emergency room.

"Two, the sex being okay? 'Okay' is a win in my book. I'll take that any fucking day of the week, sweetheart."

Having completed his trek across the room, Jackson had oozed behind her where he had taken the pistol from her hand and slid into the holster and gotten himself into a position that he could whisper in her ear.

"And third, I play poker like Seth Rogen eats the pussy."

Despite herself, Reagan began laughing semi-hysterically

at the utter nonsense coming from the mouth of her — God help her — lover.

"I don't even know if that's a good or a bad thing," she giggled.

"It's goddamn marvelous," he stated matter-of-factly. "Rogen eats the pussy like a champ."

No longer able to stay annoyed at herself or at him, wrapped up in the ridiculousness of the conversation, Reagan turned around and draped her arms around Jackson's neck, smiling as she stared into his eyes.

"And you know this for a fact, do you?"

"Oh, yeah," Jackson continued without missing a beat. "You can tell by looking at him. He's got that Jewish work ethic. Takes a sack lunch, spends the weekend down there like a goddamn lumberjack."

After another laugh, Reagan was able to continue: "A lumberjack, really?"

"Notorious cunnilinguists, the lumberjacks."

"Right."

"He also tells amusing anecdotes during timeouts to keep it entertained."

"Stop while you're ahead," she managed, stifling another laugh, kissing this court jester with whom she had been cursed to fall in love.

"Should I get my sack lunch?" he asked with a giggle.

"I'm in love with an imbecile," she sighed.

"Who is he? I'll kick his ass."

Reagan allowed him one more kiss before turning around and walking in the direction of her bedroom, never signaling whether Jackson was to follow or not. He stood motionless for several seconds, breathless, as though he were covered in mud and hiding from a Predator, waiting to find out if his life was fated to end in that very moment.

"Are you coming?" Reagan called from the other room.

"Just gonna grab my sack lunch!" Jackson exclaimed as he hurried toward the bedroom, knocking a lamp off of the desk with a love handle as he blazed by it, ignoring the shattering of glass in his haste.

"I'll fix that tomorrow!"

PART II

Fullblown Fuckery

11

Jurisdictional Clusterfuck

Kendrick was not aware that his brother had intended to close the shop shortly after he would leave for lunch somewhere around the time of eleven that morning; likewise, he was unaware that Jackson had constructed a fairly elaborate ruse that involved mentioning continually throughout the morning that his legs had been cramping up at various intervals during the previous night and that it had taken a considerable amount of effort on his part to walk at all that day. It was really overkill, truth be told, as it was evinced quite clearly by size alone that Jackson wasn't particularly fond of outdoor activities, and he was always the first to suggest driving to the diner that was only two blocks away. So the thought that Jackson would have been skulking about the shadows and back alleys of Main Street that morning in a last-ditch effort to surveil his brother in hopes that he wasn't damning Jackson himself to a predestined life of homosexuality was ridiculous for a number of reasons — the least of which was physical.

Jackson had pretended to busy himself with various phone calls to parts stores starting sometime around ten that morning, both to play up his imagined physical ailments and so that he could occasionally peek through the blinds of the office to make sure that he wouldn't miss Kendrick leaving for his so-called "brunch."

When the time finally came, Jackson had winded himself almost immediately by sprinting across the shop, dodging car parts and tools that were scattered about the floor, and had barely avoided concussing himself on the bumper of a late-model something-or-other where it rested on the forks of a hydraulic lift. He waited for Kendrick to make it half-a-block down the street in the midst of light traffic before he closed the hanging garage doors, then ran back around to the front of the shop where he closed and locked the door with panicked gusto.

Horror and crime were Jackson's favorite genres when it came to entertainment — be it film, video game, or music — and that fact served him well at that moment in his life, knowing that he needed to stay at least two car-lengths behind and that dozens of body-disposal methods were at his fingertips in the case that he was caught and forced to kill his sibling to keep him quiet. Walking instead of driving, however, created its own set of problems: how the hell far was two car-lengths when one was afoot? However the hell far it may have been, it was problematic in and of itself since Kendrick tended to keep a fast pace. Jackson found himself half-sprinting to even keep his twin in sight.

He had hoped that Kendrick would turn off Main Street at some point because, in his mind at least, the situation was bound to eventually draw the attention of the otherwise unsuspecting passersby. Much to his chagrin, however, Kendrick continued on along Main Street until it became Broadway and continued on in the direction of the high school. If it was some sort of sultry tryst that Kendrick was headed toward, it seemed destined to be a public one. Suspecting that his was a fool's errand on that particular day, Jackson was just about to turn around and head back to the shop, finish the day's work early, and go to the Watering Hole to drink himself into masculinity.

Before he had the chance to fully divest himself from the situation, however, something occurred on the periphery, just past where Kendrick was crossing the bridge across Rock Creek where Jackson's vision was partially obscured by tree branches sprouting from the side of the hill along the bridge. Though his eyesight had been getting consistently worse for some years by that point, Jackson refused to get glasses to correct the problem, citing the fact they were not the most "metal" of accessories. So, though the scene was a bit blurry to his maladjusted eyes, it looked a hell of a lot like someone had just robbed the Community Bank and was making their getaway on foot, carrying a bag in each hand and sprinting past the Buffalo toward the tree-line of the park.

A few moments later, Jackson's suspicions were confirmed as a louder-than-expected alarm emanated from the bank to fill the streets with a sense of anarchy. Without having consciously done so, Jackson had continued walking toward the crime scene, only noticing that he had done so once he bumped into Kendrick who stood, mouth agape, staring at the woods where the two men had recently disappeared.

"What the—" Kendrick had begun to ask of a stranger

before he realized that it was Jackson. "How the hell did you get here so fast?"

"What?" Jackson may have been prepared for such a question earlier, but having witnessed the audacity, the sheer size of the testicles on the men who had just scampered off into the woods in front of their very eyes, ostensibly with bags — multiple bags — of money in tow, he was unable to form a cogent response.

"Were you following me?" Kendrick asked, chest still rising and falling quickly from the excitement of the moment.

"How the hell are you going to accuse me of something so stupid when we just saw what we saw?" he responded.

Though it was not the most convincing of answers, Kendrick was unable to argue logic any further having just seen what they had seen. There was crime in Pine Creek, sure, but it was petty crime — the sort of crime that Daryl usually scared out of teenagers with a strong showing from his mustache and an un-strapping of his gun. But this was a federal crime that had just transpired before their very eyes. This was the sort of thing that transpired in Oklahoma City or Tulsa. This sort of thing might happen on the small-town streets of some shithole state like Texas, but this was Oklahoma they were talking about.

"Dude, why didn't we think of that!" Jackson exclaimed, suddenly annoyed that he had been working for the past fifteen years while two guys just concluded their get-rich-quick scheme before his very eyes.

"Why didn't we think of committing a federal crime, you mean?" Kendrick asked, brushing away the question with the ridiculousness that it deserved.

Content that he had eluded the issue of his proximity,

Jackson let Kendrick's question end the conversation as he watched an attractive female teller follow her co-workers out from the bank. God, he hoped that he wasn't gay.

IT HADN'T BEEN LONG before the bank alarm had been joined by the wail of police sirens and fire trucks — and, shortly thereafter, half of the town, it seemed, had joined Jackson and Kendrick along Broadway to shake their collective heads in awe, just as the noble citizens of Whoville had done before them. Daryl had been one of the first several professionals on the scene, but he was soon joined by the rest of the Sheriff's Department, the Pine Creek Police Department, Lighthorse Police, and the Oklahoma State Bureau of Investigation. Trying to make any sort of determination about the assailants or specifics of anything other than the fact that a crime had been committed in the midst of such a jurisdictional clusterfuck was proving problematic, to say the least.

To further complicate matters, Sheriff Reynolds — who, as head of the county law enforcement, held momentary jurisdiction — had just gotten off the phone with someone from the Oklahoma City field office of the FBI, who was sending a team to Pine Creek. It was made clear to Sheriff Reynolds that he was to contain the crime scene only and wait out the hour-and-a-half that it would take for said team to arrive. So close to retirement, however, Sheriff Reynolds wasn't in the mood to be left holding the door for a bunch of FBI bottom-feeders who were so low on the totem pole that they had been stationed in Oklahoma City; instead, he tasked Daryl with trying to discern some semblance of the events that had transpired before the FBI team arrived in hopes that Daryl would distinguish himself during the course of the investigation, thus making his transition from power go all the more smoothly.

Crime scenes were hardly Daryl's forte, and even though he was unaware of the greater ambitions that Sheriff Reynolds had in mind for him, unaware even if he had any further ambitions for himself at that point, he had seen enough cop movies over the years to know that FBI agents were dickheads to the last man and that they would walk all over him and all the other locals as soon as they set foot on the scene — not to mention the celebrity that he would earn for upstaging the FBI. There was also the added bonus of defeating and shaming his Pine Creek Police counterpart, R.J. Denny — the bastard — who had, no doubt, been given the same instructions as Daryl. If he solved this crime, he could rest comfortably upon his laurels for the remainder of his career and ride them from the Watering Hole into retirement.

He immediately set out to find Ainsley Williams, the only teller to whom the suspects had actually spoken. The bank had been cleared out so that the OSBI could start fingerprinting, so he went about trying to spot her amongst the crowd. It wasn't an overly difficult task to pick Ainsley Williams out of a crowd in and of itself; she was the sort of woman who tended to stand out in a crowd, after all, especially now that she had recently divorced her high school sweetheart of seven years.

Dating for a Pine Creek native was a treacherous affair that would see a flurry of activity during the high school years, followed by an extended dormant period and a typical resurrection somewhere near the late twenties or early thirties. There was an aura about the people who planned on leaving Pine Creek immediately upon graduation that was akin to a

Google Maps icon above their head that quite clearly stated that they were planning on going to college and would, more often than not, end up in the Oklahoma City or Dallas areas, respectively. Those were the two closest metropolitan areas to Southern Oklahoma and, therefore, the most likely designation of its denizens who were looking to shed their small-town skins and continue their evolution into something more akin to what they saw on television. Thusly, there was something of a desperate game that Pine Creek's future generations of men were playing in high school to find the most attractive of iconless women and lock them down at the earliest possible age to avoid years of unwanted celibacy. If someone had had a late night the evening before and missed the early innings of the game, it would be well into the seventh inning stretch before people began to realize that marrying shortly after high school had been a mistake — then all that was left was for the town's divorce lawyer to declare dating season open once more before the late innings.

So it wasn't the fact that Broadway had been completely closed down by that point by an assortment of various municipal enforcement agency vehicles — not to mention the two Pine Creek fire trucks and another fire truck from the nearby town of Davis — meandering in either direction between barricades and police tape that was obstructing Daryl's ability to lay eyes on Ainsley. Whereas most of the heads in the crowd were pointed in the direction of the bank and the swarm of cops who were trying frantically to look busy and thus important, there was a group of rubbernecks whose necks were pointed in the wrong direction altogether. It was in this particular group that Daryl was interested.

Making his way through the crowd, dodging the inevitable

questions of the curious townsfolk with a deft feigning of ignorance, Daryl finally came upon the group of half-a-dozen men where they were huddled around Ainsley as though she were about to call out the next play from behind a face mask.

Daryl was preparing to relive his glory days as a linebacker by bowling through the crowd of men like Dakota Lewis until he was drawn away by one of his fellow deputies yelling to him through the crowd:

"Daryl!" Megan's voice had rang out like a banshee. She had been a sheriff's deputy for a few years, and had discovered early on in her career that her booming voice was her best asset; it was particularly effective in frightening teenagers who thought that they might have more leniency with a female deputy than her male counterpart; and for attracting one's attention across large groups of people. She also swore like a sailor as a result of growing up with four brothers and working in a male-dominated profession.

Daryl sighed and turned to the find the source of the ridiculously loud voice that came in such a tiny package. He had been laser-focused in on Ainsley and getting a foot up on his competition that the last thing that he wanted was to have to fend off Megan and any attempt that she might have planned to outdo him. He saw people being pushed aside in the crowd, but couldn't yet see Megan where she was hidden amongst them like a lioness in the grass plains of the Serengeti. Finally, she emerged from the mass of bodies, slightly out of breath, but fully in control of her voice:

"Daryl," she continued.

"I'm right here, Megan," he responded, waving to where he stood a half-dozen paces from her.

"Oh," she responded, hurrying over to his side. "Sheriff Reynolds told me to come find you."

"I just talked to Sheriff Reynolds," Daryl replied, annoyed that the conversation didn't seem to be going anywhere.

"Within the last two minutes?" she asked.

"No, but—"

"Then shut the fuck up and listen," she scolded. "Some shit has gone down."

"I can see that," Daryl replied, motioning to the commotion surrounding them.

"Other shit. Different shit," she insisted. "Someone broke into and trashed the DHS office."

"Why," he asked. "Who the hell would breaking into the Department of Human Services building?"

"I don't fucking know," she answered with a scowl. "I didn't do it, did I?"

"Okay, after I talk to Ainsley—"

"And someone released the buffalo."

"What? Which buffalo?"

"All the fucking buffalo!" she yelled. "From the Buffalo Pasture! Some asshole broke the gate open and let them out."

"Jesus Christ," Daryl began.

"That's not all."

"There's *more*," he asked, dumbfounded.

"There was a sighting," Megan responded, quieter than she had been before.

Daryl could only imagine the words that were about to come out of her mouth. What sort of sighting? Alien? Terrorist? Jackalope?

"Sasquatch," she replied uneasily.

"Sasquatch?"

"Sasquatch."

"Are you fucking with me," Daryl asked, convinced that she had to be by that point.

"We got three different calls," Megan maintained.

"You're sure you're not fucking with me?" he asked again, sure that she was.

"Scout's honor."

12

Teefies

Jackson had lost Kendrick in the commotion during the aftermath of the robbery as he wandered around aimlessly for several minutes, bumping into people and wondering whether he might as well get it over with and start banging dudes.

Though he had to admit that he was absolutely obsessed with catching Kendrick in the act, in the scheme of things, he really didn't care if his brother turned out to be gay. Gay Tony had gone to high school with them and they were all friends to this day. Sure, he had received the moniker Gay Tony in school, but that was only to separate him from Fat Tony, Skinny Tony, and Dickhead Tony, all of whom had also attended their high school in varying grades below them. Jackson was the epitome of the *live and let live* kind of guy and had no interest whatsoever in who anyone was sleeping with except for himself, and the only thing that Jackson knew for a fact was that he was a big fan of the vagina — and Reagan's in particular. Sure, he could admit that dudes like Ryan

Reynolds, Matthew McConaughey, and Brad Pitt were sexy man-beasts, and who would he be to deny any one of them a quick shag in an Applebee's bathroom were they to ask? Those dudes were universally bang-able; but if Kendrick dragged him down into a life where the forecast always called for raining men? The plot had thickened when he saw Kendrick leaving the Snake Farm and Ramona, leaving open the possibility that maybe it was all in Jackson's head. Maybe his brother had just been sleeping with Ramona the whole time and was ashamed because she was an older broad; maybe she had threatened to black widow him if he told anyone.

Frustrated by his failure, it was two days later before Jackson tried his luck at tailing Kendrick again. When he did, he had been driving toward the golf course, which was strange since they didn't really interact with anyone who lived on that side of the tracks — but what wasn't strange about the events that had transpired? Once he had seen Kendrick pull into a driveway, Jackson parked his truck and ran alongside the road, ducking behind random trashcans, shrubs, and cars in an attempt to remain hidden.

Kendrick had been too focused to notice.

Jackson finally came to a stop behind a car, kneeled on the ground, and gasped for breath. He stuck his head up over the car's trunk just long enough to catch the front door opening and Kendrick about to disappear inside behind Eve.

Eve?!

Troy's Eve? Or *Ian's* Eve?

Whoever's Eve she may have been, she definitely wasn't *Kendrick's* Eve. Was she? Was Kendrick just running around town dipping his pen in anyone's ink who might have him?

Had he become some sort of metrosexual phenom the likes of which the town had never seen? He was beginning to envy Kendrick.

Deciding that it was time to end the charade and get to the bottom of things, Jackson stood up tall, sucked in his stomach, and began to walk toward Eve's house to confront the whole lot of philandering sons of bitches. Before he could get more than a few steps into the road, however, a black SUV pulled up next to him and two men in black stepped out.

THE PINE CREEK POLICE DEPARTMENT was hardly a sight unto itself. It was the same unimpressive building that it had been for the past several generations — heavily worn and dating back to the town's founding; though it had been re-bricked at some point during the Nixon Administration and the tile was regularly waxed by the inmates on work duty, it still managed to retain the Gotham-esque luster of an asylum.

Once it had become home base for the FBI field office, however, it had an air of notoriety that Jackson had never noticed during the several nights that he had spent inside its drunk tank. He was following a man in a suit who in turn was also following a man in a suit as they passed a man in a suit who nodded to both men in suits who were leading Jackson while wearing suits, leaving him to feel as though he were attending a funeral — which he hoped wasn't his own.

The agents who picked him up in front of Eve's house hadn't been overly informative as to the specifics of their request for him to come down to the police station to answer a few questions. He had seen enough of these sorts of things on

TV, however, to know that he wasn't in any real trouble yet, as long as he kept his mouth closed; that and the fact that he hadn't actually done anything and wasn't sure why they would want to speak to him in the first place.

He was led into a room that usually housed the police chief but had been repurposed as an office for the Agent in Charge. Inside, there were stacks and stacks of boxes and files, crime scene photos plastered purposefully across the walls, and three men waiting for him — all wearing black suits. Jackson wasn't sure what they wanted, but he had already decided that as long as it wasn't sex, he was going to give it to them. He felt like he was in the middle of some sort of psychology experiment designed to make him so ridiculously uncomfortable that he had no choice but to cooperate — which wasn't too awfully far from the truth.

"Mr. Brose," began the Agent in Charge. "I'm glad you could make it. We just have a few questions that we could use your help with. It shouldn't take more than a few minutes and we can get you out of here."

"Okay, yeah. No problem," Jackson answered with a mental sigh. They just needed his help with something. Of course. It all made sense — except that it didn't. Still, he took a seat in the chair that the agent motioned toward and immediately felt better about the situation. These were just dudes in suits. They had two balls and a dick under those suits just like him — with the exception of the female agent in the corner of the room — but that wasn't enough of a concern to unnerve him at that point.

"When we come to a town in crisis like this one, we have a certain set of guidelines: establish a timeline of events, scout the area for persons of interest, and so on."

"Makes sense," Jackson replied with a smile, beginning to feel as though he was in the driver's seat of the situation. "You're looking for assholes, right? I'm your guy. I know every asshole in town. Who are you looking for?"

"Actually, Mr. Brose, our questions today pertain to you."

He wasn't one hundred percent sure, but Jackson suspected that he may have peed a little bit with the last syllable that the agent had uttered. He was throwing open this door and that in the dark recesses of his brain to find whatever it was that these bionic men in suits were looking for, these androids who wouldn't stop until he had told them everything and betrayed every principle upon which he stood. And then it dawned on him: one of them was a woman; he wasn't sure why, but that frightened him all of a sudden as he glanced nervously toward her like a tweaker in Bat Country. She knew things, could look right into the depths of his soul and come up with whatever glimmer of hope he had in between her talons and rip it away without hesitation.

He was screwed.

"What do you want from me?" he screamed at them.

Being so wrapped up in his own neuroses, he hadn't noticed that all three of them had flinched at his outburst, startled by the suddenness of it.

After a few moments in which the air was allowed to clear and nerves allowed to calm, the Agent in Charge nodded to the female agent, signifying that the show was ready to commence.

"Mr. Brose, I would like to ask you about an incident in which you were involved."

"Incident?" Jackson screeched. "What incident? There was no incident. I've never incident-ed in my life."

"Do you recall your whereabouts on April 9th of this year?" she asked in a flat tone.

"It's August," he retorted. "How would I remember that?"

"On the day in question, you were involved in a minor traffic incident."

With that, Jackson sat up straight in his chair and took on an aura of desperation.

"That wasn't illegal."

"Actually, it might be," she responded. "Are you aware of the cyber-bullying act recently passed by congress?"

"Cyberbullying? That's ridiculous. I'm not a 14-year-old girl and I don't even know the woman who cut me off. How could I bully someone that I don't even know?"

"By posting it online to Facebook."

"My profile is private!" he yelled.

"I'd like to read you your response, if you don't mind."

"I do mind."

Without acknowledging his response, she produced a piece of paper and began reading its contents aloud for the room:

"If I could kill people with my mind, I would have a body-count on par with the great genocidal leaders of all time — Alexander, Gnaeus Pompey Magnus, fucking Xerxes — just mostly for people who can't drive."

Jackson, despite himself, was unable to contain the smallest of laughs at hearing his rant read in such a monotone voice, but stopped when he noticed that he was the only one smiling. He bowed his head and breathed in deeply before responding: "Granted, that doesn't sound great out of context, but—"

Without waiting for him to finish his sentence, the agent continued reading:

"I hope sincerely and with all malice of forethought that the cunt who cut me off dies in a car crash at some point today. Not only do I hope she dies, but then she's so disfigured by the sheer carnage of the wreck that they have to identify her by her dental records — only that every goddamn one of her teefies got knocked out upon impact."

"I'd just liked to stop you right there if I could," Jackson interjected gingerly. "Teefies is a vulgarization of the word teeth. I can see that you think it's a racist play on ebonics, but it's really not. It's just something I saw on a show one time and found funny."

"So they bring her parents down to attempt an identity," the agent continued, "but it looks like she's fought the fucking Mountain and her brain was just smashed out through the eye sockets. So they have to call in ex-boyfriends to verify that her old, blown-out vagina that's been pounded by the entire football, baseball, and badminton teams is, in fact, her vagina."

Jackson sinks down as far into his seat as he's able, hiding his face with his hands as his words are read aloud like a serial killer's last rights before his execution.

"So the eighty or so dudes whom she's banged over the last few weeks are staring at the vagina, comparing stories with one another, asking the mortician things like how deep it is to better ascertain whether or not it's really her. And all of this is in front of her parents! Her dad finds out how deep his daughter's vagina is at the morgue."

She stops reading, looks at him with contempt: "Shall I continue?"

"I've got nothing. It was a dark time for me."

"The fucking shame she feels watching from the ethereal plane of purgatory where she will spend the rest of goddamn eternity because mindless fucking skanks who drive like they're in a Barbie power wheels definitely don't go to heaven; and they're too fucking cunt-y for hell."

"With all due respect, I stand by that part," Jackson said with a hint of confidence finally breathed into him. "The part about the skanks who can't drive is on the money. They shouldn't go to heaven. In retrospect, I maybe shouldn't have used such graphic language, okay, but I'd really like to go back to the whole 'teefies' ordeal because I feel like I'm being unfairly judged as a racist and that's not cool."

"We can't forget the postscript," the agent continued, as if oblivious to the fact that Jackson had been speaking at all. "Which reads: if I ever see that bitch out of her car, I'm going to punch her in her stinky old cum dumpster. If I saw her drowning in a lake, I would piss in it in hopes that that last little bit of pee is what she would breathe with her dying breath."

"This isn't going well, is it?" Jackson asked.

"No, it is not," the Agent in Charge answered.

"I feel like you guys don't really understand sarcasm or even appreciate a good joke because you're missing the big picture here. No cum dumpsters were punched. No lakes were peed in. I was just venting!"

"What else do you do to vent, Mr. Brose?" the female agent asked.

"Rob banks, perhaps?" the Agent in Charge suggested.

"I want my lawyer," Jackson stated in a hushed panic.

"Of course you do. What's his name," the agent asked.

"*Her* name," Jackson corrected.

DARYL HAD BEEN DRIVING AIMLESSLY around the back roads of Murray County for the better part of the afternoon, staring ever-so-intently at nothing in particular and praying to dear goddamn Buddha or whichever deity would listen in the hope that he might stumble upon the tiniest detail that every other asshole with a badge had managed to miss. Each of the badged assholes against whom he was competing for the biggest bust in Murray County history was operating under the assumption that the perpetrators had escaped by fleeing south through the deeply wooded part of the park behind the bank to the closest access road where their parked car had been waiting some half a mile or so down; as part of his investigation, however, Daryl was traveling — both literally and figuratively — in a different direction.

Every kid from Pine Creek who played any sport from middle school to high school knew that there was a trail underneath the Rock Creek Bridge on Broadway not more than a hundred yards from where the bank stood. The cross-country team, the football team, the basketball team, the baseball team — every single one of them was sent at some point during the year to run the Buffalo Trail as part of their punishment for having chosen to be an athlete. When crossing from the high school, to avoid scampering across four lanes of traffic on their way to the park, everyone would cross the bridge on its sidewalk and jog down the Rock Creek bank to the trail beneath, coming out on the other side in the park for a short quarter-mile jog around the five-acre tract of land colloquially known as the Buffalo Pasture — cleverly named so for the fact that it was a pasture in which the park kept a small herd of roaming buffalo — for another brisk mile-and-a-half jog before returning back to the high school via the trail beneath the bridge.

For reasons unbeknownst to Daryl, none of the law enforcement agencies — even his own — were considering the possibility that the suspects could have easily doubled back to use the trail to cross underneath the bridge and wade through the creek where the bank would be too steep to spot them unless someone was standing at its edge. When Agent Douchebag had presented his profile of the suspects as out-of-towners, everyone had swallowed that pill, ignored the snake-oil aftertaste, and accepted it as gospel; and no one had given much of a second thought to the possibility that the culprits were not only local but also at least quasi-intelligent.

So while everyone else had headed south, Daryl had gone north. It had made him feel pretty damn smart in the beginning, but as the afternoon wore on, he was slowly beginning to feel less and less so. He had gotten his boots wet in Rock Creek when he was looking for a would-be exit point; had gotten a flat tire from a jagged piece of tinhorn that had become exposed during the last heavy rain; and he had to spend twenty extra minutes thereafter trying to get the cruiser to start because of a bad starter that Sheriff Reynolds had said they didn't have the budget to fix — but, by God, he was headed north.

He was about six miles north of town, having criss-crossed east and west in a grid pattern and looking for anything *out of the ordinary*. The problem was that literally anything could be either ordinary or unordinary on the back roads; they weren't particularly well-policed and people got bored. It wasn't that heinous crimes were being perpetrated on the outskirts of town — the worst of it was furniture dumping and stop sign graffiti; and though Daryl's services were occasionally commandeered to dispatch the graffiti, he typically enjoyed the creativity that the local teenagers would use in making additions to the signs with permanent black marker. *Stop humping the cows, you bastards!* had been a favorite of his, along with *Stop. Hammer Time* and *Stop, collaborate and listen.*

So aside from the random bout of vandalism or discarded couch, all was well on the northern front and as ordinary as ordinary had come to be known in those parts.

Daryl was on the verge of calling it a day. It was only three in the afternoon, and all of the assorted law enforcement personnel would still be too hard at work to notice if he spent the better part of the afternoon at the Watering Hole. It was fate, it seemed, that he should become insanely inebriated and perhaps go so far as to do something stupid in the Paulson tradition. He turned east toward the highway where it would be a quicker trip to the Watering Hole; having so recently opened his mind to the idea of the fates intervening in his day, it didn't seem prudent to make them wait. He turned on his blinker as he edged closer toward the highway, and just as he was about to accelerate onto it, he caught something out of the corner of his eye: rednecks.

Two neighbors who lived just off the highway several hundred yards from where Daryl sat had developed a system by which to determine who among them was the most handsome, cunning, virile, and all-around superior human being. There had been a time when the two men one-upped each other with home improvements, but that had grown expensive and tedious; eventually, during a moment of inspired genius, they had divined the way to test the true measure of a man: drunken lawnmower racing.

Daryl sighed as he saw the two men barreling toward him at the ludicrous speed of about seven miles-per-hour.

"Just what I need today," he announced to himself, partly to assuage the annoyance that he felt and partly in case fate was listening so she would know that he wasn't shirking his duties in the *get drunk and make an ass of himself* department.

He turned the steering wheel hard to the left to reverse course and hit the corresponding button to call the lights on his squad car into a blaze of red and blue.

When the two men saw Daryl, each not-so-deftly threw a beer can across the fence and into the tall grass on the other side, then pulled their lawnmowers into the ditch — making sure that the front of each was completely even with the other, so as to keep the other rider from a win on a technicality. Then they sat and waited for Daryl to park his cruiser and approach.

"What are you two ignorant sons of bitches doing?" Daryl began. And without giving them the time to respond, continued: "How many times have I told you that you can't race your lawnmowers on the shoulder of the highway?"

"It'd have to be a dozen at this point, Daryl," began Rhett, the older of the two. He was wearing an old, dingy white tank top which didn't do a lot to cover his budding man-boobs. His well-worn OU hat was faded fantastically more so than that of his younger lawnmower-riding adversary, which was akin to silverback status in their culture; the eyes under that hat had seen a lot of shit in their day and commanded respect; so, naturally, Rhett took the lead in the conversation.

"And not one of those twelve goddamn times sunk in? Are you two dense or just don't think I'll take you in because I went to school with you. What've you got to say about it, Trent?"

Trent was the younger of the two and had, in fact, gone to high school with Daryl. Though Trent had been two classes ahead of him, the two had played football together and partied enough together that it was unlikely that Daryl would ever take him in — especially for something so minor as drunken lawnmower racing. Still, he had to play the game and make a show of the situation, lest the word get back to Sheriff Reynolds that he was being derelict in his duty to put the fear of God into town ne'er-do-wells; truth be told, these two weren't even particularly ne'er-do-wells for the most part — just serious about their racing.

Out of habit, Rhett began to reach into the ice chest that was bungee-strapped to the floorboard of his zero-turn mower, but stopped when he noticed Daryl's watchful gaze.

"You know that technically I could arrest the two of you dumbasses for DUI or public endangerment or just book you under the new Murray County Retard Law that I'm trying to get passed with the city council." Daryl let out a sigh. "Are you at least pulling off into the ditch when cars pass?" Daryl asked with the most menacing tone he could muster.

"Of course we are," Trent answered. "We're not animals."

"One of these days, I'm going to get tired of this game we play," Daryl continued, "and I'm gonna take this to the next level."

"Waterboarding," Rhett laughed, throwing caution to the wind and popping open a beer.

"I'm gonna tell your wives."

Daryl raised his eyebrows and let that sink in for a moment before he started walking back toward his cruiser.

Shit had just gotten real — both men protesting loudly behind him as he got back into the car, their pleas becoming a sweet soundtrack to the end of his day.

"Daytona's closed for the day. Take your asses home."

He pushed the aviators down on his nose, put the cruiser in gear, gave his patented one-siren-wail, and started to take off before his brain had passed go, collected its $200, and landed back into detective mode. He hit the brakes, and yelled to the Earnhardt Brothers:

"Have you two seen anything weird lately?"

13

Fellare Non Grata

Jackson had been pacing the floors of the Pine Creek Interrogation Room for what seemed like two eternities, occasionally checking his wrist for a watch that he didn't own. He knew from experience that there had been a clock on the wall in this room at some point, but feared that he had been transported into some sort of Wonderland where clocks were accessories and time had no meaning. He had begun some time back to feel claustrophobic, but he had no idea how long ago that might have been. Was that tightness he was feeling in his chest?

Before he could remember which side of the body a heart attack creates pain in, Reagan threw open the door to the room, causing Jackson's concern about a heart attack to seem silly now that he was sure that it would seize altogether. Before he could muster any sort of relief at the sight of his savior, she launched into a tirade that made him wish he was back in Wonderland.

"What did I tell you about that stupid-ass Facebook post?"

she began.

"Oh, thank God! You don't know what's been going on in here," Jackson emoted. "They waterboarded me!"

"They did not," Reagan hissed as angrily as she could. It was going to be ridiculously hard to maintain her *adult face* with the way the conversation had already begun to teeter on the edge of absurdity.

"Not physically! They waterboarded my soul," Jackson shouted. "I've been defiled. You won't even want me after what they've done to me. I'm a broken man. How long ago did I call you? It feels like days!"

"Like thirty minutes! Sit down," she insisted. "What did I tell you about the Facebook post?" she continued without mercy.

Jackson rolled his eyes and sat down at the table like a child who had been confronted by an angry parent, crashing down to the reality that he wasn't just in trouble with the FBI but also with his girlfriend.

What he wouldn't have given for a rabbit hole.

"To take it down because if anything ever happened in Pine Creek, it would make me look guilty."

"And what happened?"

"Something happened in Pine Creek and it made me look guilty."

"Meaning?"

"That you were right."

With that, Reagan turned her back and began walking toward the door.

"Where are you going?" Jackson yelled, panic creeping back into his voice.

"I've got to call your mom and tell her that you admitted

that you were wrong about something. She's gonna lose her shit."

"You were right! You were right!" he yelled at the top of his lungs. "Now, would you come over here and help me, please?"

Reagan folded her hand and walked over to the table to sit down opposite Jackson, never loosening the annoyed stare from her face to allow him a reprieve from her disdain.

"You do realize that I'm not an attorney, right? When people are Mirandized, they aren't told that they have the right to a paralegal."

"You're the closest thing to an attorney I know. I just need someone to tell me what to do. Do I offer them an organ? They can have a kidney, maybe one ball if things get dire. Just get me the fuck out of here!" Jackson glanced anxiously around the room, realizing that by speaking so loudly, he was bound to draw the attention of one of his captors.

"I've got a way out of this, but you're not going to like it."

"I don't have to blow anyone, do I?" Jackson asked, completely dejected.

"You mean like metaphorically?" Eve asked as she stepped into the room. Despite wearing heels that echoed throughout the hallways with each step, Jackson's struggle with whether he was willing to fellate his way out of custody had allowed her to enter the room undetected. "Because you might have to get down on your knees one way or another to get out of this," she finished with a wry smile.

"What the dick?" Jackson spurted. "What are you doing here? Are you working for the prosecution? Are you here to torture me? Goddamn it, they brought in the Destroyer of Dreams to finish me off."

"She's here to help you," Reagan interrupted.

"Help me? You brought a succubus to a gunfight. How did you even know how to get in touch with her? Is there a secret bat signal with a Scarlet A?"

"We've been friends since 3rd grade," Reagan responded. "I've never stopped talking to her."

"Surprise," Eve chimed in. She was absolutely enjoying herself. Jackson had always been fiercely loyal to his friends, but especially to Troy, and she knew through her super-spy best friend Reagan that Jackson blamed her for all the wrongs in the world. Maybe she wasn't without blame in regard to Troy in the macro sense, but she was hardly prepared to accept responsibility for the state of Jackson's life.

"Just so you know, you've raped my soul," Jackson said pointedly to Reagan as he sat back down at the table, defeated.

"Your soul is going to be fine, you goddamn drama queen," she responded. "Again, Eve is here to help you!"

"It's your call, Jackson," Eve added. "I can leave if you want."

"Yes, please."

Eve stood to leave, but Reagan grabbed her by the shoulder with a hopeful apology: "He's sorry."

"I'm not sorry."

Without hesitation, Reagan reached back and slapped Jackson in the face with as an impressive a pimp hand as she could muster. Jackson was taken completely aback, shocked to his core that he had just been assaulted in so dastardly a fashion by someone so small; a building full of interrogators, a succubus across from him, and yet it was his lady love who had imposed physical violence. He wasn't sure what he was going to say, but he began to open his mouth to protest in some form nonetheless; before he could even summon any sort of coherence, however, Reagan employed part two of her (Evil) Master Plan, which was designed to disorient Jackson to the point of pacification: she grabbed him by the scruff of his neck, pulled him to within lip's reach and kissed him just as hard as she had slapped him moments before. When she finally pulled back, Jackson was breathless, which wasn't so strange a sensation for him due to being so out of shape, but more so than breathless, he was speechless — a strange sensation, indeed.

To drive her point home, Reagan added: "Now, let's get to work."

"So, the gist is that they saw that really stupid Facebook post that you made a few months back," Eve began, noticing that Jackson's eyebrows had furrowed upon the mention of his online activity. "Reagan shares the stupid stuff you post with me," she clarified, "and the FBI took notice when one of their analysts flagged you for the degenerate sociopath that you are."

"More or less," Jackson conceded.

"But you didn't rob the bank?"

Jackson just glared across the table, thoroughly unimpressed.

"I'm going to need verbal confirmation."

"I didn't rob the bank."

"Good. Then there's nothing to see here. They're just fishing and hoping that they would get lucky and catch Jaws with a Snoopy Pole," Eve stated perfunctorily before recalling to whom she was speaking. "You didn't say anything stupid to them, did you?"

Jackson lowered his head in defeat.

"What did you say?" Reagan interrupted.

"I may have alluded to the fact that Eve was back in town and that it could have been her. Or that it could have been Troy because he's acting like a dumbass since she's back in town. Or that it could have been you," Jackson surrendered with a motion of his head toward Reagan.

"Me?"

"I was just trying to cast shade to get them off of me! I named most people in town."

"Wait, what do you mean Troy's been acting like a dumbass?" Eve inquired.

Jackson, too distracted to notice that he was betraying confidences left and right, opened up about Troy's behavior: "The usual. You know, getting drunk and doing something stupid. He ran over a water hydrant a couple mornings ago, went walking around shirtless and tried to bang some British guy." It took him a moment to realize how quiet the room had become at the outlandishness of his claims. "I don't fucking know! He's just been doing stupid things because of the succubus proximity. You stole his soul and now he acts like a jackass sometimes," he finished, content that he had made his point.

A HALF HOUR LATER, the three of them were sitting in front of the collective FBI force, Eve pleading their case as though they were trying to escape through Hell's Gates.

"We just need to ask your client a few questions," the Agent in Charge began.

"It's my understanding that you've already asked a few questions of my client," Eve countered. "Without his attorney present, might I add."

"He didn't ask for an attorney. He's not under arrest."

"Though he hasn't been tested in some time, I suspect that my client has the IQ of a small child with a learning disability. Just because you didn't arrest him and weren't required to Mirandize him doesn't mean that you shouldn't have advised him that he could have an attorney present if he felt the need. Jackson?"

"They waterboarded my soul."

"The other thing," Eve said pointedly.

"They never said anything about an attorney."

"We're done, gentlemen. Jackson, let's go." Despite his misgivings, Jackson snapped to like a trained dog to follow his new master out of the room and thus out of the clutches of the machine that wished to chew him up and spit him out.

Eve stood to let him exit the room before her as she glanced triumphantly back at the agents one last time for effect, but when she turned to follow Jackson and Reagan toward the exit and had her back to everyone in the room, her demeanor shifted from one of the supremely confident big city attorney to one of the concerned ex-girlfriend. Surely she was overreacting to some off-the-wall comments by Jackson — Jackson of all people! — and her arrival in Pine Creek hadn't broken Troy to the point of federal criminality. It wasn't like she had ripped a hole in the space-time continuum by merely returning home after a ten-year absence, thus entering a parallel universe in which that action had sent Troy plummeting helplessly to the dark side.

She came home.

Her home.

Her fucking home.

I have as much right to this town as he does, she thought, righteous indignation beginning to well up inside her.

JACKSON HAD SPENT the first several hours after being released slouching in a chair by the window, peeking out into the street from between cracks in the blinds. Though Reagan had procured his liberty through the black magic of the succubi, he was sure that his was a fleeting freedom, doomed to collapse in on itself at any moment and leave him tumbling back into confinement. Even in the bright light of day, he could swear that there was something moving furtively in the shadows — had there been any shadows.

When his phone began to vibrate on the coffee table, he half-suspected that it was Satan coming to claim his due for Jackson having meddled in the macabre, but it had just been Daryl.

After Daryl had commanded Jackson to meet him downtown later that night under threat of incarceration, however, it became clear that Daryl was acting as a minion of the Dark One. He cursed his bad luck to be such close friends with a sheriff's deputy, especially one who knew all of the illegal things that Jackson did and wasn't afraid to use that information when it suited him.

Jackson would have frogged Kendrick in the arm out of spite to take his mind off of the situation, but Kendrick — once again — was nowhere to be found.

"I hate my life," he said to no one in particular.

14

Penises on the Marquee

"Who are we stalking?" Jackson asked, startling Daryl to the point that he dropped his binoculars in the dirt below the nearest shrub.

Daryl had crouched long enough that his catcher's knee had caught up with him, so he switched to a prone position where he lay amidst the various ferns and shrubberies that lined the sidewalks on Broadway. Despite his attempts to become one with and blend into the environment, Daryl was really just a guy lying on a sidewalk in woodland camouflage with a pair of binoculars. Still, he at least hoped that he couldn't be seen from the other side of the street.

He had been undercover, after all — until Jackson had shown up yelling about stalking like a drunken fool.

"What the *fuck* are you doing?" Daryl scolded. "Get down here, you goofy bastard. You're going to get us caught."

"Caught doing what?" Jackson managed while being pulled to the ground next to Daryl, fighting all the way down with a series of slaps.

"We're on a stakeout!"

Jackson was beginning to suspect that the pressure of a statewide investigation had broken his friend.

"A stakeout?"

"A stakeout."

"On Broadway?"

"On Broadway."

"In the middle of the sidewalk?" Jackson asked again.

"Yes, in the middle of the damn sidewalk," Daryl answered with a hateful glare. "Why are you here?"

"Because you said that you would arrest me for that thing — that thing about the thing, you know — if I didn't come down here."

"Yeah, I know the 'thing,'" Daryl mocked. "But what are you doing here *now*? You're twenty minutes early," he sighed. "Just lay there and be quiet," he warned.

Daryl raised the binoculars back up to his eyes for a moment before pulling them away to wipe the dirt from the lenses and casting a glare in Jackson's direction for making him drop them. He didn't like being there in the first place. It was a demeaning, bullshit assignment that he had only taken on because of the incessant nagging on behalf of one of Pine Creek's more outspoken denizens.

"Seriously, though, why are we here?" Jackson asked.

Daryl sighed.

"Somebody keeps changing the sign above the beauty parlor."

"You mean the book store," Jackson corrected.

Daryl sighed again.

"Somebody keeps changing the sign above the book store that used to be a beauty parlor."

"And that's county business?"

"No, it'd be city business," Daryl offered.

"...but Violet has been giving *you* shit about it," Jackson laughed.

"Yep."

"On account of your having taken her virginity."

"Sound about right."

"And not marrying her."

"Then there's that."

"And killing her grandma."

"'That old bitch had a heart that was a ticking time bomb,' and that's a direct quote from Dr. Stone's autopsy report."

"I love how much he hated his ex-wife," Jackson smiled. "It's inspiring, really."

Daryl, meanwhile, had continued to stew.

"We have sex one time — a decade ago! — she tells her crazy ass grandma who tries to set up a shotgun wedding and I owe her a debt ever since?"

"A blood debt," Jackson cackled.

"Dude, don't be gross."

Jackson rolled his eyes and allowed Daryl a moment to continue his self-loathing in silence. His was a precarious situation. Old Lady Hell was the stuff of Pine Creek Legend — a true Winifred Sanderson who terrorized the village and ate the bones of small children — and Violet Hail was her granddaughter. Violet hadn't yet devolved into eating the bones of small children, but she *had* been known to terrorize the village on occasion. She even opened a book store in the building in which her grandmother ran her beauty salon to maintain a lair in the middle of town.

"So we're just gonna lay here all night?" Jackson asked, content to push his luck even though Daryl was in full-on *Violet Mode*.

"Some asshole keeps spelling dirty words on the marquee between the time that Violet closes down and the morning."

"What kind of dirty words?"

"Anything that they can make out of the letters that are up there — even when there are only a few letters. The fuckers are getting creative. Yesterday, the sign said "Hi!""

"How can you spell something dirty out of *Hi*?"

"They put the lowercase *i* on a line by itself to look like a body with a tiny head, then turned the exclamation point sideways to look like a dick humping the *H* on the line below."

"That's impressive."

"It'll be a damn shame to bust them."

"So...were you just bored and wanted someone to talk to?"

"Let's go around the corner. I don't want to spook the bastards."

"You're going to abandon your post?"

"I brought my partner," Daryl said, motioning toward his ultra hi-tech, ninja-like surveillance device where it lay nearby and pointed in the direction of the bookstore. The department didn't have the budget for any sort of surveillance equipment — even if the stakeout *were* county business — so he had borrowed his sister's camcorder.

Daryl tried to stand with in one smooth motion, but his leg had gone to sleep, leaving him limping around like an old man and dragging his leg behind him. Jackson was clearly on the verge of making a smart-ass remark, but Daryl shut it down with a glance and the business end of his index finger.

Without another word, he led Jackson around the corner

and left his super duper spy device to stand guard in his stead. When they had reached the other side of the wall where Broadway intersects with 1st Street, Daryl glanced back around the corner to make sure that the coast was still clear: nine 'o clock and all was well.

Content that he had covered all of his bases, he was able to turn his attention toward Jackson.

"Have you noticed anything weird?"

"Aside from my friends laying around on sidewalks and cussing the memory of dead old ladies?"

"Specifically in regard to Troy and Rob," Daryl continued, ignoring Jackson's remark completely.

"Weird like what?" Jackson asked with a bemused expression.

He could only imagine what Troy and/or Rob had done to cajole Daryl into trolling the shallow end of the pool for information. There was an unwritten rule among the guys that helping Daryl with an investigation into any of the others would be like stink-palming the pope. It's not that they were all a bunch of blood-thirsty outlaws, running around the county committing heinous acts of barbarism; they just all enjoyed the time-honored tradition of getting drunk and doing something stupid. And though Daryl had never actually charged them for breaking any laws, he had arrested and made them spend the night in jail on several occasions, used his authority as a man of the law to influence others to exact revenge on his behalf and generally made their lives a living hell if and when they had gone too far.

"Weird like *weird*, goddammit," Daryl replied with an exasperated yawn. "Have they been acting any more...felonious than usual."

"'Felonious' as in having committed a felony?" Jackson asked.

"Do you need me to download a dictionary app on my phone?" Daryl nearly yelled before realizing that he was still technically on a stakeout, glancing back around the corner to make sure that no one had been around to hear him.

"We stick to misdemeanors!" Jackson said sternly, offended by the implication. "You taught us that."

"Have they done or said anything out of character?"

"Just come out and ask if you've got something on your mind!"

"Do you think they robbed the bank?!" Daryl finally blurted out. He could tell by the look on Jackson's face that he found the whole thing patently absurd and regretted having allowed himself to ask the question in the first place. He had planned to tiptoe around the subject like he was one of those TV detectives in the box, tricking serial killers into admitting the horrid details of their crimes; instead, he had just allowed his dimwitted friend to force his hand and reveal his suspicions far too early in the game.

"Rob?" Jackson asked in as amused of a voice as he could muster. "And Troy? I love those guys, but robbing a bank? Sure, they could probably knock off a liquor store if it came down to it — like if they some criminal mastermind held someone hostage and forced them to rob a liquor store or they would kill the hostage? I could see them getting $50 out of the register. But robbing a bank? Come on, dude."

Daryl lowered his head in defeat.

"Nothing out of the ordinary?"

"I mean, Troy has been hiding in his room more often

than usual, but it's probably just because Eve is back in town and he's jerking off a lot."

"Great. I solved the great twenty-first century mystery of Troy's empty ball sack."

"Don't be hard on yourself," Jackson cautioned in an odd moment of sincerity. "You've got a lot on your mind! Trying to solve a hand-to-God, statewide bank heist. You're basically a superhero! You just got a little turned around and started liking the smell of your own farts."

"Yeah," Daryl sighed, more down on himself than he had been in recent memory, the living embodiment of his alter-ego Barney Fife. He didn't quite get the *farts* metaphor that Jackson was going for — something that he was sure that Barney Fife would have understood — but he had to concede that Jackson was more or less right. He had spent the past several days either searching frantically for clues to a robbery that was well above his pay grade or on a stakeout in front of a book store that was well below his pay grade.

He was burned out.

He wanted to go back to sitting in his cruiser and waiting for someone to do something stupid, breaking up bar fights or scaring teenagers into thinking that he was about to execute them for petty mischief. He would even settle for catching some smart ass making lewd illustrations on marquees at that point.

He nodded to Jackson as a sign of thanks for righting his wrong, which was the closest most of the guys ever came to an apology, and leaned back around the corner one last time to check for suspicious activity before he packed it in for the night.

"Goddammit!" Daryl yelled at the top of his lungs,

running around the corner and leaving Jackson standing alone and in the dark.

The marquee that had sported a nice literary message in "Always be on the lookout for subtext" beforehand now read "Always be on the lookout for *butt sex*.

Initially, Daryl had been outraged before realizing that he had just caught the bastard on film. He sprinted over to the eagle's nest where he had hidden away his CIA filming device, only to find that it was gone.

"Motherfucker!" he screamed before laying into another obscenity-laced diatribe that lasted so long that it had impressed Jackson where he leaned against the wall behind him.

"You want to get something to eat?" Jackson finally asked after Daryl's stream of filthy consciousness had run its course. It hadn't seemed like a line too far when he had asked it, but the black eye that Jackson sported for the next several days from the right hook to his face would serve as a reminder to the rest of the group that there was a line in the sand when Daryl was in *Violet Mode*.

15

Drug-Addled Eve Psychosis

When he pulled up to the house, Daryl still wasn't quite sure what he was going to do. He wasn't even sure of what he knew; the Racing Twins had reported to him that they had seen Troy and Rob heading north of town, only having remembered because they waved to Cheryl as they passed and neither man in the truck had bothered to wave back; it had only been mentioned to Daryl as an offhand remark so that he could pass along their *fuck you* to Troy and Rob the next time that he saw them.

Though fate had attempted to cajole him into drinking the rest of the afternoon away, there had been just enough of a nagging feeling at the back of his spine, suggesting that there was something more than coincidence at play, to keep him away from the Watering Hole. And even when he had given himself the rest of the afternoon to contemplate his decision before making it, it seemed that the universe had made it for him; once his stakeout that night had gone sideways, it was such a shock to his system that it doubled his conviction to solve at least one of the crimes that he had been tasked to solve.

And that is how he found himself sitting in front of Brose Manor, wondering if his friends had committed a federal offense. Even though he was well short of anything remotely approaching proof — and knowing that the guys would never let him live it down if he were so off-base as to accuse any of them of the robbery because he lacked perspective of anything real-world outside of their group dynamic — he was going to have to follow his gut because his gut was the only thing he had.

There were a million different reasons why Rob and Troy could have been headed north, and Daryl felt certain that they were about to explain them to him.

Unless they couldn't.

He killed the engine with a turn of the key, but he didn't get out of the car just yet. He took off his aviators and squeezed the bridge of his nose like he was trying to force something out of it, snorting loudly to try and get the bad taste out of his mouth. He hadn't got out of the car yet because the moment those two lawnmower-racing sons of bitches had loosed the names of his friends from their lips, it only took the smallest of leaps of imagination to come to grips with the possibility that they could have pulled it off.

Neither of them were morally opposed to robbery, and with Eve back in town, Daryl wasn't entirely sure what Troy was capable of anymore. Something this inordinately stupid still seemed too far out of character for Troy, even with the Eve Factor — until you threw in the wild card: Rob. Daryl had been friends with Rob for as long as he had the others, but the two had a contentious relationship as adults since one — in theory, at least — was supposed to jail the other.

It wasn't Rob's drug dealing that concerned Daryl; it was that he had always been the schemer of the group.

Dealing wasn't an occupation that drew the most ambitious to begin with, and few chose it because of its retirement plan. And though Rob seemed to thoroughly enjoy his vocation most of the time, Daryl knew that he was always on the lookout for opportunities to become even lazier. And he had undertaken some particularly stupid schemes in the past in order to become a full-time slacker.

There was the time he had tried to rip off the NFL. Rob knew a guy in the city who worked at a restaurant chain which was running a promotion with the NFL in which customers got reward points for gear on their website. Through lack of foresight and appreciation for the imagination of the criminal element, there had been no limit placed on the amount of reward points one person might claim. So Rob had suggested that his friend simply steal all of the promotional material that had been delivered to his store and to the stores to which he occasionally delivered products. And though the imagination of the criminal was vast, when one and the same was involved in the drug trade, imagination often stopped just short of genius.

Though their plan had technically succeeded when an entire delivery truck full of jerseys, hats, and memorabilia showed up at the home of Rob's acquaintance in dozens of boxes, it had felt like less of a win once the FBI showed up to investigate — on account of the interstate commerce and all — the use of thousands of dollars' worth of points that had eventually been detected by the fraud surveillance company that oversaw the site.

Though it had been his (Evil) Master Plan, Rob had evaded detection in that particular instance by employing a two-step process of subterfuge in which he a) used the ever-popular drug dealer trick of burner phones, and b) enlisted the help of certain associates to create an air-tight alibi so that when his name came up as a possible person of interest through the *Guilt by Association Doctrine*, the interest of the agents quickly waned.

There was also the time that he had masterminded the attempted robbery of the local pharmacy. Had it been a pharmacy unto itself, the plan may have worked, but because it was a pharmacy inside the local grocery store, the physics pertaining to the intended mode of ingress hadn't gone according to plan.

Rob knew a guy who worked for an AC and ventilation company and had been part of the crew who did the remodel on the grocery store, including the new air ducts that were installed for the cooling system. And when that guy had made an off-the-cuff joke about how easy it would be to enter the store through the ventilation system in the roof, the gears in Rob's brain had churned themselves into a frenzy.

Die Hard style seemed like the most badass possible way to rob someone — though, of course, Rob wouldn't be going in himself. What the hell did he know about vents? He was an Idea Man, and Idea Men didn't run around committing crimes out in the open unless it was absolutely necessary.

It hadn't been.

Rob knew a guy who was diminutive, agile, and morally ambiguous. All had gone according to plan in the beginning:

the tiny criminal had been able to snake down the exhaust vent like a meth'd up Santa Claus thanks to a pair of bolt cutters that had removed the metal guard beforehand. From there, the idea was to move down the ventilation system into the pharmacy and simply run out the front door with the goods, as the security system had been set up to keep people out and wouldn't be activated by someone on the inside until it was too late. But even though he was small in stature, he soon learned that ventilation ducts weren't made to withstand the weight of a fully grown man, small though he may have been.

Die Hard was bullshit.

The next morning when the store manager came into work to find that a roughly sixteen-foot section of ventilation duct had fallen from the ceiling and destroyed a large chunk of his inventory, his first instinct was that it had been the unlucky result of force majeure. When he saw the tiny scumbag lying unconscious beneath a section of the ventilation, however, he quickly backed away from the act of God theory and realized that it had been idiocy at work.

Again, Rob evaded implication — this time simply because the guy who eventually regained consciousness but walked with a limp for the entirety of his five-year prison sentence was a career criminal, and there was no cause to suspect that he had any accomplices. And though word had gotten around town, as it inevitably does, that the suspect that the police had in custody for the crime subscribed to the snitches get stitches philosophy of criminal behavior, and so decided to keep his mouth shut.

Those were just Rob's two most recent attempts at criminal infamy — so no, Daryl didn't require a disproportionate amount of convincing to make the leap from coincidence to action where Rob was concerned. And Troy was nothing if not unstable now.

"Shit," Daryl muttered as he got out of the car, slamming the door behind him and walking at a brisk pace toward the house.

Before he could even near the front steps, however, the sound of four rubber tires screeching to a halt on nearby asphalt was enough to propel his trigger finger toward the holster that held the revolver on his hip; it was an instinct that had been drilled into him by years of training, but one that had rarely been needed. As it so happened, the pistol had never actually made it out of the holster even though Daryl had already managed to cock the hammer back while swinging around toward the street and the sound of the slamming car door.

"What the fuck are you doing here?" he yelled to Eve while simultaneously squeezing the trigger and easing the hammer back into its safe position.

"What the fuck are *you* doing here?" Eve replied without missing a step and passing him near the front steps.

Daryl managed to grab her by the shoulder and spin her around before she reached the steps — which was enough of a slight to result in him receiving a deceptively strong push with all of the 125 pounds that Eve had to put behind it, forcing him to take a step back to regain his balance.

"What are you doing?" she asked with another push that sent him a step further back toward the road. Daryl didn't appreciate the fact that he kept being pushed back toward the street and away from the house like it was protected by some sort of hoodoo witchery.

"I'm here on official business, goddamn it," he responded in an attempt to sound intimidating without incurring another shove. He had seen *this* Eve before when they were in high school, and he knew that she was capable of making him look like a fool if he was cocksure enough to arrest her; the last thing he wanted was to show up at the station with a black eye and a woman in handcuffs.

"What business?" Eve demanded. Two conclusions were being formed in her mind at that point: a) that it would be in everyone's best interest if cooler heads prevailed, as Daryl didn't want to have his ass kicked by a girl and she didn't want to face disbarment under the ethics code for fighting a law enforcement officer; and b) if Daryl was there on official business, he might already know what she suspected about Troy.

"When did you start working for the Sheriff's Department?" Daryl allowed his quip to sink in while he started walking back toward the house.

"Daryl, wait."

This time it was Eve who grabbed him by the shoulder — or at least she had tried, but she couldn't quite reach his shoulder and ended up grabbing a handful of his uniform instead. She twisted him around to stare at her where she stood, trying to figure out how to proceed.

"Am I going to have to arrest you?"

"Are you looking for Troy?"

"I'm looking to do my job, if someone would leave me the hell alone long enough to make a little headway."

"Are you here to arrest him?" she asked again, unable to contain the situation any further.

"Why would I do that?" Daryl responded cautiously.

Daryl was flashing back hard to the *Spy vs. Spy* game that

his older brother used to religiously play on the Atari; not so much because the game was indicative of his current situation in its 8-bit glory, but because his mind had begun to whirl in a vortex of paranoia and referencing any sort of big-screen spy-craft, practical or otherwise, was beyond his ability in the moment.

Did Eve know? Was she *in* on it?

The bank had been robbed right after she returned to town.

And the buffalo had been loosed all over town.

And someone had called in a Sasquatch sighting.

And someone had trashed the DHS office.

Was Eve a criminal mastermind — just running around town like the Joker with no discernible pattern to her madness? Was she stealing candy from babies and making crude sexual comments to old ladies as they left Sunday Service? Was she disabling the porn filter on the computers at the high school library? What else was she capable of and how long would it be before she showed up at Daryl's house to delete all the saves from *Red Dead Redemption 2* while he was sleeping?

Was she the one changing the letters on the goddamn marquee?!

Caught up in his own thoughts, he hadn't noticed that Eve had tired of waiting for a response and had already closed the door behind her.

JACKSON WAS EYEING Kendrick with his one good eye where he sat on the other end of the couch; ostensibly watching the same episode of *Sanford and Son* as his brother, he had instead been attempting to use the powers of his mind to bore a hole through the side of Kendrick's head in hopes that all of his secrets would come tumbling out onto the floor.

Admittedly, it hadn't been going well.

When Eve had come barreling through the door, neither brother had been altogether prepared for the suddenness of the intrusion and each had been ready to protest in his own fashion until Eve had unceremoniously cut them off:

"Where's Troy?" she yelled in the form of a question.

Before either of them could react, Eve rolled her eyes at their inability to keep up with the pace of things and continued down the hallway without a response. The Brothers Brose shared a worried glance before being taken out of the moment by another surprise visitor when Daryl pushed the door open with his typical law enforcement gusto.

"Where's Troy?" he yelled.

The brothers each extended an index finger toward Troy's room. There was no point getting mixed up in whatever-the-hell the day's events were spiraling toward.

TROY WASN'T TYPICALLY the sort to indulge in mindless apathy, yet he found himself doing just that in the moments before Eve interrupted the otherwise thoughtless absence that he had managed to find lying at the foot of his bed. He had been through some shit the past few days — mostly of his own doing, true, but *shit* nonetheless. Since he and Rob had joined the ranks of outlaw proper, Troy had developed a knot in the depths of his bowels that allowed for little to no silent contemplation. He had spent the two days since in a state of foreboding theretofore unknown, far deeper than anything he had experienced during the darkest days of his drug-addled Eve Psychosis in college.

And yet, he had been able to find a moment of peace in between the waves of desperation. Rob had already concluded his drug deal with the money they had stolen, and now he just had to sell them before he and Troy were able to leave Pine Creek for parts unknown far, far away from their problems and the fiendish women who had caused them. Though Troy hadn't believed it necessary to even be involved in a drug deal in the first place — given that they had gotten away with over $20,000.00 at the bank, which was more than enough to leave town with by any stretch of the imagination — Rob had convinced him that, between the two of them, they would blow through the cash in the first year alone, and so needed to buy a metric shit-ton of drugs at bulk and move them in smaller quantities, tripling or quadrupling their money. Rob had assured him that it would only take a week or two to move the product, which had softened Troy's mood substantially — and it was that thought that caressed his amygdala into a sense of profound security strong enough that he was on the verge of sleeping for the first time in nearly forty-eight hours.

"Troy!"

Eve's voice rang out so loud and clear and from absolutely out of nowhere that Troy initially thought that it might be the voice of God, coming to punish him for his sins. Momentarily surprised but not all that shocked that God might be a *she*, Troy snapped to attention, prepared to grovel.

When he opened his eyes, though, it was clear that there would be a different sort of atonement involved altogether.

"What are you doing here?" Troy managed between emotions that ran somewhere between equal parts terror and disbelief.

"Don't you fucking sass me right now, Troy Stephen Paulson," Eve began in a voice that surprised both Troy and herself in terms of familiarity. "You've done a lot of stupid things over the years, but this is, by far, the dumbest goddamn thing you've ever done!"

"What stupid things?" Troy countered. "How the hell would you know about the stupid things I've done when I haven't seen you in ten years?"

"Reagan tells me!" she yelled, annoyed at the fact that she was getting an argument out of him. "Like the source matters!"

"You've been spying on me!"

"Please. I've been keeping tabs on you at best. Like any concerned citizen would. And don't try to change the subject! Did you really..." Eve let her voice taper off in the middle of the sentence in an attempt at the smallest sliver of privacy before continuing: "...rob a bank?"

Troy had been baffled by the conversation beforehand, but when she mentioned the robbery, he froze completely in place, worried that her vision was not only motion-based like the T-Rex, but also capable of scanning his brainwaves for thoughts. Eve had clearly become a powerful witch during her time away from Pine Creek; and also infused with T-Rex blood at some point.

"What?" was all he had been able to meekly respond.

When Daryl threw the door to Troy's room open, Troy responded by playing the role of *deer in headlights*; he was sure that his heart couldn't take many more of these surprises. Eve, however, had reacted with the reflexes of a master samurai and slammed the door in Daryl's face as quickly as he had opened it.

"Occupied!" she yelled, annoyed.

When the door swung open again, the repeated blood-surge away from his brain to where his heart was distributing both it and adrenaline like a Pez Dispenser caused Troy to nearly pass out. And while Daryl was happy to see that it wasn't being slammed rudely in his face for a second time in so many moments, he was less enthused about the slap to the face that Eve gave him for his trouble.

"I said *fucking* occupied."

Daryl was left standing in the hallway with the door slammed twice in his face, rubbing his cheek where it wouldn't bruise nearly as badly as his ego.

This is bullshit, he thought as he started to reach for his pistol. *I'd like to see her slap me again after I fire off a few rounds for good effect*! But he was worried that she might do just that, so he decided to instead continue down the hallway to Rob's room to have words with him. "I swear to God," Daryl began as he quickened his pace, "if he slaps me, I'll fucking kill him."

"Well?" Eve asked, still waiting on a reply back in the room, hands now rested on her hips but too impatient to wait long for a reply: "Did you do it to spite me, as if somehow I would care that you were flushing what little life you had away?"

"To spite you?" Troy asked incredulously. "I did it to get away from you!"

"Away from me? You saw me once! In ten years!"

"And that one time sent me into a shame spiral so bad that I wrecked my truck and robbed a fucking bank!" Troy yelled before realizing his mistake and attempting to correct it: "*Allegedly.*"

"Troy," Eve started hesitantly. "We were ten years ago."

"I'm aware."

"Then how do I still have any effect on your decision-making process?"

"You don't," Troy answered with an annoyed sigh. "Most days, you're nothing but a goddamn interstate daydream to me, but then there are other days when..." he began before letting his words momentarily trail off into thought. "Neither of us are the same person we were when we knew each other, right?"

"Right. But..." Eve nudged.

"Seeing you just reminds me of how I fell apart!" Troy exclaimed in a moment of exasperation before sinking into himself and lying back on his bed where he stayed for several seconds before popping back up like an inflatable clown. "I was going places! I was going to one of the best football programs in the country. I was probably gonna go pro. I was gonna conquer the goddamn world, Eve! I was *Troy fucking Paulson.*"

Eve sighed and offered an empathetic smile.

"You're still *Troy fucking Paulson.* Just a little bit older. And you didn't like seeing me to remind that you that I ruined you as a quarterback."

"And a man," Troy countered.

"And a man," Eve agreed. "So much so that you *allegedly* robbed a bank to get away from the memory?"

"Allegedly."

"You couldn't have just left town?"

"With what money?"

"You know that some people actually borrow money from banks instead of just taking it."

"Bad credit."

"What about your parents?"

"I owe them money."

"And you have no savings?"

"I'm not an attorney, Eve. Who the fuck has *savings*?" Such a silly question she had asked him. Savings. Savings? *Savings?* He didn't know anyone who had savings. Who would go to work if they had savings to fall back on? Such a silly woman.

"What about..." Eve started before being interrupted.

"Look, it happened. We're past it now. It's not something I thought through, obviously. I wasn't gonna do it, but then Winona Ryder's boobs became an issue, and things just spiraled from there."

"We'll need to earmark that last part to circle back to, but continue."

"I fucked up."

"Clearly."

"So what am I gonna do?"

"I think I've got a plan," Daryl nearly yelled, swinging the door open again, dragging Rob behind him and carefully eyeing Eve all the while to avoid any sort of physical altercation that she may have been planning to unleash. "But you two goofy sons of bitches are going to owe me for the rest of your lives, and if you fuck me on this, I'll line you up back-to-back and kill you both with a single bullet."

16

Reaganomics

Reagan had spent a good amount of time fantasizing about how she might kill her boss: be it through the type of slow, agonizing torture of which the Vietcong would approve, or simply backing over him several times in her car until she felt that she restored some sort of karmic justice in the world. Though she was his paralegal, Jay Collins treated her like a secretary, which would have been bad enough in and of itself had he not treated her like she was a *bad* secretary. Her job mostly entailed menial tasks that any high school graduate could handle, and the legal work that he did assign her was the most mind-numbingly dull, pedantic drivel that one might find scouring the most obscure of legal publications. And it wasn't like he never had interesting cases with pressing legal issues that Reagan could sink her teeth into; he had plenty, but on those cases, she was relegated mostly to filing, making copies, and any other grunt work that he might think up.

She had been particularly creative in her murder hypotheticals in those instances.

She often contemplated leaving his practice, but there was really nowhere else to go. There certainly weren't any opportunities to put her expertise to use in Pine Creek, and the only thing she might find nearby would be of the same sort. If she wanted to do anything interesting or exciting in the law, she basically had two options: a) go to law school and become an attorney herself, or; b) move to one of the nearby cities of Oklahoma City, Tulsa, or Dallas and become a paralegal in a more thriving environment.

Both of those choices, however, were hindered by one simple fact: Jackson would never leave Pine Creek. So she would often cycle between competing narratives in her sanguine fantasies in which she would either kill her boss or kill Jackson; and killing Jackson seemed like it would be the easier of the two most days. She wasn't sure if it was simply that he took her back to a youth that felt like it was slowly slipping away into middle age or that when she had dated and even married "adults," they had left her with a sense of deep longing for something...else.

Jackson was, apparently, her *else*.

She had never pushed — or at least not pushed hard, anyway — to change Jackson, because it had seemed that his various quirks were the very essence of what attracted her to him; and for whatever reason, his biggest quirk was that he wanted to live and die within a few-mile radius of where he had been born. And while she could understand the desire in and of itself, it was a desire that was ultimately dragging her down into a version of herself that she didn't want to become. She was nearly thirty years old, and if she didn't push the issue one way or another, she was going to wake up at forty to find that she had pissed any opportunity that she may have had away — or that Jackson had done the pissing for her.

And so she had hatched a Plan. An Evil Plan. A Master Plan.

And though this (Evil) Master Plan had been slower to reveal itself than she would have liked, the majority of the moving parts were as follows: a) some months prior, she had discovered that part of the reason that Jay Collins had kept her at arm's length in a legal sense was that he had been both bilking clients and embezzling state funds; b) she hoped that Jackson's hatred of Jay and the fact that not only he but several other prominent members of the Pine Creek elite had participated in the graft would sour Jackson's view of the community to the point that he would leave, and; c) she could thusly talk him into moving away.

It had been an accident, coming upon the files that would damn any hope that Jay had of proving his innocence. Reagan had figured out the combination to Jay's safe, which he thought was hidden in his office behind a cheap painting, and she had used it a few times to help herself to petty cash as a way to even the karmic playing field. Nothing in the safe had ever proven useful before — just the random confidential document from the random citizen that Reagan didn't feel comfortable reading — but there had been something new the last time she had decided to help herself to some easy money. She still couldn't figure out why he had kept them at all beyond maybe using them to show the others involved that he was on the so-called "up and up," at least in terms of their involvement, but there they had been: two sets of ledgers in a large legal briefcase. One ledger held receipts of several state projects that the county had undertaken from various local businesses while the other showed the same amount of money incoming, but with a disbursement schedule to several entities only identified by initials.

It had only taken a few moments to realize that what she held in her hand was a carbon copy of her boss's testicles. As she stood over the copy machine, each image being ushered into the tray with the cosmic force of a wrecking ball, she was finally able to take a sense of pride in the menial labor of the past several years. True, she was doing it for selfish and petty reasons, but was she not making the world a better place by making sure that Jay Collins would be raped in prison? And by doing so, was she not vindicating women the world over who were stuck doing the same type of work day after day for decades? She was basically Wonder Woman.

The problem that had presented itself was that she wasn't sure how to proceed. Going to the *Pine Creek Times Democrat* didn't seem like it was going to have the juice to launch the story into orbit in the way that she wanted it to be blasted like an Apollo mission. And would one of the cable news stations really care about a small-town scandal to the point that they gave it much coverage? So she had sat on the information for two inglorious months as the urge to use it ate away at her innards like a vindictive cancer. She had, at the very least, wanted to tell Jackson to get that part of her (E)MP moving, but she was certain that he would find a way to torpedo the whole thing, so it was a secret that had stayed buried like the legendary Jesse James treasure.

She had even managed to keep the secret from her long-distance best friend, Eve. It wasn't that she couldn't trust Eve — she knew that she could — but she had found herself becoming increasingly paranoid with the information, as though someone might be listening on another line or intercepting emails; it was a ridiculous suspicion, obviously, and she blamed Jackson for rubbing off on her with his belief in every conspiracy theory that he came across on Facebook, but she couldn't bring herself to divulge her knowledge of the situation in any sort of compromising manner.

But within a half-hour of Eve's plane landing in Oklahoma City where Reagan had picked her up, Reagan had unloaded the secret in graphic detail — even while knowing that *they* could be listening in through the speakers in her car. Eve's first instinct had been to contact *The Times*, but that was quickly discarded as an unrealistic endeavor, and she finally came to the same realization as Reagan: theirs was a predicament without an easy solution. Eve pointed out that without hard evidence — the actual ledgers — and a chain of custody from Jay's safe to a law enforcement officer, it might prove difficult to actually bring charges, especially considering that he was the district attorney, which meant that a grand jury would have to be convened with the approval of the district judge — who was Jay's brother.

They had agreed that the best course of action would be to temporarily table any would-be action until they had determined a proper reaction.

It had been a little over a week since that decision had been made with no further idea on how to proceed, but while Reagan sat alone for lunch at Poor Girl's, a local cafe famous for its delightfully decent food, her phone rang. When she saw Eve's number flash onto the screen, she assumed that it had been to apologize for being late to the lunch that they were supposed to be sharing while discussing the options to keep Jackson out of jail, should he get nervous and confess to a crime he didn't (insofar as she was aware) commit.

Instead, Eve had simply said the words *Code Orange* and hung up.

Reagan's body had a difficult time processing the adrenaline that immediately flooded her veins, causing her hands to shake as she tried to reach into her purse and pull forth a small amount of cash to leave on the table. Finally, she just opened her purse, dumped its entire contents onto the table, leaving behind a few loose dollar bills as she pushed the rest back into her purse along the edge.

She rushed out the door as fast as her weak legs would allow.

Code Orange could only mean one thing: shit was about to go down.

THE SNAKE FARM rarely had many visitors. It was the kind of place that if you had seen once, you had seen a thousand times, and the locals had seen it a thousand times. Tourists on their way to the park for camping might stop by if they hadn't been to town before, and there was the occasional school trip from a few towns away that would bring in a bus-full of rowdy children. On the whole, however, there might be one or two cars in the parking lot, including Ramona's black Suburban.

So there was already enough of a disruption of normalcy to cause suspicion when Reagan pulled up into the lot to find Eve's car, Daryl's Bronco, and Cheryl alongside Ramona's Suburban. Reagan took a deep breath and prepared herself for the unknown. How the hell were all of these other people involved with *Code Orange?*

Shit was going down, indeed.

She wasn't quite sure what was awaiting her inside, but she was readying herself for some sort of Indiana Jones situation in which she might have to outrun a giant boulder or shoot a sword-wielding bad guy; she hoped it would be the latter, as her pistol was in the console and she hadn't been hitting the cardio as hard as she could have in recent months. And now that she thought about it: should she take her pistol in with her? Eve's text had just said to meet her at the Snake Farm, but given that it was *Code Orange* and the Bennetts looked to be somehow involved, it was possible that she might need it. *Better safe than sorry*, she thought, placing the snub-nosed .38 that she referred to as her "car gun" in her purse.

Her gun-toting adventure came to a quick halt, however, when she noticed Eve out of the corner of her eye, still sitting in her car and frantically motioning for Reagan to join her in the passenger seat. Reagan jogged over and hopped in the car as quickly and covertly as she could manage, scanning the scene for bad guys that might need to be shot as she closed the door behind her. She had been so focused on the specter of evil-doers outside the car, however, that she had wholly missed the evil-doer inside the car.

"Thank God you're here!" Jackson blurted out from the backseat.

Reagan nearly jumped out of her skin at the suddenness of it all, slapping Jackson's hand where he tried to hug her from the back seat.

"What the hell is he doing here?" Reagan yelled at Eve. "You told him about *Code Orange?*"

"It's this *whole thing*," Eve began before Jackson interrupted.

"Tell me you brought your gun," he nearly yelled. "Eve wouldn't let me bring mine."

Reagan wasn't sure why he would need a gun, even if he knew about the unknowable, so she slapped his hands away as he tried to reach in her purse, looking for her gun.

"What the hell is going on?" she continued with Eve, bypassing Jackson and going to the source.

"The short version is that some things went down and we need to initiate *Code Orange* because we might need it as a backup plan."

"What sort of things?" Reagan asked breathlessly, still slapping at Jackson.

"Rob and Troy robbed the bank and now Ramona might kill us all," Jackson spewed forth, drawing a gasp from Reagan who momentarily stopped fighting against Jackson.

"What?"

"Sweet, you did bring it!" Jackson yelled, pulling the pistol from her purse and checking to see if it was loaded.

"We probably won't need it," Eve said uneasily. "But you should probably keep it out just in case. And for sure take it away from Jackson either way."

"YOU ROBBED THE BANK?" Ramona asked calmly.

Rob and Troy glanced back and forth between themselves before looking back to Ramona with lowered eyes, as though they were two school children being called before the principal; the difference, however, was that the principal didn't even have the power to spank unruly children anymore, whereas Ramona, at least according to legend, had literally disappeared people who committed senseless crimes in town that might draw the unwanted attention toward other criminal enterprises such as her own.

"Yes," Troy answered.

"Yes, ma'am," Rob countered.

"Yes, ma'am," Troy parroted.

"And you were aware of this?" Ramona asked, glancing past the two of them at Daryl, who stood light-footed behind them.

"Just found out," he answered.

"And now the FBI and every state law enforcement agency is trying to turn any traffic ticket in the last ten years into a federal charge."

They couldn't bring themselves to answer that question, as it seemed to imply more than they had hoped it might, so they just nodded silently in unison as Ramona sat quietly for several unbearable moments.

"Well, you two are fucked," she laughed, breaking the silence with an even more uncomfortable sense of frivolity. "I'd say that all that's left for me to do is to call the cops, but lucky for me and brevity's sake both, here stands a cop within my very sight." She then turned her attention fully to Daryl to wait and see what sort of game they were playing.

Daryl sighed, looked to the floor, then back up. He wasn't quite sure how he wanted to proceed. There was a time when even a man of the law was reluctant to throw shade in the direction of the Bennett Family, but that time had largely passed over the recent decades under the direction of Ramona and her grandmother; still, even though theirs was a peaceful enterprise on the surface, he didn't want to get caught up in the middle of something that could either flush his career down the drain or maybe worse. He almost wished it were the olden times so that at least he knew where he stood, as Ramona's mystery operation left too many things to the imagination.

"We're just looking for some help, Ramona," he finally answered.

"Help?" she asked, playing as if confused before finally continuing: "*They* did it," she said with a smile, pointing in the direction of Rob and Troy. "Police work is much easier than I would have thought."

"That's not what I meant..." Daryl began before being cut off in a tone that didn't instill confidence.

"Isn't it?" Ramona hissed, dropping her otherwise charming facade. "Because if it isn't, I'm afraid that you're about to ask me to do something illegal, deputy."

She let that point waft through the air as she walked back toward her desk, sat down, and propped her legs up on the clutter, settling back into her friendly face with a smile before continuing: "An upstanding member of the community such as myself, approached by a man in uniform, asked to help him cover up a crime committed by two of his childhood friends. The impropriety of it all is enough to make a lady blush," she finished with a heavy Southern Belle accent for effect.

"Ramona," Daryl began before being cut off again.

"Lucky for you, I'm not a lady," she offered curtly. "State your business."

"I basically want to give the money back," Troy answered after a nudge from Daryl. "Like it never happened."

"Then give it back," Ramona replied. "You don't need me for that."

"We already spent it," Troy answered with a glance in Rob's direction.

"On drugs, no doubt," Ramona quipped, drawing a nod from Rob. "Robert, you silly bastard. You know that I allowed you to deal for all of these years because it was just a little weed and you had the common sense to be discreet *enough* about it. I'm assuming you bought more than weed, then — to what end? What were you two trying to accomplish? Not trying to become Murray County Kingpins, I presume?"

"No," Rob quickly answered, noting the seriousness on Ramona's face before correcting himself: "No, ma'am. I was going to try to move it to some guys I know in the city so we could leave town."

"You realize that you could have just left town, right?" Ramona asked. "I don't charge a fee."

She sighed, clearly bored of what had devolved into the trivialities of the common folk — at least that was what she was conveying to the room. The wheels were turning in her mind as to how she could make this work for her. Keeping in mind that they were civilians, even Rob for as little as he rocked the boat as a drug dealer, she wasn't looking to make an example out of them the way that she had done with others who had broken the cardinal rule of committing senseless crimes within Murray County, and specifically within Pine Creek itself. There was a reason that the town had been largely spared the type of small-town crime that had swept the area in the last decade: the pill-heads and meth-heads stealing everything that wasn't nailed down, the large-scale drug shipments moving through that were sporadically stopped by the police, or really any of the problems that similar towns had to the point that people had begun to lock their doors at night.

The reason that none of those things had come to Pine Creek was simple: it was bad for business. Ramona had learned the lesson that her grandfather had failed to heed. The men in her family had always been in open and notorious control of the town, and everyone knew it; they kept the petty crime down the same way that Ramona did because there was only so much that a townsperson would accept before the many would turn on the few — but while her grandfather would drag a thief into Main Street in front of the whole town to beat the ever-loving shit out of him, Ramona preferred to conduct her affairs in private. Better to have whispers about how she may have killed a man who had dropped off the face of the Earth than to have two-dozen witnesses to testify in federal court. And peoples' imaginations usually conjured up things more horrible than even reality could produce.

Still, this was an unmistakably giant fuck-up of epic proportions, and she couldn't let these two fuck-ups and their friends off lightly.

"If I had to guess," she began, "I would presume that you want me to give you money for the drugs so that you can do some sort of anonymous-tip ordeal and give the money back that way?"

"Yes, ma'am," Troy and Rob answered in unison.

"How much did you get from the bank?"

"About twenty-thousand," Troy answered.

"More or less," Daryl chimed in.

"Was it *more* or *less*?" Ramona asked.

"More," Daryl responded. "Twenty-thousand and a little over two-hundred. Are you gonna help us or not?"

"I take it that the drugs are in the duffle bag?"

Rob carried the bag over to Ramona and laid it down on the desk. She peeked inside the bag, rummaged around for a moment before zipping it back up and throwing it back at Rob.

"No thanks," she said in a nonchalant tone.

"Ramona," Daryl began.

"I said 'no thanks,'" she reiterated in a tone more suited to the situation. "It's too much risk for too little in exchange. Our business is concluded, gentlemen. I won't expect to see you in my presence again regarding this matter."

"What if we had something to sweeten the pot?" Daryl asked. "Something that would take the heat off of everyone else in town, including you?"

"I'm listening."

AFTER DARYL HAD EXPLAINED that they held damning information on a certain number of Pine Creek's more illustrious members in regard to a state embezzlement scheme, Ramona softened her tone and agreed to give them $21,212.37 in exchange for the drugs and the damning documents. Daryl assumed that she would use them for blackmail or just to oust the members that she didn't like, but that was beyond his pay-grade; he was only interested in keeping his friends out of jail so that he might kill them himself, the ingrates.

And though Ramona had agreed to help, it wasn't with the easy terms that Troy and Rob had hoped for; instead, she had imposed a fee in the amount fifty percent interest that would make any loan shark proud. They had tried to protest the exorbitant fee, but Ramona had replied with "woe to the felons," which closed the matter. It had been *take it or leave it*, and they had had no choice other than to take it with no idea how they would ever come up with $10,000.00 to repay the debt and worried that they had just unwittingly become employees of the Bennett Family.

17

Tsk Fucking Tsk

Sheriff Reynolds hadn't been in a particularly pleasant mood for the past several days. Things had been going on in his county that typically didn't go on in his county, and he didn't like it. Aside from the robbery that had created a Texas-sized headache which lasted from dusk till dawn by way of the jurisdictional mess that it had created, there was still one buffalo missing from its pen, he had yet to find any leads on whomever-the-hell might have vandalized the DHS Office, and there were still people calling dispatch to report fucking Sasquatch sightings. He was too close to retirement and thusly *too old for this shit*, in the vein of Danny Glover.

However, he had gotten a call that afternoon that had put some pep in his otherwise cumbersome step.

The good sheriff had known for a few years about the goings-on of the upper echelons of Pine Creek. Judge Collins, his brother, and three other members of Card Game had been syphoning off money from state funds for the past decade by awarding contracts to companies that they owned in one manner or another and doctoring the books. It's not that it wasn't a well-kept secret: it had only ever been discussed by the members involved; however, one of those members had been Freddy Wade, a curmudgeonly old man, late of Card Game, who had divulged the secret to Sheriff Reynolds a few years prior after having been unsatisfied with his take in the profits. Sheriff Reynolds had promised to keep him out of it, and had been preparing to take some sort of action when the old man had up and died on him. Suddenly lacking a witness and without hard evidence, Sheriff Reynolds had decided to sit on the information until it might prove to be of use to him.

But now that he had recently come into possession of evidence and had something that he wanted to accomplish that would require help, it seemed like as good a time as any to finally act on his knowledge.

When Old Man Frazier peered through the peephole in the back door of his Barber Shop, he became momentarily flummoxed. It wasn't like the Old Man to be flummoxed; in fact, he was rarely at a loss for words or an insult, but when he saw Sheriff Reynolds standing two feet away from him with just three inches of rickety steel separating them, he wasn't quite sure how to proceed.

Sheriff Reynolds was breaking the rules. The rules were that Card Game was sacrosanct and that the men of local law enforcement were to look the other way. Sure, it was technically illegal through lingering bible belt laws to host backroom card games, but the main gist of the reasoning for its off-limits nature was that it was an avenue for Pine Creek's Betters to decide policy. There was also the adversarial relationship between the good sheriff and said Betters due to his refusal to climb on board the money train with the town's ticketing racket that made the visit unseemly.

Old Man Frazier hadn't been privy to the corruption that certain other members of Card Game were, but he still was no fan of Sheriff Reynolds.

"Private game," he grunted through a puff of smoke before sliding the rusty piece of metal shut to close Sheriff Reynolds out for good and hopefully send him on his way.

Sheriff Reynolds, however, wasn't so easily put off as Old Man Frazier had hoped:

"Open the goddamn door, John."

When the door slowly creaked open, Sheriff Reynolds glanced at Old Man Frazier with a shake of his head to convey the futility of his obstinacy. "Didn't think that one through, did you?" he mused before walking past him and into the back room to find the remaining members of Card Game doing their best to ignore him while projecting their focus on the game.

"You need something, Sheriff?" Judge Collins asked with apathy dripping from his voice. "You're interrupting a private game."

"I won't be staying long," he replied, tossing a folder down onto the table, sending the random poker chip flying.

"What's this?" the judge asked.

"Confidential information," Sheriff Reynolds answered. "Pertaining to certain business dealings of certain individuals in this room."

Judge Collins shared a disturbed glance with his brother before responding: "Oh? And how did you come across this confidential information, Sheriff? Extralegal means, I'd assume, since I haven't signed any search warrants recently."

Sheriff Reynolds smiled. He had worried that he might have to elongate the situation by the need to play a long round of word games, but the judge was getting quickly to the point.

"Anonymous tip from a concerned citizen, if you like," he replied with a grin. "Regardless of how I came about it, it's now in my possession. And I know that your first instinct is to fight it in court, but I'm too old to play that bullshit. It'll go straight to the press, with a copy also going to the state and federal AGs. So let's just skip the part where you bluster and threaten to have me arrested because the only person in the state who can arrest a sheriff is the governor, and I'd be just as happy to talk to him as you would."

"What the hell is he talking about?" Old Man Frazier asked in the direction of Judge Collins. He had already been annoyed that Card Game was being interrupted in the first place because he had started the night on a heater, but he was equally irritated by the fact that he had no idea what all the prattle entailed. And he hated prattle.

"It's none of your concern, John," Judge Collins hastily answered. "Sheriff Reynolds has overstepped his mandate and he should think about walking out of here before he says something that he regrets."

"The thing is, John—" Sheriff Reynolds began to address Old Man Frazier, already tired of the bullshit that had begun to be peddled. "—some of your colleagues have been embezzling state and county funds. Did they ask you to be involved or were you just out in the cold?"

"You goofy bastards," Old Man Frazier said in between shakes of his head.

"Everyone who wasn't involved should leave now," Sheriff Reynolds urged. "My business tonight only pertains to those who were."

Of the nine men seated at the table, four got up to leave, including Old Man Frazier, who turned back to look at those who remained, reiterating: "Goofy bastards."

"Now," Sheriff Reynolds began, once the last man had left and the door had closed behind him. "We've all had our differences over the years — partly because I see the job of law enforcement to keep people and their property safe and you see it as a way to add money to the town and county coffers. Which makes sense, since you've been pillaging money from those coffers for the past fifteen years. From what I could tell, given your extracurricular activities, the city would have been broke years ago without all the money from traffic tickets, city code violations, DUIs, and the like. Stop me if I'm wrong."

He stopped for a moment to emphasize his point and wait for any would-be objection from his audience. None were forthcoming, as he had expected, and he took a moment to take in the situation. He had loathed the position that these men had created long before he was aware of how they had created it. Speed traps, checkpoints, strict enforcement of trivial city codes had all been hallmarks of the Pine Creek Police Department for so long that people had just come to accept them as having always been there. The city had tried to level a citation on Sheriff Reynolds himself for lawn clippings blown onto the city street by his lawnmower, but he had made such a fuss over the $25 ticket that it was eventually dropped once he started pulling members of the city council over and issuing them citations of his own; others just paid the fine because ongoing city fines could be used to levy a lien against a person's property and to eventually force foreclosure in order to pay the fines.

He *really* hated everyone involved in the racket that had been created, but his was a plan that would take patience to implement. He couldn't replace the city council, the judge, the DA, the police and so forth; it was so well-entrenched that he was going to have to begin by planting a Trojan horse — which is where Daryl would come in. His plan had been to have Daryl replace him as sheriff with the hopes of creating such a popular candidate that Daryl could either run for mayor or get him back-doored as police chief. But now that he had actual evidence, there was no point in pussyfooting around. He could just front-door Daryl as police chief and start the reconstruction from there.

"So here's the deal: I'm willing to overlook things on my end in exchange for a few — let's call them considerations. Each one of you on the city council or county board aren't going to seek re-election next year. Neither is the mayor. Neither is the DA. Neither is the judge," he said pointedly to Judge Collins. "And you're going to fire your puppet of a police chief."

"To be replaced by you, no doubt," Jay Collins nastily interjected.

"Have you not been listening to a word I've said? I don't want the goddamn job."

Not that they had been pleased with the proceedings beforehand, but now those being shaken down were beside themselves. They understood Sheriff Reynolds making the move to give himself more power, but what was the point of all of this if he was just going to oust them and give their power to someone else who could abuse the power for himself?

"You're out of your goddamned mind," Judge Collins declared. "On our side, we have a judge, a district attorney, the mayor, the chief of police. You have copies of some papers that could be anything. No chain of custody. No confessions. Basically nothing."

"I wouldn't say 'nothing,'" Ramona announced, walking into the room from the darkness of the barbershop front. "He does have me."

The five men at the table shared worried glances. They weren't sure how things were about to proceed, but they couldn't be good. They were each keenly aware that the Bennett Family had been the de facto law in Pine Creek for half-a-century before Ramona's grandmother had relinquished control back in the '80s, which is what allowed them to gain their positions in the first place. They had tiptoed around Ramona's grandmother just in case it had been a ruse, but after she had died without imposing her will and Ramona had, likewise, never made a power play, it was generally assumed that the Bennetts were best to be treated as *out of sight, out of mind*; and they largely had been. But there she stood in front of them, wearing sunglasses and a smile.

"And I come bearing gifts," she said with a smirk. "I assumed that none of you were stupid enough to leave a paper trail and that me and mine were largely spared from your little Soviet-era reign of terror — thanks for that, by the way — and I had been content to let things lie. But, since Sheriff Reynolds is a friend and you *were* stupid enough to leave a paper trail, I decided that maybe it was time for the Family to poke its head back out to see what's what."

Ramona dropped a repurposed feed sack onto the card table in front of the largely petrified men.

"You won't believe the kind of shit I found, Sheriff," she grinned.

"Anything interesting?" he asked, playing along.

"Extremely."

She opened the feed sack and started dropping folders full of paper onto the table.

"Not only did every one of these goofy bastards have at least some sort of record detailing their involvement in the embezzlement at their houses, along with making bank deposits that matched the numbers on their ledgers, but there was all kinds of weird shit in closets, basements, and search histories. Isn't one of you a deacon?" she asked with a false tone of disapproval. "Tsk fucking tsk, boys."

"That all?" the sheriff asked.

"Aside from the aforementioned perversions," Ramona replied with a smirk, "one of them was dumb enough to leave a paper trail in their text messages to an acquaintance who robbed your little card game. Seems like he was light on cash. I'll let you boys figure out who."

Sheriff Reynolds walked over to the table, picked up one of the folders, and made a show of flipping through it before tossing it back down. He looked each man in the eye in turn as he walked around the table to stand alongside Ramona.

"I think we understand each other," he said.

Earholed

The back roads of Murray County were, at times, capable of inspiring a sort of tranquil ambivalence about the world around a person in which they weren't being torn this way and that by anxiety or guilt; and there were even times in which ambivalence could find itself softening into something close to serenity. Not that Pine Creek was a bustling metropolis of civilization, but it was still capable of the occasional panic-inducing neuroses when it bared its teeth and a federal crime was being committed.

Eight miles north of town and two miles east of Highway 177 on County Road 1538, Daryl's aunt owned eighty acres of land. It was mostly pasture that was home to a few head of cattle, chickens, guineas, goats, and a donkey. The house sat about a quarter-mile off the dirt road on which Daryl sat in his cruiser, but though the hills may have aspired to mountain status in their youth, they had barely managed the humble rank of "rolling" in their late adulthood. Daryl could just make out the shape of his aunt where she sat on the front porch and waved when he stopped his cruiser. If he stayed long enough, she would eventually call his cell phone to see if he wanted to stay for dinner, but she knew that he liked to park on the road when he needed to think, so she generally left him to his business.

He had spent a large chunk of his childhood on that tract of land. He could see the smallest of the three ponds on the property just this side of the barn where rows of giant round-bails stood watch; and every time he saw them, it reminded him of playing hay-tag with his friends and the time that Jackson nearly lost a foot trying to jump from atop one of the bails and land on the back of the passing four-wheeler that Troy had been driving; or the time that he had fallen through the ice on the farthest pond one winter and had nearly frozen to death by the time he walked back to the house; or the time that Kendrick had flipped a dirt bike trying to jump a cow from a nearby ramp and the others were certain that he had broken his neck; and that was all before they had started drinking in their teens. The sheer number of stupid things that they had gotten up to as kids out there was mind-boggling. It seemed a miracle that any of them had survived.

Daryl wasn't particularly sure if it was the death-defying theatrics that made this his Happy Spot. For all he knew, it could just be regular old nostalgia, wrapping itself in the guise of danger to lessen the damage to his masculinity that didn't like to admit that he was getting older.

All he could say for sure was that when his mind was behaving abnormally, that is where he liked to come to reset it. It was usually a quick process: he would park on the side of the road where he had helped Jennifer Allen change a flat tire, which jumpstarted a summer fling that he held dear in the depths of his spank-bank — that in and of itself would sometimes do the trick. He would then play through the greatest hits of his childhood and the aforementioned death-defying theatrics, as he had been doing for the past several minutes; and eventually, if all else had failed, he would sprinkle a generous helping of Coors onto the recipe, which would typically work its frothy magic to finagle and caress the reset button from where it was stubbornly stuck somewhere at the back of his brain.

There was growing concern, however, that the button may have disappeared altogether.

His mind was too tightly wound for ambivalence.

It was a strange feeling to know that there was a satellite somewhere in orbit over the Earth capable of changing the direction of his life — just floating aimlessly about with no thoughts to spare for the trivialities of gravity or federal prison, content to sunbathe as if it were simply floating on its back in middle of the lake with little neon floaties around its arms.

Daryl envied that satellite in that moment.

But when the small flip phone that was riding shotgun began to ring, his mood immediately went from envy to disdain. Damn that evil, soulless, commie satellite straight to hell.

Daryl sighed and picked up the burner phone that he had driven three towns over to purchase in order to avoid leaving any sort of digital breadcrumbs. He glanced at the unfamiliar number on the Caller ID, which was from another burner phone that he had driven a further three towns over from the first three towns over that he had visited. It had been an incredibly long trip because he drove around all six towns on the back roads to avoid being seen on the highways in his old K5 Blazer, but a dull panic began to creep in as he worried that he hadn't done enough to conceal the trip now that he was holding the phone in his hand.

Goddamn that satellite.

"Yeah," Daryl said cautiously once had opened the phone.

"Go," was the only response that he received — at which point Daryl closed the phone, opened the back, and removed its battery. He tried to take a deep breath, but it was a longer process than he would have liked, requiring a double take to coax into his lungs the air that was hellbent on not becoming carbon dioxide. Much as the air around him was suddenly aware that it was doomed to become zombified, Daryl was suddenly very aware of the fact that there was a duffle bag with roughly $20,000.00 in the trunk of his cruiser that threatened to zombify his own life as a ward of the state.

He finally managed to sweet-talk the air into his lungs before leaning back hard onto his seat with his eyes closed and silence ringing in his ears. When he opened his eyes, he had meant to take one last glance at his aunt's house, but at the last moment, he decided that he didn't want to sour the memory in case things didn't work out as planned. So he sighed, began to turn the key where it rested in the ignition, and froze.

As he grabbed for the keys, he caught sight of something in his rearview mirror just about the time that he had noticed the sound of an approaching vehicle. He was sure that it was in his head, but the rumbling of the nearing engine began to sound like the rusty steel hinges of a jail cell the closer it came. There was never a lot of traffic on this road, and he would typically recognize the vehicle of any traffic that there may be, but he didn't recognize the '80s model truck kicking up dust in his direction.

This could be the butterfly that started the hurricane.

Daryl's first inclination was to lean back into his seat so far that he couldn't be seen in hopes that whoever it was would think that he was sleeping, but Daryl's curiosity at that moment was on par with *Ghost Troy's* incessant nagging. He was mentally preparing himself for whatever scenario might come his way so that he could temper his reaction to suit, but whatever those scenarios may have been in his head, they were nowhere close to what reality provided.

The two men in the beat-up '83 Silverado had their own curiosity to satisfy and were too stupid or willful to try to conceal their identity — both staring directly at Daryl as they passed; and there was a mutual recognition as Daryl recognized the Brown Brothers and the Brown Brothers recognized him. Each man was sporting chest-length long hair that was wildly different than he remembered, but Daryl would never forget their faces. Johnny and Ronnie Brown were denizens of the next town over from Pine Creek where they had played football against Daryl in high school, developing a reputation even in those days as being ne'er-do-wells and for general hooliganism. Since their high school days, they had devolved into petty criminals and all-around lowlifes, in and out of prison with the regularity of a high-fiber diet and never far from sight when trouble was to be found. They weren't seen much in Pine Creek anymore, though, not after the trial that labeled them as public enemy number one.

A little over two years prior to the day, someone had broken into Daryl's aunt's home. There had been a string of similar burglaries in the surrounding counties over those several months in which the perpetrators rarely took anything beyond what was in the medicine cabinet — the junkies having realized that it was much easier to move unidentifiable prescription pills than stolen personal property.

So it was typically the homes of the older generations that were hit, as they had almost universally had the best pills that would move quickly on the black market. The pattern was that they would simply wait until the homes were empty and rifle through the house for prescriptions, then leave the same way that they had come in with little or no fanfare. It was an easy racket — until the evening that they had broken into Daryl's aunt's house expecting an empty home but not having taken the time to properly surveil and know that her car was in the shop. When they opened the front door and found Helen standing at the kitchen sink, the story was that they panicked and nearly tripped over themselves trying to get back to their truck. Daryl's Aunt Helen, upon seeing the two masked men enter the home that she had shared with her late husband, had immediately set upon them with the knife that she had been at that very moment cleaning, content with the idea that she would have to clean it all over again to get the robber's blood off it. But the two scumbags wrestled the knife out of her grip and proceeded to stab her twice and leave her where she lay as they hurriedly ran through the house looking for their score.

Helen was able to call 911 and she was patched up in the hospital to the point that she would be nearly as good as before, with only a few scars to show that the incident had occurred. Though she was a strong woman and had taken to open-carrying a nine-millimeter pistol on her hip, Sheriff

Reynolds made certain that at least one squad car drove by her house twice a day.

The whispers around town had been prevalent before the incident that the Browns had been responsible for the string of robberies, but since the county and Daryl's jurisdiction ended two miles outside the city limits of Davis, home of the locally-renowned scumbaggery that were the Browns, it hadn't been enough to incite any sort of action on behalf of Murray County. With the incident with Daryl's aunt happening inside Murray County, however, and because of the nature of the crime, it had very much become part of the consideration of Sheriff Reynolds and his deputy, and the Browns were quickly apprehended with the cooperation of the Davis Police Department. Though the evidence was circumstantial, the public outcry was enough to push the District Attorney into bringing charges against them, but it ended in a hung jury and the Browns hadn't been seen again within a three-county radius since they left the courthouse that day.

Before Daryl had time to process what was happening, his cruiser started and followed closely behind the Silverado as if the car had taken it upon itself to initiate an incident on behalf of its driver, like KITT or a slightly less-demented Christine. He wasn't sure what he was doing in that moment, but he had forgotten all about the duffel bag full of money in his trunk and his mission to deliver it to an abandoned house where he was to stumble upon said duffle bag through an "anonymous tip." He was instead flipping the button on his siren and trying desperately to prepare himself for whatever was about to happen.

He half-expected the truck to keep driving once he turned on the siren and that he was going to be led into a high-speed pursuit for the next twelve miles down back roads until they reached the next highway, but the truck almost immediately pulled over to the side of the road as Daryl pulled his cruiser up behind them. Still unsure what his move was going to be, he exited the cruiser with as much speed as he could muster and had his gun drawn before he took a step.

"Get out of the truck!" he yelled as stood in a defensive posture with his gun pointed at the head of the driver. He wasn't sure if they would be armed, but he wasn't prepared to take that chance before he got to talk to them. The next few moments seemed like an eternity, but he breathed a sigh of relief when both brothers exited the truck with their hands in the air. "You, go stand beside your brother," he commanded to Ronnie, the passenger.

Ronnie did as he was bid and Daryl took the moment to contemplate his next move.

"Lift up your shirts and turn around," he commanded.

"You wanna see our dicks, you can just ask," Johnny said with a wry smile, but the smile quickly evaporated when Daryl fired a single shot into the dirt a few feet in front of them. "Shit, okay," he replied with a nod to his brother as they both lifted their shirts and turned around to show that neither had a weapon.

Daryl was finally able to relax for the time being, content that he was in control of the situation.

"What do you want from us?" Ronnie asked.

"Just to talk!" Daryl answered with a forced smile.

"Haven't seen you boys in a couple of years. Wanted to see what you were up to. Where have you been holed up at?"

"Here and there," Johnny quickly replied, still unsure what was happening.

"Here and there," Daryl echoed. "Two worldly travelers I'm dealing with, I guess. I haven't seen you boys since — fuck, when was the last time? Was it that time I dropped your ass on that sack to win the state championship in high school, or when you stabbed that old lady?"

"Why you bring up old shit, man?" Johnny asked. "The past is the past. We're just in town to see some family and then we're leaving. No one's doing anything that requires a police escort."

"What family do you have in Murray County?" Daryl asked, knowing that the answer was none.

"He ain't blood. Just an old family friend," Ronnie responded. "Not that it's any of your concern."

"I see. A family friend," Daryl echoed again. "Two world travelers in my county to see an old family friend."

"Can we go?" Ronnie asked again. "We've got shit to do. We have jobs and shit. We don't get to just drive around in a car all day like an asshole."

Daryl responded with a laugh. "Yeah, it is a pretty cush gig. Mostly just drive around, eat donuts, and shit like that. Every now and then, though, if we're really good, they'll let us shoot somebody." Daryl raised his eyebrows with that last bit to let the situation sink in as the brothers exchanged worried glances. "And believe it or not, I've been pretty fucking good this year."

Daryl waited several moments before releasing another round of raucous laughter.

"Hell, I'm not gonna shoot you boys! Why would I? Fine, upstanding citizens. World travelers just in my county to see an old family friend. Shit, pillars of the fucking community."

When the brothers exchanged relieved glances and a shit-eating grin, it was in that very moment that Daryl decided that there was a line. And that he was going to cross it.

"It's not like you stabbed an old lady or anything, right? Found innocent by a jury of your peers."

"That's right. We didn't do that. It was some pill-heads," Johnny responded with confidence.

"Right! Some goddamn pill-heads running around my county stabbing old women. It was a fucking travesty," Daryl answered before leaning up against his cruiser and crossing his arms. "Well, you boys better be on your way. I just wanted to pull you over and see what you were up to on account of having not seen you for all that time. Make sure that you were okay."

"We appreciate your concern, Daryl. And we will be on our way," Johnny managed to say with a somewhat civil tone despite the fact that the grin on his face was anything but civil. They turned to get back into the truck, but were stopped short by—

"Just one more thing."

When they turned back to Daryl, they didn't have time to throw any sort of quip in his direction once they noticed that his gun had been drawn again and pointed in their direction.

"Did you two stab that old lady?" Daryl asked calmly. "Just between you and me. Who am I gonna tell? And even if I wanted to, it doesn't matter, right? Double jeopardy and such. You boys can't be tried for the same crime twice."

The Browns exchange nervous glances again but kept their thoughts to themselves.

"So between friends," Daryl continued, "did you do it?"

He waited for about ten seconds while the Browns stared at him with the sort of look that made him glad that he was holding a gun; because he wasn't sure that he could take both of them — even with his night stick. But he did have his gun, and he used it one more time to fire a shot into the bed of their truck a few feet from where they stood. Though they had dropped their death-stares in favor of a more concerned demeanor, neither brother appeared as though he was ready to betray any sort of secret.

"I'm getting bored, boys. And when I get bored, I shoot shit," Daryl advised. "So for the last time, did you stab that old lady?" After a few more seconds, he pointed the gun at Johnny and appeared ready to loose another round from his chamber before—

"Goddammit!" Johnny yelled. "Yeah, we did it, you fucking psychopath. You happy? Shit, I can't believe this fucking county lets you carry a gun! She came at us with that knife first! We don't just run around stabbing old ladies for the hell of it!"

"See, how easy was that?" Daryl said with a smile. "Kinda pisses you off that it took that long to come out with it, doesn't it? All that effort wasted for no reason. Now that you've satisfied my curiosity, I gotta get back to my donuts."

Daryl started to turn around to get into his cruiser, but stopped short again.

"Oh, shit, I know that I said the last time that it was one last thing, but there was another thing. This will be the last one, I promise. See, you boys probably didn't know this, but that old woman's maiden name is Lumley," Daryl said as he reached back toward the gun on his belt. "Which might sound familiar, because it's also my last name."

"Shit," Ronnie exclaimed, finally realizing what was happening; and instead of waiting around for it to happen, he started to sprint in Daryl's direction in hopes of getting his gun before his gun got him. That hope was ill-placed, however.

Daryl shot him twice in the chest, watched him drop and trained his gun on the remaining Brown brother.

Johnny, for his part, hadn't taken the bait, but was fuming where he stood. "You won't get away with this!" he screamed. "You can't shoot two unarmed men with no consequences."

"That's why I've got this," Daryl responded, tossing a small revolver that he pulled from the back of his belt in Johnny's direction.

Johnny caught the gun and stared down at it, checking to see that there were bullets in it before glancing back to his brother lay.

"I'm not gonna do it, Daryl," he responded. "I'm not gonna let you get away with it. You'll have to take me in."

"I've already got away with it, you goofy bastard. Your white trash brother was running toward me when I shot him. I even fired a few warning shots into the dirt and into the bed of your truck before I shot him," he said, motioning toward the bullet holes. "So if you don't—"

Daryl had gotten so caught up in trying to goad Johnny into shooting at him that he was taken completely by surprise when he began shooting at him; so even though the first couple shots whizzed by his head, as Johnny was just dumb enough to try for headshots, he corrected course with the next round and caught Daryl in the shoulder. The pain was even worse than he would have imagined, but he would be goddamned if he was going to be killed by a Brown, so he used the adrenaline that he was base-lining through his veins to flash back to his firearms training. He pushed himself away from the cruiser where the force of impact had thrown him and emptied his revolver.

MINUTES HAD PASSED before Daryl was fully able to recover from the shock of the situation. He had killed Johnny — or at least he assumed that he had. After emptying his revolver and hearing several more clicks emitted from his pistol as he tried to empty what was left of his hatred, he fell back toward his cruiser again, though this time he missed the side and fell through the open door, against the seat, and onto the ground. He had tried to peer over the open door and through the window, but the adrenaline had begun to wear off and his muscles were shaking like he had contracted MS from the whole ordeal. He had fallen back to the ground and he lay like that until he was able to catch his breath enough to push himself up against the rear tire of his cruiser and assess the situation. He still couldn't see over the door, but he was able to glance underneath it and see that neither man was moving, so at least he had that going for him.

He was going to have to drag himself to the front of the car and use the radio to call for help, as the small mouthpiece on his shoulder had been damaged at some point during the debacle. He really didn't want to pull himself so far as the front of the car, however, and he contemplated whether just lying there and dying wasn't the better option. At that point, he felt that it was 50/50.

Either way, he was spared the choice of an impending suicide by the sounds of an approaching car, but when he turned his head to see who it was, he was struck by another moment of panic when he didn't recognize the car heading toward him. For all he knew, this was some of the Brown cousins coming to finish the job that their asshole cousin Johnny had started; and since he wasn't sure that he had the constitution for suicide, Daryl figured it was just as well if it was.

By the time the black SUV had stopped alongside Daryl, he was prepared for the worst, but at least being killed by throngs of Brown Brothers would make for a better eulogy than being killed by the Browns proper, so he was thankful for that. The driver of the SUV killed its engine, which could be either a good or bad sign in and of itself, and the window motor hummed into life as the window calmly responded, mocking Daryl as he lay awaiting his fate.

"Oh, what the tits?" Daryl exclaimed upon seeing Ramona smiling back at him. "What the fuck are you doing out here?" he continued, wincing as he pushed himself up from the ground.

"Hey, Cowboy," Ramona responded as she pushed the sunglasses down to allow her to take in the whole of Daryl's situation.

"'Hey, Cowboy,' my swinging dick," Daryl further exclaimed. "I asked what the fuck you're doing here." The situation had somehow devolved into a worse course of events than summary execution. He knew that there was no way in holy hell Ramona was there by accident, and that her involvement could only be bad news for him.

"I figured you'd be in a better mood," she answered, getting out of the car and walking around the front to where Daryl stood, then leaning back against her own car with a casual demeanor.

"After being shot?"

"After getting to exercise your God-given right for revenge."

Daryl thought about trying to play the situation cool, but he didn't really see the point. She obviously knew more about the situation than he did.

"Revenge?"

"Daryl," she said with a smile. "Look who you're talking to."

Daryl hung his head and winced again when he tried to move his shoulder.

"What do you want, Ramona?"

"I just wanted to see the look on your face, darling. That's all any proud parent wants to see on Christmas morning." She cocked her eyebrows to drive home the point before walking toward Daryl's cruiser.

"What is that supposed to mean?"

"Sweetie, what do you think those scumbags were doing all the way out here?" she asked with a glance in Daryl's direction as she reached underneath his dashboard and popped the trunk.

Daryl sighed and watched her walk back toward the trunk — not bothering to fight the fact that she was going for the duffle bag full of money.

"I'm guessing you sent them."

"Called in a debt," she answered with a smile.

"You knew where they were this whole time and you didn't bother telling me?"

"You didn't ask. Them's the rules. You want something, you come to me and ask. I'll help you if I can, and you scratch my back at a date to be decided later."

"Jesus, Ramona, I'm a cop."

"I've always had a soft spot for a man in uniform," she said playfully, running her finger across Daryl's collar as she walked past him with the duffle bag and plopped it down on the hood of his cruiser.

"So how and why? Why *here* and why *now*?" Daryl asked, exasperated.

"'How' was easy. I banished them after what they did to your aunt."

"Banished them?"

"From my territory. Nothing goes down in Murray County. They knew the rules, they broke the rules. They got banished and, as you can see—" she said, reaching over to where Ronnie lay on the ground and pushing back the hair from his face to expose a nub with a hole where his ear used to be, "—I punished them accordingly."

"Goddammit," Daryl exclaimed, looking away from the grotesquery of the open ear hole.

"People've gotta know that they can't break rules, Daryl. It's a key aspect of personnel management," she answered, going back to the duffle bag where she unzipped it. "You should keep that in mind."

Daryl didn't know nor did he want to know what she was talking about with that last remark, so he turned his attention to Ramona as she removed several stacks of money from the bag.

"What am I supposed to do now? I was supposed to find the money to take the heat off the guys."

"Ta-da! You found it," she said, throwing the bag into the bed of the Brown's truck.

"But—"

"Look, Daryl, you're gonna have to be a little quicker on the uptake in the future." She took some money and threw it into the front seat of her SUV. "I agreed to buy a certain product from your friend Rob wholesale — at your urging. Because of the added risk involved with moving this product out of your county, there was a fifty percent interest rate attached that Rob agreed to, so he still owed me a not-unsubstantial amount of money," she said, holding up the last stack of cash and tossing it into her SUV. "Which he has now paid in full. And you've got two dead bank robbers in place of your friends."

"This was your plan all along?"

"Of course it was. Would have been a bad investment otherwise. How were those two ever going to come up with this kind of cash to pay me back?" She slapped Daryl on his non-injured shoulder. "Buck up, Cowboy. You just killed two bank-robbing, woman-stabbing pill-heads that eluded capture by the fucking FBI and recovered whatever money they didn't spend on smack and whores. You're a goddamn rock star."

She smiled again, walked around the front of her car, got into the front seat, and slipped her sunglass back on.

"Ramona?"

She slid the glasses back down onto the end of her nose. "Daryl?"

"How'd you know where I'd be?" he asked, utterly defeated.

"You're nothing if not predictable, babe." She started the car, put it in gear and blew Daryl a kiss before taking off. "I'll see you soon."

"God, I hope not," Daryl said as she drove away.

PART III

Post Fuckery Cuddles

19

Codeine

Daryl groaned as he pulled the door open to the Sheriff's Office, annoyed at how much it had hurt to get shot. He had always expected that he would be the sort of man to brush off a gunshot like Mel Gibson or Clint Eastwood, but he felt closer to Betty White than either of the aforementioned paragons of virility. He felt old, which was partly due to the pain-killers that he was still on from the surgery to remove the bullet and partly due to the fact that there was a gaping hole in his shoulder. He had serious doubts as to whether he could win a fistfight against Betty White at that moment if she had strolled in and called him a pussy.

It had been four days since he had shot and been shot, and he would have come back into work the next day if the doctor hadn't advised against it — or had he been able. In fact, he had disregarded the doctor's advice and tried to force himself out of the hospital bed that morning, but he hadn't realized just how heavy the medication was — or how much the bullet wound still hurt despite the weight of the medication. So he had sat and received visitors in his loopy haze like some drugged-out Don. He remembered his friends coming through at some point and laughing heartily as he told them in detail about his plans to kill them all for getting him into this. He vaguely remembered Sheriff Reynolds. And he thought that he had dreamed Ramona's visit, in which he kept grabbing at his waist for the pistol that wasn't hanging from the belt that wasn't there, but he had woken up to find a floral arrangement with the message: "Buck up, Cowboy" signed simply with an overly flowery "R."

He pushed through the second set of doors with a grimace before slowly making the trek to Sheriff Reynolds' office, hoping to find a sense of closure by spilling his guts and letting the cards fall where they may. He had been content to keep his friends' secrets before he had realized that there was some sort of vast criminal conspiracy with the Bennetts at the head of it that somehow included Reagan and Jay Collins and maybe Judge Collins. There was something fucky lurking in the shadows, and he intended to bring it into the open.

He found Sheriff Reynolds at his desk, puffing on a cigar with his boots propped up on his desk, and though his position implied relaxation, the scowl on his face betrayed that entirely.

"You're aware there's a parade going on for you right now," he pointed out. "Why is it that every lazy son of a bitch from this office is out there, but you're not?"

"I'm not really in the celebratory mood, Boss," Daryl responded, lowering himself into one of the chairs across from the desk and attempting to find any sort of comfortable position.

"Nonsense. You solved the crime, killed the bad guys, took a bullet for the town. They'll replace that buffalo with a statue of you wearing the duster from *The Good, The Bad and The Ugly*."

"They can keep their fucking buffalo," he managed before taking a deep breath to counter the pain in his shoulder from simply speaking too loudly.

"You'll never make mayor with that attitude," the sheriff said with a smile, trying to take Daryl's mind off the pain.

"Look, Sheriff, there's something I need to get off my chest," Daryl began, shifting the tone of the conversation to one that his mentor didn't want to have. "The official story—"

"—is the official story," Sheriff Reynolds interrupted. "It's a fucking story to make all the good townsfolk feel good about themselves and about their town and about you. Let them have it."

"Things didn't go down the way that I said they did."

"I have a pretty good idea about how things went down," he replied, offering a cautious stare in Daryl's direction. "Let's just leave it at that."

"All due respect, sir—" Daryl tried to counter before stopping when the sheriff shook his head and held up his finger in a gesture widely known the world over to mean *shut the fuck up*.

Though the office was empty with no signs of life besides the two of them, Sheriff Reynolds stood up, walked over to the open door that Daryl hadn't seen the need to close, and pulled it tightly shut before returning to lean up against his desk only a few feet away from Daryl.

"When I say I have a pretty good idea, I mean that I have a pretty good idea," Sheriff Reynolds said in a hushed voice. "Meaning that I don't need you to go into detail."

"But, sir—"

"'But, sir,' my ass," he said with a shake of his head. "Fucking kids these days."

Sheriff Reynolds took a glance back out toward the office to make sure that they were still alone before leaning in close to make his point: "Only a fucking moron would believe your story. The scumbag Brown Brothers show up back in town after robbing the bank and you happen upon them on the back roads with some of the money?"

Daryl furrowed his brow and felt his heart starting to race, which made the pain in his shoulder begin to throb almost in unison.

"I know that you know who robbed the bank, and I know why the Browns are dead just as well as you do. And I know that a mutual friend of ours was part of the solution."

"Our *mutual friend* is the one who set all of this in motion."

"They're the one who robbed the bank?" the Sheriff asked with a faux tone of surprise. "The one who decided to instigate a cover-up and frame a couple of assholes?"

"No, but—"

"You're too young to remember, but do you know what this town was like in the 70s and before? It was a rough fucking place with one or two murders every year and all sorts of violence. Nothing like it is now. You ever notice how easy your job is?" he asked. "How you mainly write speeding tickets to out-of-towners and deal with kids' pranks? How what happened to your aunt was such a fucking travesty because it's the first time anyone can remember something like that happening in thirty years?"

Daryl nodded, waiting for the punchline.

"You never wondered why that's the way it is here when all of the surrounding areas have the druggies and the perverts breaking into everyone's houses and the goddamn white trash or homeless moving in to drag everyone else down? It's because in the '80s, I made a deal with the grandmother of our *mutual friend*. She would keep that sort of element either out of town or in their place. And I would look the other way and occasionally facilitate certain of her enterprises."

Daryl couldn't believe what he was hearing. There he was about to try and report a minor criminal conspiracy only to be told that a much wider criminal conspiracy had been ongoing for the past thirty years. Should he be reaching for his handcuffs — and even if he should, how would he manage with a hole in his handcuffing shoulder?

"I can see on your face that you disapprove," Sheriff Reynolds observed. "I couldn't give two shits. I made a deal to keep the peace, and I'd do it again."

"What about the surrounding counties where the crime does take place?" Daryl asked, incredulous.

"Fuck them," Sheriff Reynolds replied. "They should have had the sense to cut their own deals. I'm not sheriff of the state, just of this county, and I run the safest goddamn county in the state."

"So what do you expect me to do?" Daryl asked, dejected and completely overwhelmed.

"I expect you to do what's right for the town," he replied. "Truth is that I was grooming you to run for sheriff when I retire next year."

"Sir—" he began before being cut off again. Daryl was beginning to resent the frequency with which his speech was being interrupted, but he was still unsure how to respond.

"But that's off the table now. You're going to be offered the job as police chief. It's not my decision, but if I were you,

I'd take it. Clean up that viper's nest and work with the new city council to run the town the way it should be run."

"And our *mutual friend?*"

"Also not my decision. But if it were, I'd accept their offer of friendship. The laws they're passing today are there to protect the criminals, not the citizens; and it's a lot easier to run a town when the criminals have their own code of conduct being enforced."

"What about you?" Daryl asked.

"What about me?"

"You said you were going to retire."

"Ah, hell, I'm too young to retire. Young pup like me. When I find the right replacement, I'll let them run for election and ride off into the sunset. Until then, I'll have to settle for having a good guy in the Pine Creek PD. So what do you think?" he asked, hoping that Daryl would commit to the plan on the spot.

"Sir, I'll be doing good if I remember this tomorrow on account of the codeine. You might have to run it all by me again."

The laughter helped to ease the mood of the room, and both men felt that things might just end up okay.

20

Winona Ryder's Boobs

The Summer Soiree was a festival that Pine Creek held each summer to commemorate the founding of the town. Though there was great pride in its undertaking, there was really little else to separate it from any of the festivals of the surrounding communities. Just like the Sandbass Festival in Madill, the Okie Noodlin' Festival in Pauls Valley, the Water Festival in Sulphur, or the Peach Festival in Stratford, the Soiree was a collection of artisan booths, fried food, and the same carnies working the same rides who did the carnival circuit every year.

Still, there was music and alcohol, so it drew a crowd.

There was also the yearly performance by Wylie Hurst, a local musician who was a legend on the Oklahoma and Texas Outlaw Scene, but to everyone's chagrin he hadn't been able to make it back to town in time, so there had been some poor band from the city who had to step in and fill his shoes last-minute. They were setting up their equipment on the recently erected stage where it stood in the middle of Main Street, noisily tuning their instruments while absolutely no one paid attention to them as they passed with a beer in one hand and cotton candy in the other. Main Street was shut down for a solid six blocks to accommodate the festivities, and it would take a combination of three city workers and several kids who had received public service for bad behavior nearly two days to clean up the aftermath.

Jackson was sitting alone at one of the dozens of picnic tables that had been brought in and placed along the edges of Main Street. He was drinking beer and eating something fried, though he really couldn't remember or tell what it was by that point. He was supposed to be meeting the rest of the guys there, but they were running late, which had thrown him into fried-food frenzy topped off with Budweiser and shame.

It had been about a week since all of the excitement had subsided, but there was still a hint of something strange in the air — a sort of restlessness that all of the commotion had caused by removing one of the more precarious blocks from the Jenga Tower that felt like it could come crumbling down at any moment.

Brose Manor, in the short time since all had been well, had seemingly become a shell of itself. Troy had largely remained holed up in his room while Rob had already begun his stint in rehab — a condition which Daryl had imposed in exchange for allowing him to live. Kendrick had been mostly absent with little explanation as to why. Jackson had been so excited to have the group back together that he had pre-gamed more extensively than he had planned and found himself rather day-drunk, watching everyone else enjoy themselves with the hatred of a Sith growing inside of him.

"Bastards," he said to no one in particular.

"Who?" Reagan asked as she sat down alongside Jackson, kissing him hello on the hairy cheek.

"Everyone. Bastards, all."

"You're in a good mood," she replied with a smile.

"I'm thinking of dropping an A-Bomb on all of them."

"You don't have an A-Bomb."

"That's why I'm just thinking about it," Jackson lazily replied, taking another gulp from his beer while pushing the fried surprise across the table. "That's disgusting."

Reagan rolled her eyes. Jackson had been depressed in the wake of the happenings, and his depression was that of a petulant child's. Instead of seeing the opportunity to change the stagnation he had fallen into, he mourned to no end the potential passing of the way of life that he, for one reason or another, had come to cherish.

"I'm leaving town," Reagan blurted out, much more quickly and with less subtlety than she had planned.

"Your yearly visit to see your sister and that butt-ugly kid of hers?" Jackson asked with little interest.

"First of all, fuck you. My niece is interesting-looking at worst."

"Ugly as fuck," Jackson replied, still with little effort or interest. "I feel bad for that kid. If I won the lottery, I'd pay for her plastic surgery. And they spelled her name with a *Y*. I think your sister may have Downs."

Ignoring the slight against her family, Reagan continued: "And second of all, I'm not going to my sister's. I'm going to law school. In Tulsa."

"Like, for the weekend?" Jackson asked, finally beginning to pay attention to the conversation that had theretofore held less significance than having his friends abandon him.

"Like, for law school," she replied, throwing a knowing glance in Jackson's direction.

"Why? I figured you would just work with the Succubus now that she's opening a Succubus Law Firm in town." Jackson felt the initial pangs of panic begin to set in, but knew that he had to keep them under control lest they be used against him.

"I talked to Eve about that, but we agreed that law school presented the best opportunity for me."

"Are you lesbians now?" Jackson asked, hoping that she wouldn't notice the slight crack in his voice.

"Yeah, we're lesbians now, and I'm going to come back to town after I graduate so we can run a Lesbian Law Firm and handle lesbian cases." Reagan felt like Jackson was on the verge of collapse, that she might actually be able to talk him into leaving town with her against all odds. He had a crack in his voice for God sake.

"I can't pretend that's not hot," Jackson answered.

"I want you to come with me."

"I don't think they'll just let me into law school when I didn't go to college."

"I meant to Tulsa, asshole," Reagan responded, knowing that Jackson was attempting a game of distraction and that it was time to drop the pretense. "Leave your friends and your brother, at least for a couple of years, and come with me. You know, the way that we had planned after high school."

"What the fuck would I do in Tulsa?" Jackson asked straightforwardly. To that point, he had relied on humor to keep the conversation from delving too deeply into consequence, but Reagan kept pushing him back into the deep end like she was hoping Jaws might be swimming to devour him and his soul.

"I don't know. They have cars in Tulsa. You can keep being a mechanic or you can go back to school or you could fight crime. You've always wanted to fight crime like Batman."

"That's true. I would make a sweet Batman," he conceded. "But what about Brose Manor?"

While Jackson couldn't see himself leaving his namesake behind, Reagan couldn't see leaving Jackson behind, so she continued with her argument as though he hadn't been continuing with his: "Maybe we get married."

"Kendrick can't keep the place running without me. He's about as close to Downs as your sister, and Rob would just turn the place into an opium den."

"Maybe have kids."

"Have kids?" he asked, quickly being taken out of his argumentative trance. "I am a kid."

"You're twenty-nine-years-old."

"In some cultures, you can't breed until you're fifty."

"That's not true."

"It could be true."

"Besides," she began with a hopeful sigh before releasing a tiny smile, "you better get ready. Because I'm pregnant."

Here, the conversation had come to a complete halt. Jackson had been so wrapped up in winning the argument and the prize of getting to stay in a Pine Creek that he had missed the subtext of the argument itself.

"Don't fuck with me," he scoffed. "You are not."

"Scout's honor."

"You weren't in the scouts."

"You were," she said while holding up her three-fingered

scout sign to illustrate her honesty. She had expected him to either fake falling asleep or to run away by that point in the conversation, so she was really doing better than she would have thought.

"I'm not raising another man's baby."

"It's yours."

"You can't know that."

"I do."

"God, I hope that your sister's baby takes after her husband. I can't love an ugly baby. I'll abandon it."

"So you're coming to Tulsa?" In that moment, she felt like she was destined to become a great trial attorney. She might as well have been arguing with Flat Earthers about how the Moon Landing was the greatest achievement of our time, and she had gotten them to sail right over the edge of the world.

"I'm not shaving my beard."

"Why would you have to shave your beard?"

In the scheme of things, Jackson wasn't sure if it was the mention of a baby or the fact that his circle of friends was beginning to fade before his very eyes like McFly in that picture or maybe even that he had hit the proverbial wall years earlier and had been ramming his head against it ever since; maybe he was just tired of the headaches or maybe he remembered the last time that Reagan had left town without him and had married some jackass. The more that he thought about it, the more he was sure it was the latter, and he couldn't see himself allowing her to marry some jackass all over again, especially if she was carrying his demon spawn. But he couldn't just give up without a fight.

"They don't know about manly shit like this up there in the city. It'll scare the poor bastards."

"They have hipsters there."

"This isn't a bullshit hipster beard. This is a Chuck Norris beard." The conversation had remained mostly playful up until that point, but she was coming awfully close to crossing the line.

"You can keep the beard. Are you coming?"

"Winona Ryder's boobs," Jackson sighed.

"Winona Ryder's boobs," she agreed, never so happy to hear a reference to breasts in her life.

AS JACKSON APPROACHED the front steps of Brose Manor an hour or so later, flush with the type of unadulterated excitement that only alcohol and testosterone could fuel, he felt the sudden urge to stop and examine his behavior. His gait was so uncharacteristically loose that it nearly had a skip to it; his mind had wandered away from leaving everything behind and focused on the prospects before it; and he had even momentarily forgotten why he was home in the first place: to break the news to Kendrick.

A rush of uninvited sensations began to creep over his body, leaving him feeling strange and vulnerable in a way that he didn't appreciate. He tried to focus on the fact that the universe had taken him to the woodshed over the last hour and that it would require him to cut ties with everything he had ever known, but his brain wouldn't cooperate; it was still churning furiously to wrap itself around the fact that he had agreed to abscond to lands unknown with his lady love and their bastard love child. Where would they live? Where would he work? Would those city hippies be scared of his beard? Was this what introspection felt like?

Was this what *adulthood* felt like?

If so, he didn't like it one damn bit, but he didn't have the time to iron out any specifics as Kendrick opened the front door to Brose Manor and started descending the steps before Jackson could get any further.

His plan had been to try and formulate the best angle of attack with which to approach his brother in regard to his impending exit from Pine Creek in the last few steps before he entered the Manor — maybe sitting on the front porch with a beer before going in — but that plan had been blown to hell now and he would have to think on his toes. He had spent the past few weeks following Kendrick around town, thinking that the situation might be easier to deal with if he were to spontaneously combust, and now he was beginning to feel as though might actually miss his brother were he to mysteriously implode; he might actually miss him if he were to not see him for more than a few days at a time. He hadn't been away from Kendrick for more than the month that he had spent at OU before being unceremoniously dismissed, and it had been dreadfully boring having no one to fight. Jackson had a lot of hate in his heart, and it was only with Kendrick that he was able to let it out.

More than that, though, all of his other friends were notoriously flakey in their own right, and Kendrick was the only one on whom he could actually rely to be there when he needed him; true enough, *needing him* usually only accounted for having someone to play video games with or to drive him somewhere when he was too drunk, but there was a lifelong symbiosis there that Jackson wasn't keen on having to replace.

What was he supposed to do: rely on his girlfriend as a life partner? Now that he had had time to think about it, perhaps committing to Tulsa hadn't been the most prudent of moves, but Kendrick was, by that point, standing a few feet in front of him with a quizzical expression on his face as he watched Jackson's brain try to work out the conundrum.

"What are you doing?" Kendrick asked, uninterested.

"Fuck you! How about that?" Jackson asked with a huff.

"I hope your dick falls off," Kendrick retorted before beginning his descent down the steps toward his car.

Jackson watched him for a few steps before feeling it was *now or never* with his announcement.

"I'm leaving," Jackson blurted out.

"Yeah, me too," Kendrick responded with a jangle of his car keys for proof.

"I mean for good!" He hadn't meant to scream his follow-up like a drama queen, but there he stood.

"So you're actually going to go to Tulsa?" Kendrick smiled.

"Did you just read my mind?"

"Yes," Kendrick dead-panned. "And Reagan told me that she was going to ask you."

"Why would she do that?"

"To see if I thought you would actually go if she asked, dumbass," Kendrick offered. "Of course, I told her that there was no way you would leave your cozy little life here for the unknown, but look at you: proving me wrong."

"Yeah, well, I'm full of surprises and shit."

"And shit," Kendrick agreed. "Look, man, it's just as well because I've been trying to find a way to tell you that I'm leaving, too."

"The Watering Hole?"

"Ada."

"That's a long way to drive for a beer."

"But not a long way to drive to go back to school."

"What the fuck is in the water today? Why is everyone going back to school like there's going to be a goddamn test next week?" Jackson spat. "What does that even mean 'you're going back to school?'"

"That I'm going to take classes in hopes of attaining a degree."

"You're going to leave me," Jackson yelled.

"You're going to leave me," Kendrick yelled back.

"Yeah, well, you were going to leave me first, dickhead, because you obviously had this planned for a while, where I just decided an hour ago! And I'm not even doing it for myself, so ha!"

"Ha!" Kendrick echoed.

The two brothers stared accusingly at one another for a few moments, each content to let their stare continue the conversation for as long as it could.

"You really leaving?" Jackson asked.

"Not tonight, but yeah," Kendrick responded. "You really leaving?"

"Not tonight, but yeah," Jackson dittoed before they stood in an awkward silence for a few moments. "Wow. Ain't that some shit?"

"Shit, indeed."

"Is this why you've been acting so weird lately?"

"Yeah," Kendrick answered with a shrug of his shoulders. "Maybe I was feeling guilty about leaving you for school again. Or maybe I just didn't want to let you guys know until it was definitely happening. Or maybe I just hate you and wanted it to be a surprise. Who can say?"

"Well, whatever the reason, I'm happy for you, brother," Jackson said with a sincere nod of approval. Kendrick was taken aback when Jackson began to move toward him, preparing to fight off some sort of attack before Jackson wrapped his arms around him in the first hug the two had shared for as long as either could remember. Both felt weird about how it had started and how long it was lasting, but neither wanted to break it so soon; even they had both agreed that neither was leaving that night, each felt as though letting go might begin the process.

"I thought you were gay," Jackson let slip.

"What?" Kendrick asked, pulling back from the embrace.

"I thought that's why you were acting so weird lately. I thought you were running around banging dudes in the shadows or something," Jackson said with a smile and a dismissive wave of his hand. "And here you are, just going back to school like a nerd!"

Jackson moved in to hug his brother again before Kendrick put his hand in between them to stop the motion.

"Actually, now that you mention it—" Kendrick began, sensing his own *now or never* moment and ceasing his speech in favor of a revealing nod and shrug of the shoulders.

"Bullshit."

"Not bullshit."

"You've been banging dudes in the shadows?"

"Not as lewd as all that, but yes," Kendrick responded. "I'm gay."

"Bullshit," Jackson repeated.

"Not bullshit," Kendrick repeated.

"Then why were you at Ramona's the other day?"

"To try and get money for school," Kendrick answered with a frown. "And how did you know I was at Ramona's? Did you follow me?"

"Then why were you at Eve's the other day?"

"To try and get a recommendation letter for school," Kendrick answered with a frown. "And how did you know I was at Eve's? Did you fucking follow me?"

"Then when were you banging dudes in the shadows?"

"I'm not..." Kendrick angrily began before calming himself. "...banging dudes in shadows. Jesus, Jackson. I'm not seeing anyone right now, if you must know."

"But you have seen someone?"

"Yes."

"But not in the shadows."

"Not in the shadows."

"So you're gay."

"We're going in circles here."

"Banging dudes."

"In the shadows," Kendrick finally concluded with a nod to shut him up.

Kendrick's ruse had worked and Jackson did stop running his mouth for a bit. Kendrick was trying to read his expression, but he appeared to be *beautiful minding*, so best to leave it until he worked it out for himself. Finally, it had been quiet for longer than Kendrick had expected. He really hadn't foreseen any of his friends or Jackson having a problem with his revelation, and he had only really kept the secret for so many years because he had eventually reached a point some time after realizing his sexuality that he was embarrassed for not admitting it to them sooner. Now he felt silly even having let it slip because it was like he had some drama queen's sense of whimsy.

"Good for you, man," Jackson finally responded before grabbing his brother for another hug that Kendrick wasn't quick enough to stop.

"You're not mad?" Kendrick asked, unsure if Jackson would have been angered by the subject or because he had kept it from him.

"Fuck no! I approve of your deviant lifestyle wholeheartedly. Pissed that you've kept it from me, but okay with it."

"As long as you approve," Kendrick said with a shake of the head. "I thought you'd be...weirder about it."

"No, I mean, there was a time when I thought that if you were gay, that meant that I was gay and I really didn't want to bang any dude other than, like, Ryan Reynolds, but then I'd miss vagina and I didn't think I'd want to be a bottom or maybe I would after some wine and all that, you know?"

"No, I don't know."

"Fuck it. You don't need to know," Jackson declared. "Water under the gay fucking bridge. My brother, the fag!" he yelled for the world to hear.

"That's grossly offensive," Kendrick said, pulling out of the embrace with a smile. He hadn't imagined things going nearly this well.

"What, you're gay now, so you can't take a little shit?"

"I'm still leaving, you know," Kendrick reminded him, bringing the conversation back around to the first bullet point.

"Yeah, well, who the fuck's not?" Jackson asked before turning toward the Manor. "Try not to suck any dick on your way to the car!" he yelled with a smile.

"Try not to stroke your fat ass out climbing the stairs," Kendrick yelled back as Jackson flipped him off.

When Jackson closed the front door behind him, Kendrick took in the sight one last time. When he had walked out the door before realizing that Jackson was waiting outside, he had still been unsure if he could bring himself to actually leave Brose Manor, let alone Pine Creek, and now found himself on the verge of being out of both — and the closet to boot.

The house looked tiny where it stood on the corner lot, as if it had never been more than a dollhouse in someone's attic; and in that moment, Kendrick was certain that he wanted to explore the attic.

21

Oklahoma Breakdown

Troy had been late to meet Jackson and the guys at the Summer Soiree — so late, in fact, that the sun had begun threatening to set on him as punishment. He had been lying low ever since *The Incident*, as the only person with whom he might commiserate was Rob and he had been unceremoniously shipped off to rehab as though he were a class three heroin addict. He had tried to avoid even Jackson and Kendrick insofar as he was able, but Brose Manor didn't allow for the type of solitary existence for which he longed. He had even taken to ducking Eve, which he would have never considered in the years leading up to then, going so far as to turn his cellphone off and even fleeing through his bedroom window when she had made the pilgrimage to Brose Manor.

He couldn't bear to face the others — not just because he had gotten them all caught up in what could have devolved into a life-or-death situation, but because the embarrassment that he had brought upon himself by being so ridiculously myopic and childish was going to take more than a few days to outlive. He felt like he had developed something of a thick skin when it came to embarrassment — being that he wasn't only a local but also a regional embarrassment from the meteoric crash of his football career — but having gone so far as to commit a felony to avoid having to relive those moments had been a step so far past common sense that he felt like he needed to keep his head buried in the sand for at least a month longer.

But Jackson had cornered him when was trying to tiptoe toward the restroom the night before and had made him promise upon penalty of a tittie-twister that he would show up for a group-bonding experience at the Summer Soiree. Troy had no desire to go to the Soiree or to bond with the group, but those were outweighed by his desire to not have one of Jackson's world-famous tittie-twisters.

And though his third nap of the day had lasted longer than he anticipated, he had shown up at the carnival and was scanning the crowd for any of his friends — and especially for Jackson in the event that he was hiding behind a food booth, doing finger exercises. The crowd was typical, and it would be difficult to distinguish it from any of the previous twenty iterations that Troy had attended over the years. The only difference was that it was the first in which he wasn't joined by his friends, spending ten times the worth of some "prize" and drinking their body-weight in beer.

He sighed with a shrug of his shoulders.

He thought about grabbing a beer and maybe wandering aimlessly for the remainder of the afternoon in attempt to fade softly into the universe and bleed away his shame altogether through a fantastic degree of inebriation, but though almost everything in the scene held the familiarity of a decade's worth of banality, he finally spotted something that caught his gaze long enough to stop his wandering mind in its tracks.

The sun was carrying through on its warning and was beginning its descent over the horizon, showering half of the scene with glistening embers of radiance and casting the rest into a darkness that threatened to leave them behind. Troy welcomed the coolness of the shade and it was enough to weigh the scales in favor of inebriation, he had decided, but when he glanced around for the closest beer vendor, he saw *her*. The sun, that sadist, had singled out Eve for the silhouette of a lifetime just to rub Troy's face in it; he could barely make out the flowered pattern on her sundress that was flirting with the idea of transparency, and her red hair looked blonde with the fractals of light glancing from it until it escaped the glare and lay across her shoulders and the small straps of her dress.

The sun had done its part, and now the universe had taken its turn to twist the knife as Troy watched her push up on the tips of her toes, wrap her arms around the neck of and kiss the very man of whom Troy had suspected either wanted to bed or murder him some days before.

That sealed the deal: Troy was going to get drunk and do something stupid.

But before he could even force himself to take his eyes of Eve, she finished her kiss and laid her head upon her husband's chest with her face staring right in Troy's direction. When her eyes locked with his, Troy was mortified; not only had he been spotted when she was the person he had most been trying to avoid, but he had been spotted in what looked like the midst of voyeurism; he might as well have had his hand down his pants.

Immediately abandoning all intentions of getting drunk and stupid, his body had initiated *fight or flight* mode and had instinctively chosen flight, as it had done so many times before. He turned to make his getaway, content with the fact that he might make a scene by sprinting through the crowd like he'd spotted a xenomorph before anyone else, but before he could even take his first step, Jackson appeared as if by some form of fat bastard magic and grabbed both of Troy's nipples in unison, twisting with all of his might.

Troy screamed at the top of his lungs, tried desperately to toss Jackson aside, but Jackson used his superior size to push Troy down to his knees where he urged: "Say you're sorry, dickhead!"

"Let me go!" Troy screamed again, worried that he might pass out and piss himself in front of the whole town.

"Say it!"

"I'm sorry!"

"Okay, sweet," Jackson said in a calm voice, releasing Troy's nipples and helping him up from the ground. "See that wasn't so hard, was it?" he asked, brushing the dust off of Troy's clothes as though he hadn't just violated him.

"I'll get you back for this," Troy warned.

"Bring it on, bitch..." Jackson began, but he let the word bitch trail off for longer than was necessary, staring over Troy's shoulder to where Troy could hear someone approaching.

Please don't be— he thought seconds before:

"Speaking of bitches," Jackson began.

"Fuck off, Jackson, or I'll tell Reagan to punish you," Eve threatened.

"Yes, ma'am," he responded, in no mood to ruin what was working so well between him and his lady love. He scampered away, leaving Troy to deal with whatever he might be about to deal with.

"Troy," Eve said to get his attention once he hadn't turned around for several moments.

Troy sighed, turned around, still holding his hands over his aching areolae. It was this exact situation or one somehow unthinkably worse that he had been trying to avoid ever since Eve had come back to town. He was beyond being reminded of his own shortcomings by that point and onto being relentlessly embarrassed.

"Yeah," he acknowledged.

"I see Jackson got you with one of his world-famous tittie-twisters," she observed with a motion of her hand toward his chest.

"He did."

"I had a few of those — back before I had boobs, so it wasn't weird," she quickly corrected. "They hurt."

"Yeah," Troy agreed, looking for a way to sneak away from the situation and wondering if she might fall for Jackson's *pretending to be asleep* trick.

"I've been calling. And I came by once," she offered. "Jackson said that you were in your room, and I thought I heard something, but your room was empty when I opened the door."

"I climbed out the window," Troy admitted, seeing no point in lying at that point. He suspected that he had finally hit the mythical *rock bottom* that people were always talking about, and that there would be nowhere to go but up from there.

"I saw you watching us."

He had been wrong. He had somehow dropped through the bottom and into the upside down.

"I wasn't watching," Troy exclaimed with what little dignity he could muster. "I noticed you. There was the sunlight and it was bright and confusing. And I was just looking for a beer. And then you were kissing that guy."

"That guy's my husband."

"Yeah," he said, preparing to drop to the ground in a false fit of narcolepsy. "I didn't think you were just running around kissing randos at the Summer Soiree."

"He confirmed that he hit you with his car," she offered.

"I've got to go," Troy finally managed when he started to have his doubts about being able to fake narcolepsy and the possibility of having to wait several minutes until she tired of the game and left.

"Wait, Troy," she said, grabbing him by the shoulder before he could scurry away. "Why are things so weird between us? I thought we sorted all of this out the other day. It wasn't me, just the way that I reminded you of your fuck-ups."

"Yeah, well then there's the added fuck-up of getting everyone involved with the local criminal element to fix the last fuck-up, and now having seen you make out with your husband," he finished, exasperated. "I need to go take a nap."

"Stop," she cautioned, having again taken her serious tone that seemed to scare Troy into behaving. "Not to sound like Jackson, but you've got to stop being a little bitch."

"A little bitch?"

"A little bitch," she agreed. "Your life didn't turn out the way you wanted it to. Boo-fucking-hoo. In case you didn't realize, I had my heart broken when I was 17, just like you, but whereas I left town and grew the fuck up, you moped around for a decade-plus until you committed the dumbest crime that any high school kid would know to avoid."

"I technically got away with it," he said, momentarily finding a backbone inspired by the verbal beating that he was taking.

"You got away with jack and shit," she said with a forced laugh. "Aside from Daryl having to agree to become the chief of police, I had to agree to run for District Attorney as part of the deal to get you guys off, with an understanding that there's a *look the other way policy* when it comes to the Bennetts, so spare me your self-pity. And Jackson has to pay to fix the damage from when he got nervous and accidentally shot holes in Ramona's building with Reagan's gun, so we're all doing something we don't want to do because of you."

"You had to—?"

"Yeah," she said, pushing the hair from her face. "I've got to run and serve at least a term and then I can go back to private practice. And you better be fucking grateful because I went to law school to help people, not prosecute them."

"Thanks," Troy muttered, more self-conscious about his situation than he had been before.

"Yeah, well," Eve began, "what am I going to do, let you and Rob go to jail?" She let the moment sink in before continuing: "Irk me though it may, you were my first love. And you'll always have a place, however small, in my heart. So I couldn't just sit around and watch you go to fucking jail, could I?"

The two shared a forced smile. Troy wasn't sure what to say. The embarrassment was so much worse than he had even originally suspected. He went from trying to escape seeing Eve because it made him feel stupid to owing her his very freedom.

He wasn't sure that Hallmark made a card for *that*.

While Troy was searching desperately for a way to defuse the tension and fighting the urge to rub his sore nipples, it seemed that the universe was on the verge of throwing him a bone for the first time in recent memory. As the sun had begun to duck behind the horizon, the band had taken that as their cue to initiate the hootenanny. The singer began to introduce the band to the crowd, which would ostensibly give Troy time to string together a few words to say *I'm sorry*, *thank you*, and *I'm not a pervert* all in one go.

But the band wasn't a fan of lengthy introductions or getting to know the crowd, and said only: "Hello, we're *The Batshit Crazy Blues Experiment*" before breaking into song. Though the name didn't inspire confidence, their choice of opening songs proved to be sublime. It was an old Stoney Larue song that both Troy and Eve recognized by its third note.

"No," Eve said with a laugh. "Are you fucking kidding me?" she yelled at the band, who couldn't hear a word she was saying. She could barely get them out between bouts of laughter.

Oklahoma Breakdown had been *their* song. It had been played ad nauseam, insofar as their friends were concerned, the summer that they had gotten together, as it was almost always queued up on an iPod Shuffle in Cheryl's cab where it was played through a connected cassette tape.

"I can't even remember the last time I heard this song," Eve admitted. "Probably not since *that* summer."

"Yeah, me neither," Troy lied. Aside from being able to

occasionally hear the song on some of the local radio stations or at the local bars, Troy still had the same iPod Shuffle in Cheryl to the very day and had probably listened to it a thousand times over the past decade. Still, it was quite the coincidence that a band called *The Batshit Crazy Blues Experiment* would open their set with it. And to top it all off, with the setting sun came the illumination of an assortment of white Christmas lights strung along both sides of the street to the telephone poles and through all of the assorted food carts and makeshift buildings. He was sitting next to Eve beneath the soft glow of Christmas lights, listening to *their* song. He was going to have to figure out what he had done to deserve the assist and do it again.

Not one to ignore the universe when it was being so generous, he stood and held out his hand as an invitation for her to dance with him.

Eve stared at his hand for what felt like an eternity. Her husband was getting them something to drink; *them*, as in her and her husband, not her and Troy; she was a married woman looking up at the face of her high school boyfriend; she wasn't *that* girl; and yet it felt like it was an event ten years in the making. With a reluctant sigh and an unsure smile, she took his hand and began dancing with him there on the sidewalk to their song.

At first, they fought to keep enough space between them so as to remain proper, but by the second chorus, they were cheek to cheek and her arms were around his neck. She was fighting the urge to allow any pent-up emotion through and he was fighting the urge to allow any blood to flow to his penis.

God, she smells good, he was thinking.

He smells like he hasn't showered in a few days, she was thinking. Still, it was nice and familiar. She pulled back a few inches to look him in the eyes.

"This is nice," she said.

"Marry me," he said out of nowhere.

Eve laughed wholeheartedly at the suddenness and ridiculousness of the proposition, at once dismissing and also wondering if he meant it.

Troy laughed, too, surprised by the suddenness and ridiculousness of the proposition and wondering if he meant it. He hadn't really meant to say it out loud, but it had slipped out somewhere between a heartbeat and a memory.

"I'm married," she responded, holding up her wedding ring for proof.

"Yeah, but he's British," Troy responded.

"While your argument is foolproof," she said with a smile, "I'm not leaving my husband for a boy I had a crush on in high school."

"Yeah, probably not the best idea," he conceded. "If he were to die of cancer or just mysteriously vanish with no one in particular to blame..."

Eve shook her head and rolled her eyes. "I'll keep your number."

Their song was coming to an end as Eve pulled back from the embrace. "Are you gonna leave town now? Reagan says that you've gotten pretty good at it."

"Reagan is a goddamn succubus," Troy answered. "And I haven't decided yet."

"Let me know when you do," she added before kissing him on the cheek. "With Reagan leaving town, I need all the friends I can get."

With that, she turned and walked back toward the food booth from whence she came, spotting Ian as he walked toward her with *their* drinks. Troy watched her walk away, taking one last mental picture of the moment before cautiously turning around with his hands, ready to block an attack in case Jackson had been standing behind him.

"Well *fuck*," he said aloud before turning around and noticing the Buffalo staring back at him with the same stare that it always had. Troy felt that he had something to do with the events that had transpired, but he didn't want to push his luck by trying to assault the statue; he had done that once before and broken his big toe.

22

The Buffalo on Main Street

Two weeks had passed since the Summer Soiree. The carnies had packed their rides and wares and blown town as they were wont to do, the city workers and juvenile delinquents had cleaned up the mess, and life had gone back to normal. Jackson — to everyone's surprise — had remained committed to following Reagan to Tulsa, Kendrick had begun to pack for his first semester at ECU, Daryl had been hired as chief of police, and Troy had remained noncommittal about his plans for the future. With all of the upheaval, he would have been able to slip out of town fairly easily while everyone else tended to their affairs, but he told himself that he at least needed to see everyone off before he might leave.

Jackson and Reagan were leaving town on Thursday night to avoid the weekend traffic for the three-hour drive to Tulsa. The guys decided to meet up one last time before they all were split apart like a single-cell organism going through mitosis. Daryl was even able to get Rob a day pass so that he could join in the parting festivities. The *festivities* were light on the festive side, though, as it was really just all the guys meeting up on Main Street one last time where they used to brazenly flaunt their delinquency to now flaunt their responsibility.

Troy, as was fitting, was the last to arrive to find the others already there and waiting. When he turned the corner from Pecan Street and made to park in the fifteen-minute parking spaces in front of the bank, he saw that the Buffalo, too, had been awaiting his arrival; the statue had its face painted like Gene Simmons as an homage to *Dazed and Confused* — a group favorite.

Maybe they hadn't quite mastered the concept of responsibility.

Troy approached the others with his head held higher than it had been in the previous weeks. He had been doing mental calisthenics in an attempt to work on his deep-seated Eve issues and to return to a state of normalcy that perhaps he hadn't known since before Eve — though he admitted that he should probably stop short of becoming the entitled asshole he had been while a star athlete.

"Boys," he said with a nod.

"About time," Jackson yelled.

"Couldn't find parking," he said with a grin.

The five friends gathered around the buffalo on the assorted lawn furniture that they had brought along as Daryl opened the ice chest and started distributing beers.

"Is this kosher now that you're chief of police," Kendrick asked.

"Haven't been sworn in yet," Daryl responded.

Everyone chuckled at the outright impropriety of it all.

"Rob, it's good to see that you're still alive," Troy

observed. "And sober," he mentioned with a motion toward the beer in Rob's hand.

"I'm in rehab for weed, not beer," he responded spitefully. "Besides, it's not even rehab, it's like a day spa. Really, I could just not go—"

"You're going back," Daryl said loudly, cutting him off.

A round of laughter erupted, everyone having known that Rob would try to weasel his way out of going back and that Daryl would cut it off at the pass — which is why he is the one who had picked Rob up and would be the one who dropped him back off. By all accounts, Rob had been doing well in his rehabilitation so far; and according to Rob, he didn't even need to be there since weed was non-addictive, but the therapy had proven to be beneficial in helping him to get past some of his more neurotic tendencies. Jenny had even visited him during his stay and he hadn't tried to escape through a window in the Paulson tradition.

"I still can't believe you're going to leave," Troy said to Jackson. "And that you're going to leave," he said to Kendrick. "Neither Brose Brother staying behind in Pine Creek to keep it from floating away."

"What can I say?" Jackson asked. "I've wanted to get away from Dickless here all of my life. He followed me out of the womb and hasn't stopped following me since."

"If you'll recall, it was you following me all around town like a psychopath," Kendrick retorted.

Jackson grimaced, but didn't feel the need to jump from his lawn chair to slap his brother, which was an odd feeling for him. Given that he was about to be away from him for the longest amount of time in either of their lives, his need to physically assail him had dimmed.

"Besides," Jackson continued, "when you're in love with a goddamn evil genius, it's hard to let her leave town without you."

Reagan had confessed a few days earlier that she wasn't really pregnant, but had used it as a ploy to get Jackson comfortable with the idea of moving before pulling the rug out from under him. He had been so impressed by her ruse and so turned on after she had slapped and then kissed him when he tried to argue with her that he hadn't been able to form a cogent argument as to why they shouldn't go. The others had teased him mercilessly, but he maintained that escaping the clutches of a bloodthirsty succubus was more than should be asked of any one man.

"And you," Troy said to Daryl. "You're going to be the chief of fucking police."

"And you'll be the prisoner of the fucking month if you step out of line again. Don't think I'm going to look the other way now that I'm chief. I'm an important man, and can't be seen rabble-rousing with troublemakers."

"Drinking beer on Main Street," Troy reminded him.

"Starting tomorrow, dickhead."

"No more cops and robbers," Kendrick asked.

"Alas," Daryl responded.

"Shit around here really is going to change," Rob chimed in.

"Shit really is," Daryl agreed.

They all sat in silence for a bit after that, no one wanting to spoil the moment that they wanted to hang onto for the rest of their days. The five of them had been friends since grade school, and because none had moved on from Pine Creek, they had developed a weird symbiosis that had turned into full-blown Peter Pan Syndrome. But now they were finally about to be leaving Neverland for the real world.

Eventually someone cracked a joke, someone threw a beer can at someone, and the scene devolved into a giant wrestling match. And after that had been broken up by a group truce that was broken several times, Jackson announced that it was time for him to leave, as Reagan had been texting and threatened to drive up like an angry mother to embarrass him in front of his friends. He was mocked relentlessly as a way of saying goodbye, no one actually bringing themselves to use the words. And shortly thereafter, Kendrick had announced that he, too, must be off because he was still trying to get his new apartment over in Ada in order while the other guys promised to come help him over the weekend, as a way of saying goodbye, no one actually bringing themselves to use the words. And finally Daryl announced that it was time for him get Rob back to the rehab facility because he had already kept him out past curfew and was pushing the bounds of his newfound authority — even though he wasn't getting sworn in until the next day — as a way of saying goodbye, no one actually bringing themselves to use the words.

Troy stood alone, surrounded by lawn furniture and beer cans, only just realizing that he had been the last man standing and thus saddled with the responsibility of cleaning up. He slowly began picking up the cans and taking them over to the nearby trashcan, then picked up each of the lawn-chairs and trekked them over to Cheryl's bed where he tossed them in without much ceremony. He walked back over to check the area over one last time, knowing that Daryl would spend the required amount of time on his first day as police chief to write him a ticket for littering if it hadn't all been picked up.

Content that he had accomplished his mission, Troy was ready to leave, but began to wonder if he was content to *leave*. He had spent his life trying to get away from Pine Creek where he knew every person and every inch of the town. There was no mystery or adventure to be had, and nothing that could surprise him at that point. Should he just hop in Cheryl and leave at that very moment with a bed full of lawnchairs and the clothes on his back — content to stay in whichever town he was passing through when he ran out of gas?

Though his head had seemed clear for most of the day, he found himself in a familiar situation when his mind clouded like it was trying to rain. He was hesitant to make a decision in that mindset, worried that the wrong choice would doom him to a life of not knowing if the other would have turned out. Feeling as though he needed to make the decision in that moment or that he may never be capable of making such a decision again, he reached in his pocket for a coin to flip. When he came up empty without a single coin to his name, he glanced up at the buffalo and laughed out loud. The universe was fucking with him again, but the difference between then and now was that he had begun to see the humor in it.

"You did this, didn't you?" he asked the buffalo with a laugh. He laughed harder until he could feel the muscles in his abdomen begin to threaten pain. He still didn't have an answer, but at least he had made a new friend.

So wrapped up in his own amusement, he hadn't noticed the sound of something approaching from behind; when he had quenched the last bit of laughter and wiped his eye where a stray tear had landed, he turned around to leave, but between him stood a buffalo — not *the* buffalo, but *a* buffalo. The lone remaining buffalo that the park service hadn't accounted for was the biggest of the bunch that they called Hercules, and though Troy had seen Hercules dozens of times in the park when he drove by, he had never been close enough to realize how he had come by his name.

The animal towered over Troy, its head about level with his own. Troy had frozen in place upon seeing the animal and couldn't find it in himself to facilitate any sort of movement. Perhaps if he had seen it coming, he could have brought himself to run, but being face to face and nearly eye to eye with the animal as it stared at him with a gaze that seemed to be trying to determine whether he was friend or foe — Troy had nothing. Moments passed in which Troy began to formulate a plan: if he was going to run, in which direction should he go? The animal was between him and his truck, so did he want to try to make the tree line? Or maybe try to make it the two blocks down to the Snak-Shak?

Still undecided which direction he should take, Troy decided that it didn't really matter and that action in of itself was required if he were going to live to see another day.

He tried to relax and flex the muscles in his legs a few times so that he didn't pull anything when he made his move and make an easy target, but in the moment before he was about to try his luck, Hercules licked his face.

Troy wondered if that was like a double-dog dare, the buffalo trying to push him over the edge so it could chase him down and maul him. But then it licked him again, and then a few more times with a slimy tongue that left a film over Troy's face. Content that he had made his point, Hercules turned and walked away — right down the middle of Main Street as though he didn't have a care in the world aside from maybe finding more faces to lick.

Troy waited for him to get a few steps away before wiping the saliva from his face. He shared a look with *the* buffalo, who seemed to be just as surprised.

"Well, that settles it."

Acknowledgments

To the memory of my Papaw, Jerry, to my Grandma, Louise, to my Nana, Carol, and to the memory of Papaw Ken. Without the guidance of that generation, our parents would likely have let us free-range into traffic and extinguish the human race. Also, to Grandma, sorry about the time that I had that party when y'all were gone for the weekend, broke the cabinet door and then switched it out with one behind the ice box. It was totally Steven's fault.

Also to my dad for my sense of humor; growing up being told stories about how he killed a grizzly bear with a pocketknife while I crawled through the sliding-glass window into the bed of the truck to get him and Johnny Wilkerson another beer no doubt had an impact on my ability to bullshit. And to my mom for instilling me with a devout sense of road rage that scared me as a child, but without which, I wouldn't have written Jackson's Facebook post (a real post that I made on Facebook, by the way).

To my first cousins — far too many to list here with the

proficiency of breeding in the previous two generations — half of the things I wrote about in this book inspired by or lived through with you guys.

Okay, I'll name a few. Jake: all the backroading and shit-talking accounts for half of the characters herein; also **BUSTED IN BAYLOR COUNTY!**; Trent: the bar fights are cool in retrospect, but goddammit, man, you're lucky you made it into the book after the time that guy kicked my ass at the strip club with those shitty wheeled chairs; Steven: you poured rubbing alcohol into the gaping hole in my shoulder after getting stabbed with that beer bottle and the doctor said he'd never seen such a clean wound; Dakota: the time that Casey shit in that mailbox may have been the funniest thing I've ever seen in my life; Aaron, you didn't make the book because you made me ride in the back of that goddamn CRX when we were fifteen and ALWAYS ramped that hill on Sunshine — 22 years later: vengeance is mine!; Shandy, fuck you, it wasn't that funny the time that I didn't use the parking brake in that Dodge and it went rolling down the hill where my fat ass had to chase it. Fat man caught it, didn't he?

And to everyone else who played a part in my getting here: that was nice of you.

Made in the USA
Columbia, SC
21 February 2023